DEMON GAMES I: DARK MESSIAH

LUCIFER ARISES, A NAVY SEAL AWAKENS TO A NEW REALITY, & THE U.N. TAKES CONTROL OF THE NATIONS

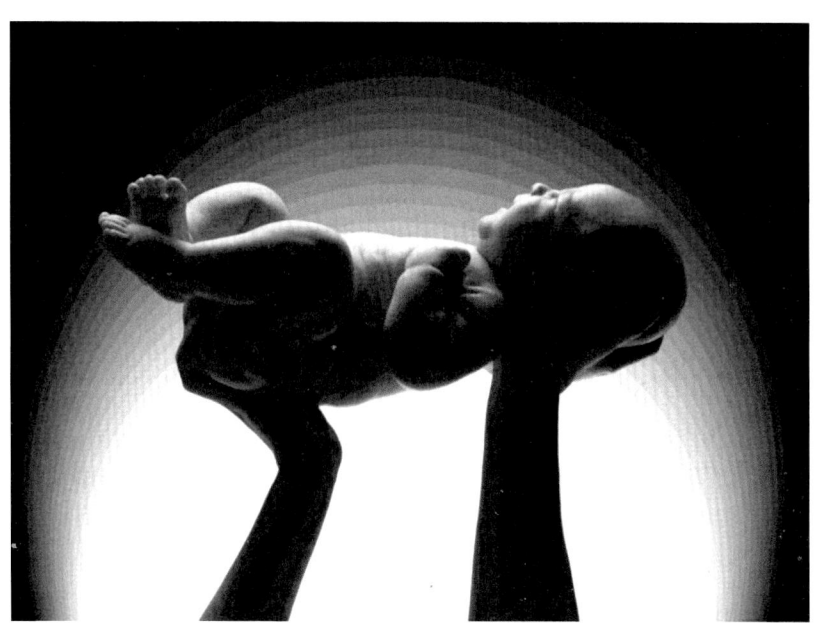

MALLOW SHERIDAN

This is a work of fiction. Names, places, and incidents are either products of the author's imagination or are used fictitiously. In most cases, the masculine pronouns represent all people.

DEMON GAMES I: DARK MESSIAH

© 2020 by Mallow Sheridan. All Rights Reserved

ISBN: 978-1-64921-743-1 (print)

ISBN: 978-1-64921-747-0 (ebook)

Also available:

DEMON GAMES II: THE GAME OF EVIL

DEMON GAMES III: NEW WORLD ORDER

Published by New Realm Publishing

Nashville

mallowsheridan@sheridanpodcasts.com

Library of Congress Cataloging-in-Publication Data Available upon request

Printed in the United States of America

...AND GOD CHANGED HIS MIND

EXODUS 32:14

MALLOW SHERIDAN

TABLE OF CONTENTS

EPISODE I: SNIPER

1. Sniper ... 9
2. Yemen ... 15
3. Enemies ... 21
4. Victim ... 25
5. Death ... 29

EPISODE II: LEAD DEMONS

6. Lucie ... 37
7. Kali ... 41
8. Demons ... 49
9. Tactics ... 57
10. Almighty ... 65

EPISODE III: DESIGNER BABY

11. Cohens ... 73
12. Benchmarks ... 75
13. Idea ... 79
14. Virgin ... 91
15. Stranger ... 95
16. Scientists ... 101
17. Humanetics ... 107
18. Reappearance ... 117

EPISODE IV: MASTER

19. Substitute ... 123
20. Surrogate ... 125
21. Bethlehem ... 129

22. Awakening 133
23. Exit 137
24. Bat Mitzvah 141
25. Possession 145
26. Harvard 147

EPISODE V: AMBASSADOR

27. Janet 155
28. Benjamin 163
29. Agendas 167
30. Mandates 173
31. Decree 187

EPISODE VI: HEAVEN

32. Seneca 193
33. Trust 199
34. Dimensions 205
35. Warriors 215
36. Strategists 221
37. Heaven 229
38. Idealists 239
39. Samaritans 247
40. Saints 259

EPISODE VII: MISSION

41. Preparations 271
42. Superpowers 277
43. Jerusalem 281
44. Warfare 291
45. History 297

...CONTINUED IN DEMON GAMES II: DECEPTION

EPISODE I:

SNIPER

(GRAYSON'S STORY)

MALLOW SHERIDAN

1.

SNIPER

January 4, 2029, Socotra Island, Yemen

"It's not personal."

I say it aloud hoping it will clear my conscious. This time I say it while loading a gun. The years of telling myself, "I don't choose the victims; their blood is not on my hands," is failing on a subconscious level. Soon, the artificial barrier I hide behind will be punctured by guilt and I will be done. In my line of work, reflection and soul-searching do not get you ahead — they get you fired.

I have no idea why I am being hit with an extra dose of guilt today. I have killed in these humble conditions before. I am familiar with the torturous heat and blood-sucking gnats of the Middle East. I got up early and picked this spot while the temperatures were still reasonable, and the gnats were still sleeping. It is now glaringly obvious that calling "dibs" did nothing to improve my condition. The minute the sun crept onto the edge of the horizon I began competing with the little vampires for the only visible shade in the area.

If I had a sense of humor right now, I could laugh at the irony of being armed with a super-powered rifle capable of killing two hundred-pound men while having nothing to combat these minuscule gnats. My flailing gorilla arms are obviously not posing a significant threat to them. They dart in and out of my personal space like this is the greatest game they will play in their pathetic, ten-day lifespans.

Even before I let the heat and the gnats get under my skin, I was dreading another day of watching men die. Sometimes I feel like a player in a pointless game — one that offers nothing more than dark options and tragic endings. Even worse, every player in the game sees himself as the "good guy" battling the "bad guys". We internalize our convictions deeply enough to risk our lives. We meet on the battlefield armed with our respective talents and physical fortitude and play to the death. Though we have never met, we are driven to kill each other - because killing bad guys - is what good guys do.

The wars of today are much different than the ones of my grandfather's day. Now that country borders are defended by the United Nations, wars for the purpose of expanding territory have pretty much ended — Russia excluded, of course. Today's wars are about religion and human rights. It is nearly impossible to know when wars based upon the social sciences end — and who gets to claim victory when they do.

I may not choose the victims, but I did choose to play the game. I'm the best rifleman in the U.S. Armed Forces. An admiral convinced me that my talents with a gun obligated me to be on the frontline. I wish that I hadn't bought into that. Now, I'm little more than a compensated killer who can't be convicted because of the uniform I wear. Every day, I tell myself I'm the good guy. Mostly, it works. Sometimes, it doesn't.

In between swatting gnats, I watch the six men I was sent to kill. I am perched atop a rocky knoll directly in front of the cave they are guarding. The men are using the cave to illegally retain six American soldiers, and I am a Navy SEAL whose job is to protect American interests. In short, they deserve what's coming to them.

My job is to get the American soldiers out of Yemen without drawing international attention. This mission is "Classified." It is one of thousands of classified operations sanctioned by the U.S. military every year. Classified operations do not make the evening news – which is probably a good thing. If kids still tune into the evening news, I can imagine one watching me pick off a "bad guy" with a single shot and telling his father he wants to grow up and be a sniper like me. After all, the thing he just witnessed, aligns his real life with his video games.

The father, wanting to abolish the dream of a career choice that comes with high risk and low reward, would tell his son the sniper is not as cool as he looks. "He may not even be on assignment," the father might say, "He could be nothing more than a lone wolf on the run." He would be wrong about the being 'on the run part'. If I were on the run, I wouldn't stay in a bug-infested war zone. He would be right about the lone wolf part though - and if the boy is anything like me – he will be sold on this point alone. I consider the isolated lifestyle of a sniper to be a serious *upside* of the job.

Even if only adults watch the evening news these days, I'm not sure *they* could handle the truth either. The truth is that every branch of the U.S. military now has thousands of professional killers doing hits all over the world. We snipers, and the leaders who commission us, move in secrecy in the private sector. The things we do now could be pulled from a *Mission: Impossible* movie. When dead bodies surface, they are quickly swept under the rug by sealing files and hiding behind uniforms.

It's no secret that I prefer to work alone - which makes this mission less appealing than most. I am leading a team of six ground troops who are waiting in the brush behind the cave. They will go in for the rescue after I clear a path. It's important to keep them hidden as well. The clever military officers in Washington advised me to avoid detection "at any cost." Evidently, a treaty the U.S. is negotiating is on the line. I try not to think about what that means. After the Benghazi incident we troops in the field feel a lot less protected by our leaders.

When the seven of us arrived at midnight to Socotra Island from the USS America assault ship, we buried our SCUBA gear in protective bags to be retrieved by the cleanup crew and set up a base camp. The camp is halfway between the prisoner cave and the plateau where the helicopter will land to transport the rescued soldiers out of Yemen. I gave the troops their instructions for the day and moved on alone. Having one man moving through the shadows of the trees trying to avoid detection is better than seven.

Once I found the perfect spot, I set up the swivel bipod for my rifle and checked conditions — weather, lighting, wind velocity, distance — with the N2300. When this hot piece of technology dropped into my hands last year, I named it "Kool-Killer-Kalculator." I had to change the name after some officers compared the acronym to the KKK hate group. After agreeing with their logic, I shortened it to "Kool Killer." These days, KK is my only companion at the front. It's my *Wilson*.

Not every part of prepping for a mission is as high-tech as positioning my rifle and programming Kool Killer. A good sniper knows the importance of having a solid set-up routine that covers everything within his site range. Before I consider myself to be locked and loaded, I systematically dart my eyes from detail to detail looking for any points of exposure.

Points of exposure change depending on the mission. For this one, it's as simple as limestone pebbles. The white prickly rocks are plentiful on this rock ledge. To neutralize the risk they present, I spent the better part of an hour gathering up the small, loose stones, placing them into a handkerchief-sized cloth I carry, and relocating them to an area ten feet behind me. I don't want to jeopardize an entire mission by accidentally knocking a pebble off a ledge and letting the targets know I'm here.

After finishing with the rocks, I studied the weather forecast for the hours I expect to be in a holding pattern. Weather patterns change quickly on the islands of Yemen. If I do not prepare properly, I could be forced to change locations. Changing locations after setup can be a critical error for a sniper - the mission would probably fail. I used a reversible camera attached to an expandable metal wand to test the effectiveness of my camouflage. I also planned a quick exit in case something goes wrong. A sniper needs to be able to vacate an area in seconds without leaving any evidence he has been there.

The last thing I did was empty my bladder. I am going to be flat on the ground for hours watching these men through a scope. The less

I move, the better. I made sure to pee downwind from the cave, so the smell of my urine doesn't give me away — or attract the wrong kind of wildlife.

The men are enjoying some after-dinner conversation. My Arabic is limited, so I'm not able to understand most of their exchange. They seem happy tonight. I figure that's a good thing since they only have minutes left to live.

If I have learned anything about himself [myself] as a sniper, it's that I need to get to the killing before I develop sympathy for the targets. I don't want to know any more about these six men than the others I've killed in the past. I just want to know how to best position myself to take six clean shots, which "kill order" gives me the best chance of survival, and the fastest way to get out of here when I am finished.

I have done this 127 times in the last six years – a number that stays in my head. The running tally makes for great conversation at parties. Everyone wants to know how many "evil bastards" I have taken out as a sniper. The growing number of successes also increases my confidence each time I site another target in my scope. I refer to the men I kill by the order in which they die — never by name. Right now, I am watching numbers 128 through 133.

For my professional killing services, I receive an annual salary of $250,000. In six years, I have earned 1.5 million dollars, which works out to be a little more than $11,000 per target. From my calculations, I am looking at about $66,000 outside this cave. Many eyes are watching me stateside today. The expectation is high, and I will not disappoint. I intend to earn my salary. Good guys do as they are told.

MALLOW SHERIDAN

2.

YEMEN

Staring through a scope for hours at a time is the hardest part of my job. Patience has always been a challenge for me. Only years of insane training have made it possible for me to sit still with this much adrenaline pumping through my body. When I sit still, my brain goes into overdrive. Mostly, I reflect on my career choice — well, *question* my career choice might be a more accurate way of putting it.

I will be forced to retire on my next birthday. I will be thirty-two years old. In the world of Navy SEALs, that makes me an old man. I have already received two exceptions to the rule on age, but this is the end of the line. Navy SEALs are ideally commissioned between the ages of seventeen and twenty-eight. Only snipers and officers receive exceptions. Even so, I have been one of the *lucky ones*. I find it ironic that Navy SEALs and Miss America contestants share the same exit age. I bet some beauty queens have also wondered at the age of twenty-eight, *"What am I supposed to do with the next fifty years of my life?"*

Being back in the chaotic Middle East is adding to my frustration today. It is almost impossible for anyone who lives outside this cesspool of evil to remember which countries are enemies and which are allies. At times, I have to Google uniforms and flags to know where to point my gun.

In *Art of War*, Sun Tzu warns men of the cost of entering wars they "do not intend to win." Every time I read the book I worry about my country. The United States has a habit of rushing to provide troops when there is a breach of its definition of "human rights."

As far back as 2017, Russian President, Vladimir Putin warned America to stop forcing its morals on the world. That was a big statement — and it caused me to stop and think. I cringe when I hear the stories of children being raped and sold into slavery at the hands of dictators. I have nightmares about men and women being drowned in giant cages for disagreeing with their governments. I cannot process the level of evil necessary for men to do such things.

No matter what I think, I realize that until there is a worldwide governing body with more power than the United Nations currently wields, hands are tied. Human rights are at the whim of the nations.

Though I don't want to live in a world where such heinous acts go unchecked and unpunished, I accept that my thinking is as about as American as it gets. The United States is always out to correct the evil in the world. The question that begs an answer is, "Who gets to define 'evil'?" That question will have to be answered by the philosophers and theologians. I am simple. Though I like my paycheck, I mostly come here because I want to do my part to free POWs and protect citizens who are being used as pawns by fascist governments. Even though I consider my motives to be noble, I admit that my reasoning — and many times the reasoning of the United States — does not pass Sun Tzu's litmus test.

Covert operations such as this one further confuses the issue. I'm not even sure if I am participating in a war with today's assignment. Most Middle Eastern nations do not consider themselves to be at war. They do not feel the need to register papers with the United Nations or to justify their actions. If they have an army, it usually doesn't have a clear objective. If they have a government, it usually doesn't have a definitive strategy.

The one thing many of these nations seem to have in common is hate — and hate only goes so far in giving soldiers the motivation they need to risk their lives year after year. My experience has convinced me that the amount of passion necessary for a nation to sustain itself through a long war must be borne from the pain of its people. And, if so, I wonder if the citizens of these despotic nations would be bolder — and rise on their own — if they knew no one was coming to rescue them. It's entirely possible that America is hindering them more than it is helping them. I'm glad these are not my decisions to make.

    To us outsiders, the core cause of unrest in this part of the Middle East is easy to see. The less-enlightened governments spread hate-driven propaganda to their people — often in the name of religion. Since their governments lack definitive objectives, the only thing the people have left, is hate. Hate without a strategy for change becomes internalized and surfaces as erratic terrorism. I smirk at my brilliance. I never have a pen and paper in the field to write down my deep insights. Kool Killer does not allow for life footnotes. When I get back to the barracks, I will add this stuff to my war journal - a journal which is much longer than I expected it to be.

    I have been on assignment in sixteen of the twenty-two nations that make up the Arabian world. Some of the nations are in Asia and the rest are in Northern Africa. The citizens of most of these countries are devastated and weary from war. Many of them are weak from hunger and sick from disease. Other nations here are wealthy, well-armed, and connected to the rest of the world through the World Wide Web. Their citizens are free to participate in social media and pursue information at will. These "more enlightened" countries are active in the United Nations and respected by the leaders of Western Europe, Russia, China, and even the United States.

    These nations don't concern me. It is the independently operating renegade nations that keep me looking over my shoulder. Rumors abound that two of these rogue countries have nuclear weapons. From what I have seen, it is not conjecture - they have nukes. I doubt there is anything more threatening to the future of the planet than the combination of nukes and unenlightened hate.

Within the last decade, this nation of Yemen has also become problematic for the rest of the world. It is one of the poorest nations in the Arab League. Fifty-four percent of its population lives in poverty. The nation is experiencing severe water shortages – something that is now being weaponized. If things do not improve soon, starvation will follow. Heavily in debt to the One World Bank, the Yemeni government only affords its citizens eight hours of electricity a day. If this were happening in the United States, millions of X-boxers would probably march on Washington and rally for change.

Yemen does not have much of a government to rally against. A deadly civil war threatens its stability. Because of its vulnerability, this tiny nation makes money by agreeing to be a hideout for leaders of Al-Qaeda, the new ISIS, and other terrorist groups. Though the nation's limestone plateaus are poor for growing vegetation, the Karstic Caves located just beyond them are excellent for hiding terrorist operations.

In 2011, the United States military saw an opportunity for a bargain and built an Air Force base here for testing its classified war weapons. These are mostly massive drones built for spying operations and for sinking battleships. The newest drones are much smaller - the size of hummingbirds. They are undetectable, untraceable, and programmed with facial recognition software to seek out and explode the heads of their targets. It won't be long until drones replace most snipers. Drones are reinventing the entire weapons industry based on research being done here - in a nation that cannot afford to pay its light bill.

While the United States is constantly redesigning the future, many of the twenty-two Arabian countries seem frozen in time. They purposely ignore the scientific and social advancements of the world. Most insist women remain in the traditional roles. Not much changes from one day to the next. Their *preferred* idleness adds to their underlying resentment of the Western nations that constantly push the world forward. Conversely, from a Westerner's perspective, much of the Middle East is a gigantic landmine that is unpredictable and deadly to navigate — mainly because its mines of religious prejudice were set centuries ago and have yet to be disarmed.

Some may think this an oversimplification of the problem. Many believe this entire mess is a holy war between the Judeo-Christian and Islamic religions. They say it tracks back to the days of Abraham and his two sons. They also believe this unrest will not end until life on Earth is over. If this is true, my career choice was a lousy one, but one with indefinite job security.

There are opportunities for me to contract as a sniper in the Middle East after the SEALs kick me to the curb on my next birthday. If a nation cannot afford drones, hired assassins are its weapon of choice. Sniper hits can remove corrupt leaders with a single shot and send strong messages to the other side. A one-man hit squad is discreet and doesn't incite wars and international conflicts. Like the U.S. these nations can bury a story as easily as they can bury a body.

Most modern-day Americans have little experience with the extended conflicts of the past. Today, when the United States military invades foreign lands, it takes what it wants and repairs a minuscule amount of invasion damage on the way out. This means it does only what is necessary to stay on good terms with its allies.

When my grandfather was a soldier, the United States would restore hospitals, schools, major roads, and leave behind peace-keeping troops for a decade or so after a conflict ended. Times changed when the Millennial generation assumed leadership. The United States no longer places troops in foreign nations and has pretty much relieved itself of the responsibility of policing the world.

Middle East policy has also shifted. The United States has not been an enthusiastic participant in Middle Eastern affairs since it stopped buying crude oil here. These days, America is a reluctant ally at best. It only comes when it needs to support Israel or when it needs to ensure that terrorism remains on foreign soil. The decreasing military budget in America encourages the Brass at the Pentagon to keep its troops at home.

In the past, America routinely participated in wars it did not intend to win, and the cost was mounting. Now, it puts its military money into two things: Space Force satellites and stealth aircraft to keep tabs on Russia and China, and specialized forces such as scientists, engineers, computer hackers, and snipers. My mission today called on the talents of all four specialties. Working together, they located the prisoners, devised a plan to get the team in and out without detection, broke the code to scramble Yemeni communications, and positioned stealth drones to surveil the entire operation. After the team leaves, these same specialists will erase all digital and literal footprints. In time, they will send a follow-up crew to retrieve the SCUBA equipment. The entire operation is being run from a conference room in the Pentagon — over 7,000 miles away. My grandfather calls this the warfare of the future.

3.

ENEMIES

Twelve hours in, I have collected useful data through my scope. I have confirmed there are a total of six Yemeni soldiers here. I have also been able to identify the ranking guard by the black band on the left sleeve of his uniform. I will take him out first. He will be number 128. When the ranking officer goes down, the rest of the troops will be confused. These men are soldiers. They rely on orders a little too much for their own good. Their training does not teach them much about individual survival. This makes my job easier.

Two of the remaining five are sharing a cigarette every twenty-five to thirty minutes. They are due to light up again in about ten. I will take them out last. They will be numbers 132 and 133. It will take them longer to drop the smokes, get the rifles off their backs, and locate a safe spot from which to return fire. The next match they light will be the last of their lives — and my signal to start firing. I will kill numbers 129-131 from left to right. There is no special reason for this order; I just happen to prefer shooting from left to right.

The smoking buddies do not disappoint. They light up right on schedule. The ranking guard is on his radio wrapping up the day with his commanding officer. His pacing will make his shot a little more difficult. I scan my infrared scope over each of the six targets, hesitating for a second on each man's neck to check for the clearest shot. Everything appears to be ready. I still have not seen the prisoners. It helps that they are not outside where a stray bullet could hit them or where they could end up in a hostage situation. The ground team is on standby. They will rush the cave to get the American prisoners out as soon as I finish my job.

The ranking guard finishes on the radio and puts it back in his gear box. It's "go time." I take in a long breath and release it slowly as I settle into marksman position. I am lying on his stomach with my elbows supporting my upper body. My .300 Win Mag rifle is resting on the swivel bipod, which gives me steadiness and ease of mobility. With my scope locked onto the neck of 128, I gently touch the tip of my finger to the trigger and re-check conditions: no wind, lighting is adequate, no precipitation, and all six targets are in view. I slightly pulse my finger on the trigger to take it the rest of the way. The gun kicks a bit. The silencer contains the sound. The leader drops.

As expected, the other five begin to scatter. Guards 129 and 130 rush to check on their captain. They pull him out of the line of fire — as if he could still be alive. I refocus on the one on the left. Another swift pull of the trigger and he drops as well. Guard 130 catches on now and looks in my direction. He opens his stance for a second and I pull the trigger again. He drops on top of 129. Guard 131 runs for the cave. I must stop him before he gets to the prisoners. I do not like shooting men in the back, but I have no choice now. Luckily for me, the guard is not wearing a helmet. I take out the back of his skull.

The smokers now have their guns off their backs. They jump behind separate boulders for protection. I hold tight. After all, I have the advantage. I can see them, but they can't see me. They are afraid; I am not. After a few minutes, I see 133 send a signal to 132. Though I cannot make out the hand motion, I know he has assumed leadership. He just jumped to the top of my short list. I do not worry myself with their plan; it is always the same. One will try to distract me by either running in my direction or diving for a piece of communication equipment. A good sniper ignores distractions and keeps his eye on the target.

I must give the Yemeni soldiers credit for originality. They go with the suicide distraction — a tactic popular with the Japanese and Islamic armies. It is tougher to anticipate and almost impossible to diffuse. Guard 132 jumps out from behind the boulder with his Mini-UZI aimed in my direction. His Israeli-built submachine gun can hold up to thirty rounds. I assume it is full and that he is not worried about accuracy. I must move quickly, or risk being hit by the spray of the guard's aimless bullets.

My scope has not left the boulder where 133 is hiding. If he is going to run, he will either go for the brush behind him — where he will meet up with the rest of the team — or for the cave. I bet on the cave. I aim my gun at a spot just to the right of the boulder. Based on his height, I estimate where his head would reach if he were bent over running for the cave. I choose a spot fifty-four inches above the ground and wait. My calculations are correct. Guard 132 moves directly into my line of fire. Forced to shoot another coward, I blow off the back of 132's head. Blood sprays all the way to the cave opening.

With an immediate straight three-inch drop of my gun, I lock the suicide shooter into my scope just as he reaches the base of my perch. It will be an easy shot. Like his buddies, 133 is not wearing a helmet. I could go for the face, but I will choose the neck instead; I prefer the bigger challenge. I squeeze the trigger. 133's head drops, and he falls backwards. The area goes quiet.

I signal the ground troops. They come in cautiously, guns ready. Four of them head into the cave with bolt cutters to free the POWs. Two stand guard outside. I watch over the area in case backups were deployed. Since we are on an island under surveillance by Navy drones, the chances of there being anyone else in the vicinity is extremely low.

I reach for my backpack and pull out my binoculars. Feeling relaxed now, I drop my rifle and stand up to take a better look around the island. I feel the warm ocean breeze across my face. I hear the helicopter approaching to pick up the American prisoners and ground troops. I congratulate myself on another job well done. As I drop my binoculars, I feel a sting on my neck. My legs collapse under me, and I hit the ground hard.

MALLOW SHERIDAN

4.

VÍCTIM

In six years of being a sniper for the United States Navy SEALs, it never occurred to me that I could be the one lined up in the scope of a sniper. That thought could not co-exist with my massive ego. This same ego allows me to kill a man from a hiding place, leave without facing him, and still accept props for being brave. Now it appears as if *I* am a victim and soon-to-be casualty of war.

My death certificate is set — and it will not be impressive: *Terminal ballistics in the line of duty*. Those seven words will undercut my accomplishments, including the one hundred percent accuracy of taking out any man sighted through my infrared scope. Death certificates and headstones do not record the victories of man. Such is the fate of humans. After you are in the grave, people who read the marble slab put over your head will only learn two details about you: the date of your birth and the date of your death. Every other detail of your life will be reduced to the dash between the two.

In addition to earning myself an unimpressive grave marker today, my death will be fodder for the body count banner during the evening news. Viewers use this banner to gauge how well U.S. troops are faring in the multi-nation conflicts of the world. They lose interest in about six months. Eventually, soldier deaths become little more than visual noise. The sad truth is that if you are going to be a casualty of war, it's best to die early in the game, so your story gets some screen time. If a soldier dies on a classified operation, things are even worse.

He is given a single line that says something like, he was "killed by friendly fire," which makes him look like a complete moron.

Like TV viewers, soldiers also get over the thrill of war in six months. From that point on, they are just hoping to be alive when it's over. I can relate to the apathy. Dropped right into the center of this front-line action, I am guilty of playing along without having measurable passion for any of it. Sun Tzu would tell me this is the real reason I am dying.

Though I didn't make eye contact with the sniper who took me out, I know he was a worthy opponent. He contained his emotions long enough to deliver his hate-driven bullet with flawless accuracy. He took the shot I perfected and called the "Adam" because the bullet enters the neck exactly one inch from the target's Adam's apple. It takes out the carotid artery; no man can survive it. The bullet initiates a fatal blood loss as it enters the body and shatters the spinal cord as it exits, paralyzing the victim from the neck down.

When sniping, you rarely get a chance for a second shot. Every single one must be exact, hitting a spot about the size of a BB pellet. The Adam is the best shot to take if you intend to kill. Helmets block the head, and bulletproof vests cover the torso. Legs and groins are vulnerable but hitting them only increases the chance of failure. You end up with an injured shooter who is mad as hell that you hit him. He will tie off the wound and come after you. There is a good chance that the ineffective bullet you sent his way will help him pinpoint your location.

Even if you get off the field alive after a botched sniper assignment, you will not hear the end of it in the barracks. As far as snipers go, hitting a target and failing to drop him earns you the title of subpar marksman. For the rest of your career, you will not be able to shake the fallout of that single shot. Your salary will nosedive, and you will find yourself facing the reality that there are zero jobs awaiting a sharpshooter who failed to take out a target — especially after age twenty-eight.

Tonight, the Yemeni basecamp will celebrate the sniper who just put a bullet through my neck. He perfectly sliced through the artery. I will bleed out in three minutes — five minutes tops. I will hope for five but prepare for three. SEALs are acutely aware of every second when executing a mission. There is an expected protocol for using time, even when dying.

The first thing the Navy's best must do in a situation like this is to assess if any of his men are in the line of fire. They are not. By now, they should have cleared the red zone and disappeared into the brush. They will be boarding the chopper soon.

The second thing a SEAL must assess is the likelihood of capture. This is a zero. The Yemeni sniper will need to climb a sharp limestone terrain to get to me. I have no doubt that he will come to ensure his target is no longer a threat, but this will take twenty minutes. I will be dead before he arrives.

The third thing a SEAL needs to do is decide if he should destroy his gear and backpack. This isn't possible, but all I have left is my rifle which is locked by a code, binoculars, and a few rounds of ammo. I'm not carrying anything the shooter can use. There are no grenades or classified information here. The checklist is complete.

The only question now is whether I can do anything to prolong my life. This is also a zero. Even if I could lift my arms, there is no way to stop the bleeding from my neck. It is the one place where a tourniquet cannot be tightened. The only thing I can do is slow my breathing and stay in control of my head. A quick assessment tells me that I am breathing too fast and too shallow. If I don't take the air in slowly and push it deeper, fear will consume me.

As luck would have it, controlled breathing is a mandatory skill for SEALs. We spend weeks in the training pool pushed to the brink of losing consciousness before earning a small amount of oxygen from our tanks. It would be just enough to keep us from blacking out. We did this repeatedly for hours at a time to expand our lung capacity. I can still hear the commander shouting at me through his underwater headset, "You're not breathing on count, Cunningham! Breathe in for five, out for five...in for five, out for five. You can either do this right, or you can die. It's your choice." There is no grand reward for doing it right. The only prize is the minimum amount of oxygen needed to protect you from having permanent brain damage.

After surfacing from training sessions, I would go for a long run up to the highest elevation I could find just to take in as much air as I wanted. It put me back in control of oxygen — and my head. Most days, I would close my eyes and focus on the sweet smell of the air as it passed through my sinuses on its way to my lungs. Ironically, restricted breathing from an underwater tank is where I learned that fresh air has a sweet aroma. The smell of air is something you take for granted until you must fight for it.

Here I am again — fighting for air. This time, I am fighting for just enough to keep me alive for a minute or two. Some positive news: my controlled breathing is beginning to work. The panic pushing its way to the surface is subsiding. I cannot move my head, but I can look around a little with my eyes. I want to know more about the place where I am taking my final breaths. I like that it is peaceful and quiet here. Soldiers rarely get such a serene place to die. Again, I appear to be the *lucky one*.

None of my body parts are responding to my nervous system. Not being able to move is a very vulnerable feeling, especially behind enemy lines. I push that thought out of my head and focus on my surroundings. White limestone boulders cover the hillside on which I am lying. These beautiful rocks line the beaches of most of the small islands of the Arabian and Red Seas. It would be nice to hear the ocean right now. I cannot think of a better sound to hear when you are dying than waves breaking on boulders. Unfortunately, I am too far inland to hear the soothing sounds of the sea.

5.

DEATH

It is quiet here — so quiet that I can hear each breath as it leaves my lungs. The shots and falling bodies have silenced the birds. I am lying at the base of three Socotra dragon trees. Ironically, their nickname is "dragon blood tree." They get this name from the red sap that runs down their trunks; it is the same color as human blood. Right now, I seem to be competing with the trees to see which of us can turn more of the pale rocks from white to red.

Raindrops begin to fall from the sky. They are lightly misting my face, but thankfully not affecting my vision. They are cool and soothing as they run down my cheeks. A few drops run towards my neck and mix with the blood. I cannot feel them after they reach my neck. If it were not for the rain on my face, I would not be feeling anything right now. The rest of my body is just tingling with what feels like an electric shock. I am not sure if I will get any feeling back before I die.

I am surprised to find myself completely accepting of my fate. Either I am in shock or the Navy has done a fine job of turning me into a piece of military equipment. I do not have time to analyze everything right now, but I am determined to summarize and file the details of this day before I slip into unconsciousness.

From the day I entered active duty, I have found peace by cataloging and permanently filing everything that happens in a 24-hour period. It helps me sleep and keeps me from dragging old baggage into the next day. I credit this habit with keeping me sane for six years lived in various war zones.

For some reason — perhaps the realization that I only have a few minutes to live — I am struggling to shut things down. There is a debate inside my head, and I feel like the third party to a conversation between the two cerebral hemispheres of my brain. The two are battling to control the few thoughts I have left.

The hyperactive right brain, known for processing emotion and self-reflection, is insisting I feel something. It begins the discussion: "You are a war hero, and sometimes heroes get shot. You knew this when you signed on. Be proud you are not dying in vain. You just freed six prisoners of war — well, not of a *war* per se, but a *conflict*. No, that's the wrong word to use with you. Your grandfather was a soldier in what the political machine likes to refer to as the 'Korean Conflict.' When you were a child, he would tell you that he did not spend 18 months trudging through rotting rice fields and dodging bullets to settle a 'pissy little conflict. If your life is on the line, by God, it's a war!'

"You always agree with your grandfather. You admire him. You share his name. When you were a child, your mother told you to feel honored by a name modeled after such a great man. When she wanted to guilt you into accompanying her on the drive to the country to visit her father, she would be sure to mention he could teach you how to be an American war hero. That was a big burden to carry at thirteen.

"In the interest of full disclosure, you weren't actually told you had to carry this burden. There was no discussion of your responsibility to rise to anyone's expectations. Teenage boys just think this way — especially the responsible ones like you. In the early years of your basic training, you told your bunkmates someone should warn the mothers of the world not to drop this kind of 'war hero' info-bomb on a teenager. A simple, 'You are named after your grandfather because you resemble him' or 'You are carrying on a great family heritage' would be enough to get a kid into the car.

"If your mother had not bound you to your grandfather's legacy by giving you his name, you might not be here right now. You might not have felt obligated to join the U.S. Navy. You might not have set our sights on becoming a Navy SEAL. You might not have volunteered for the secret mission in Yemen to free the POWs. And you might not be here dying with a bullet hole in your neck."

I stop the right brain like a judge overseeing my death from a court bench. "Stick to the facts, Mr. Cunningham. I will only warn you once. This is not a theatrical stage laid out for your emotional outbursts."

The emotion packed right brain responds carefully, "I retract that last tirade, Your Honor. As I stated in my opening remarks, 'Grayson, you have received a fatal gunshot wound and are dying. Know that you are dying a war hero.' Your mother will be proud of you. She will not cry when they take the flag from our coffin and place it in her arms; she does not cry in public. 'It just spreads the grief. Heroes detest grief that is spread for their honor.' That is what she told you at your father's funeral when you were only six years old.

"Your grandfather will be proud, too. He will hold your mother's hand as they lower you into the ground. He will salute as the trumpet plays Taps. He will make sure no one labels your final mission as a 'military exercise.' You saved lives today, G-man. May you rest in peace. Your Honor, I rest my case."

I am fighting to control my emotions. I'm not comfortable with emotion in any situation, especially when on duty. I push my feelings deep and open the channel to my left brain where pragmatic logic efficiently settles matters. "Admiral Cunningham, difficult or not, you must face what you did that cost you your life. You knew you were supposed to keep your head down and expect weapons to be aimed at you. The purpose of the bullet on the ground was to end your life. It, and its shooter, did just that. The sniper from the Yemeni tactical team saw you as a threat — a very capable and significant threat — to his mission. He had his sights on you while you had your sights on the guards. He was aware of you, but you were not aware of him. This is the reason he was able to take you out. You deviated from protocol and are paying the ultimate price.

"In your defense, you kept him from succeeding as well. His assignment was to thwart any rescue attempts for the American prisoners. You made your operation a success with a flawless execution of the details on the rocky ledge. You took out the Yemeni guards one by one with a silencer and they fell with six quick shots. Your accuracy and pace did not allow the guards enough time to return significant fire. Your ground team got in, loosed the men from their chains, and are getting them to the chopper the Navy grounded on the Plateau. The Yemeni government is none the wiser — and will not be until after all the Americans are safely back on the ship.

"Sadly, after your successful mission, pride got the better of you. You stood up to scan the area with your binoculars to make sure this was a contained in-and-out job. That is when he hit you. You made the mistake of ruling out a sniper on their side. You did not think anyone could out-do you when it came to rescue missions — certainly not a Yemeni soldier. This is the reason you are dying, my man. Let's pray, for the sake of your honor, that your team does not hold the chopper for you. We will hope they come to the quick conclusion that you have dropped and get out of here fast. Your Honor, I rest my case."

Normally, I thrive on tough love when dished out by the logic of my left brain. It has kept me alive on more than one occasion. Right now, though, it seems pointless to assign blame or to accept criticism. Since I cannot decide which version of my situation serves me better, things will have to go un-filed today.

I can feel the warm air as I struggle to pull it in. It hurts now — just as it did in the training pool. I feel as if I'm breathing through a heavy wet towel draped — no, glued — tightly on my face. It's a blessing that my labored breathing is weakening me. It's keeping my panic in check. The slowing heart rate tells me I am down to my last minute. I feel a few tears pushing their way from my tear ducts. They join the trail of raindrops and blood. This is really the end. For the first time in my life, I am thinking about my death.

For as long as I can remember, I have believed in life after death. I have never doubted there is a Creator behind all of Earth's madness. Raised by a Christian mother who revered the Bible, I spent most childhood Sundays in church. I pray — maybe not as much as I should — but it seems to be a good idea right now. As my grandfather used to say, "Can't hurt; might help."

I see a small ray of sunshine cutting a sharp line from the clouds directly to the limestone near my head. This seems to be a good thing to focus on as I say my final words. I am trying to speak, but my voice is gone. Desperately, I try to mouth the words of my final prayer. My body is refusing to cooperate.

Father, it's me, Grayson. I'm out of time here, but I'm sure you know that. As men go, I'm far from perfect, but I'm sure you know this too. I tried to do you proud today by getting those men home to their families. I hope you don't judge me for killing 133 men in battle. It was the duty I was given - and the one I accepted. Thank you for my family and for my war buddies. I would thank you for love, but the one girl I cared about slipped through my fingers before I could tell her how I felt, and before I could protect her from her fate.

I hope you'll accept me into your Paradise. Take care of my mom and my grandfather. Heck, I am coming there to be sure you do. I don't know what happens next, but I am not in pain — and I am not afraid. I figure that's a good thing – since I only have seconds to live.

MALLOW SHERIDAN

DEMON GAMES I

EPISODE II

LEAD DEMONS
(KALI'S STORY)

MALLOW SHERIDAN

6.

LUCIE

January 4, 2029, Hades, Center Earth

Lucie leans over the brimstone to get a closer look at the image that has just arrived from the surface. She drops her long black fingernails on the sulfur surface one by one. *Click. Click. Click.* "They have the soldier," she says to no one in particular. I am watching the image over my boss's right shoulder but say nothing. Over the years, I have learned not to speak unless asked a direct question. I know the foggy scene will unhinge Lucie and I brace myself for the verbal tirade to come.

Taking a step back and straightening her six-foot, lean figure, Lucie flips her waist-length hair off her shoulders to hang down her back. Today, her hair is fittingly red and full of ringlet curls. She rubs her hands together as is her habit when she is conjuring up evil. She brings them up to rest on the large pillows of her glossed lips, which today, are painted black.

She narrows her eyes, their color morphing from brown to yellow as she clenches her teeth. Her yellow eyes signify hate — and her hate in unparalleled. She sees it as her duty, and privilege, to hate every single creature on Earth. "This soldier, Grayson, is the one they have chosen to lead the mission. They are holding him in the time dimension - hoping we would not notice. Idiots! They should know by now we do not miss the details. The countdown has begun. We must get everyone into position. The strategy is about to change."

Lucie turns to glare at me. "Get the Lead Demons into my chambers immediately! I have seven years to rule the world, and I will not lose a single minute." She pivots on her high-heeled boots revealing the razor-sharp blades that line the back of them. Her tail stretches long behind her as she moves towards the door. Its stinger tip is aglow — ready to strike. She wears a white bodysuit that clings to her perfect form. As I watch her leave, I cannot deny that Lucie is as beautiful as she is evil. Her stunning beauty is something she negotiated before the Great Game began. She also insisted that her Lead Demons be made beautiful as well. The imp demons are the definition of grotesque. It is difficult to look at the hideous creatures.

Stopping at the threshold, she faces me a second time. "Kali, do it now!" This time, the words leave her mouth laced with flames. I bow and quickly slither up the stairs to the Communications Tower. I hate my boss and her demeaning leadership style. For now, there are no options for escaping. Lucie can have me tortured eternally if she is not pleased with my performance. I am not about to be her next victim.

It takes every bit of strength I have, to open the heavy gate that protects the large viewing screens used for communicating with the outside world. The other six Lead Demons are on special assignment on Earth's surface, so I am about to ruin their day by calling them back to the heat and darkness of the core. They will be indignant of course. Not hiding my anger of Lucie's treatment, I slap the six torbernite caps hard to open visual communication. While I wait, I run my fingers back across the caps' surfaces and smile. The size of these torbernite caps makes them toxic enough to kill any human who dared to touch them. It makes me feel powerful to be stronger than mere mortals. My smile disappears when I see the six images of my sister demons before me. I bark out my command, "She wants you in her chambers immediately!"

Their response is typical. Abaddon smirks, Lilith spits in my direction, Valentina gives me the middle finger, Azazel turns her back, Amy triple snaps her fingers in mockery, and Jezebeth voices a sarcastic, "Yes, Your 'Lowness.'" I hate them, too. It is a stiff competition between the seven of us. We are fighting for position and the opportunity to do as much damage as demonly possible on Earth. Since we are bound to the confines of this forsaken place, hate is all we have.

MALLOW SHERIDAN

7.

KALI

I slam furniture into place as I set up the meeting room inside Lucie's chambers. The other Lead Demons will be arriving soon. I huff as I think through Lucie's stupidity for tying up my Lead Demon time to set up a meeting space. In the pecking order of demons, I hold the same rank as the other six who will be attending — which most assuredly proves this task is beneath me. As I shove Lucie's throne into place, I scream at the top of my lungs, "This is a job for an Imp — not a Lead Demon!" No one hears me — and no one cares. Such is my lot in Hades.

Though Lucie hates everyone, I know that she hates me on a whole different level. The hatred began long before the creation of man — and before demons were women. In that space, Lucie was Lucifer, Almighty's highest-ranking angel. He was plotting his revolt against Almighty and hosting a secret meeting in the basement auditorium of the Crystal Castle. The castle was the ideal setting for planning a coup, and for drumming up the support Lucifer needed to pull it off. Almighty built the luxurious residence for His angels and granted us privacy within its walls. He designed us with "free will," and gave us the freedom to discuss any topic without His knowledge. To make this possible, He willfully placed a restriction on His omnipresence.

Taking advantage of the free will agreement, as well as his God-given right to rebel, Lucifer presented the ten reasons why angels could — and should — challenge Almighty's power over them. He also presented the ten reasons why he should be their new leader. As Lucifer was Almighty's favored angel, hearing his plan to overthrow the established leadership sent shock waves through the room.

After three hours of debating and discussing options, the issue was ready for a vote. Lucifer insisted all votes be given orally. I objected but was overruled. Even before this vote, I was aware of Lucifer's longing for power. Some of the angels feared that if Lucifer knew who voted against him, he would retaliate. This put us in a precarious position. Lucifer was asking us to turn our backs on our Creator when, for the most part, we were content with our lives. Some changes might have been nice, but they were not the kinds of changes that required a restructuring of leadership. Almighty had given us the free will we enjoyed. Using the gift against the giver seemed to be a major overstep to me.

On the other hand, Lucifer was popular with his angel peers. He looked out for us. He was our spokesman and had successfully negotiated removable wings, assignment choices, and additional discretionary space within which we could exercise our freedom.

At the time of the revolt, there were twelve billion angels in heaven — separated into twelve groups of one billion each. The twelve groups each sent twelve representatives to the meetings on voting days. One hundred forty-four voting members could attend these closed sessions. On the night of the infamous vote, all 144 voting angels were present. To have a majority for the coup, Lucifer would need seventy-three votes.

Given the room's setup, I would be the last angel to vote before the presenter himself. Though the chances of a tied vote were slim, it was exactly how it played out. The vote was 71-71 when my turn came. If I voted for the revolt, the tally would be 72-71. Lucifer would cast the last affirmative vote needed for him to win. If I voted against the revolt, it would make the tally 71-72. Lucifer would cast the last affirmative vote and push the matter to a tie. Tied votes were tabled indefinitely.

When he observed me hesitating to cast my vote, Lucifer walked to where I was sitting. "What say you, Angel Kali?"

I sat up straight in my chair, took a deep breath, and answered, "With all due respect, Lucifer, your plan is merely a spin of Almighty's. The only difference this change makes for us angels is we would answer to you rather than Him. I think it is too risky. We have no idea how He will respond."

My answer angered Lucifer. "My, my, Angel Kali, I did not peg you as a coward — this is a new layer of you we are seeing. Tell me, why do you call my plan a 'spin'?" I did not respond. I was very aware of Lucifer's volatile temperament. For the first time in the three-hour meeting, Almighty's favored angel began to lose his composure. He turned to walk away from me, but then suddenly spun around in anger and slammed both of his fists down on my desk. Leaning over to place his face within inches of mine, he spit out his question: "Do you have anything else to add?"

It was probably a rhetorical question, but I decided to push through his sarcasm and seize the opportunity to comment openly. "Your plan, like Almighty's, gives little power to the rest of us. In time, the angels who side with you will tire of your leadership and want more power for themselves. When they do, they will exercise *their* free will and cause another revolt. The cycle will continue. Eventually, both sides will be looking for a 'savior' of sorts - and relief from suffering which was largely self-imposed. Why not just meet with Almighty and work through the issues that are causing you to consider challenging His authority?"

Lucifer stood up slowly — all the while keeping his eyes locked on mine. He turned and faced the audience — obviously wanting every angel to hear what he has to say. "I want to thank you, Kali, for having the courage to question my plan. Every leader should have someone like you to challenge him and point out the fallacies within his visions. Though I disagree with the conclusions you have drawn, I respect your candor. You are fearless. I admire this. I would like to keep you close when the revolt ushers in my kingdom. I officially extend you an offer to be one of the Lead Angels in my inner circle. You will be at my side as I lead. You will be the only one who is privy to my everyday activities. What say you?"

I swallowed hard and looked around the room. Every set of eyes was on me. This was the first time I had ever been the center of attention. I felt powerful and relevant, so I accepted his offer. "I am honored by your invitation, and I cast my vote *for* the revolt." The angels applauded. Lucifer smiled as he interlocked my hand in his and raised them high for the cheering crowd. To this very day, I wonder why I gave in so easily.

Within a week of the meeting, I felt regret. I was Lucifer's personal assistant and running senseless errands. To test my loyalty, he insisted I be his second-in-command in the challenge of Almighty. One-third of the angels joined the revolt on that fateful day. We were defeated, banished from Heaven, stripped of our wings, and burdened with animal-like tails. We were sent to inhabit the dark hollow core of Earth. Almighty called the place Sheol. The Greeks named it Hades, which remains unto today.

The Creator downgraded his fallen angels and labeled us as "demons". The eight billion angels who remained in Heaven maintained their male gender. The four billion of us who fell to Earth assumed the female gender. All seemed to be lost, but Lucie was not one for giving up. She promised she would find a way to get us out of Hades. We could only hope this was true.

Centuries later, we banished demons are still living in Earth's horrific core. We spend our days in complete darkness, except for the flicker of the flames and the glow of the lava river. The temperature exceeds 120 degrees in the highest levels and continues to rise as we move closer to the Earth's core. Tempers constantly erupt in this perfect storm of miserable conditions. Lucie pretends she is queen of a kingdom in Hades. She has convinced us she has a special relationship with Almighty and is bargaining for something better. We are desperate, so we play along with her delusion.

Running a kingdom — real or imagined — of four billion inhabitants requires regular meetings with your inner circle. Sometimes Lucie calls an emergency meeting, like this one. When she does, I have the mind-numbing job of preparing the room. This is my punishment for complaining about a room setup in the past. After arriving late to a meeting last year, I made my way to my assigned seat and noticed an Imp had forgotten to put my name on the back of my chair. I looked around to see that all the other demons had their names on their chairs, so I refused to sit down until this was corrected. I interrupted Lucie mid-sentence to draw attention to the oversight.

Lucie's response made it glaringly clear that the only arrogance she would tolerate in Hades was her own. After being interrupted, she silently locked eyes with me and moved in my direction in the snake-like slither she uses when she is about to strike. Her elliptical eyes turned bright yellow as she pressed her face close to mine. All the demons in Hades fear Lucie's yellow eyes. To mentally escape, I closed my eyes tightly and stiffened my body to accept whatever Lucie might do to me to make a point. She slowly pressed the long red fingernail of her left thumb deeply into my windpipe. She wrapped the other four fingers around my neck and sneered. "Look at me!"

I forced my eyes open to a squint. Lucie stared deeply into my eyes searching for the fear she craved. I could not think of anything to say to improve my situation. Even if I could come up with the words, Lucie's fingernail was pressing on my vocal cords making it impossible for me to speak.

After a minute of weakening me by obstructing my breathing, Lucie shifted her weight to her back leg and, with her free hand, slapped me hard across the face. I recoiled in pain. Before I could right myself to respond, Lucie turned and rammed her speared stinger tail into my abdomen. The force knocked me back into the chair that had no name. I doubled over and vomited all over myself. I wanted to strike Lucie — to kill her. I looked around the room at the other demons. No one came to my defense. There is no compassion in Hades.

The Lead Demons snickered as I pushed my hair away from my eyes to peer up at my attacker. I knew this episode was not over. Lucie pulled my hair tight — lifting my head to where she could look me directly in the eyes. "You think you deserve your name on a chair, do you? What makes you think you are even fit to sit in the same room with me? You should be bowing at my feet. You are nothing but what I make you to be.

"Do you think you are better than the Imps? You are nothing more than a gullible demon who fell from glory. Look at you now — cowering before me like a helpless lamb. Know this: Your condition is set. There is no hope here, no bargaining for anything better."

Barely able to breathe or stand, I knew what I had to do to save myself from banishment to eternal punishment. I wiped the vomit off my lips and found enough oxygen to force a whisper, "Please forgive me my lord, I remain your faithful servant."

Lucie released my hair and stood up slowly — vertebrae by vertebrae — uncoiling like a snake until the entirety of her six-foot frame towered over my small and battered one. Watching Lucie rise was like watching a cobra lift to the music of a snake charmer. As part of Lucie's curse in the Garden of Eden, she turns into a black serpent when she is at her most evil. Only by controlling her anger can she stop the embarrassing transformation.

Struggling to avoid turning into a serpent, Lucie took in a long breath and stared down at me in disgust. She began pressing her metal boot deeply into my right foot, increasing pressure until I cried out in pain. With the pressure of the boot restraining my movement, Lucie smirked at me as she belittled my feelings, "A little chair with your name on it doesn't seem so important now, does it?

"I'm not going to banish you, Kali. I am much too busy with the Great Game to stop and look for an untrained Imp to take your place; but since you seem to believe you are the authority on the topic, you will set up the meeting room for the rest of the year." She removed her foot from mine but thrust her spiked boot blade deep into my thigh, drawing blood. The room erupted in jeers.

MALLOW SHERIDAN

8.

DEMONS

Even after a year, the memory of Lucie's attack causes my heart to race. I know I must push the ordeal out of my mind and focus on the six demons making their way to these chambers. Lucie put a condition on my punishment: If I prepare the meeting room perfectly for a year, I will be relieved of this soul-crushing job. Today makes exactly a year. Things must go smoothly.

I run through a mental checklist as I finish moving the furniture into place. The Demons of Privilege will arrive first. Azazel and Lilith are the most arrogant of all the Lead Demons. Azazel, aka "Bug Girl," is the Demon of Insects and Parasites. She rules over the creepy, crawly, and winged insects that inhabit Hades and Earth. She demands a footstool for her ugly feet and then allows her disgusting little bugs to run around the meeting room floor and over the toes of the others. At the last meeting, I took action to stop this nonsense. I set up roach motels around the room. The bugs went in, but they did not come out.

The others laughed when Azazel looked for her pets and found them dead inside the bug traps. She was livid and vowed to get even with me. Every demon knew what this meant. Azazel has all the weird, stinging locust creatures at her beck and call. In the alley after the bug-killing incident, she had one of the four-foot locusts sting me on the bottom as I walked by. Though it hurt for days, I am sure my bug murders were worth the pain.

Lilith, aka "Man Eater," will arrive right behind Azazel. She is the Demon of Relationships. Next to Lucie, Lilith is the most beautiful demon in the underworld. Like Lucie, she uses her looks for evil and often flaunts her knee-length, auburn hair. To meet Lilith's demand that her hair never touch the ground when she sits, I raise her chair five inches higher than the other demons' while also being careful not to raise it higher than Lucie's chair at its usual twelve inches above the others.

When setting up the first meeting for which I was responsible, I purposely placed Lilith's chair higher than Lucie's. Lucie was so angry she lit Lilith's hair on fire with a flaming spear lobbed at her head. Three of the demons laughed so hard they fell out of their own chairs. Lilith had to run down the stone path and dunk her head into the Dark Well to put out the flames. Lilith got me back by snaring my human boyfriend into an affair with one of the Imps.

Lilith, the so-called relationship expert hates all women. For that matter, she hates all men. She claims displacement from the Garden of Eden, telling anyone who will listen she was Adam's first wife. She accuses Adam of being unfaithful to her. Whatever the truth, Lilith's hatred of both Adam and Eve prepared her for the assignment Lucie bestowed upon her — destroying relationships.

Lilith has a great record of ruining marriages throughout the centuries, and her power is just beginning to spike. She beams with smugness when she tells the others how the Millennial generation mocks the notion of true love. She says they are becoming addicted to easy thrills such as pornography, prostitution, and affairs. Though Millennials are not shying from marriage and the traditional roles of spouses, neither sex seems willing to be faithful.

Lilith believes modern women just want "equal rights to cheat." She is well-versed — and opinionated — on the sexes. One of her most persistent beliefs is that demons are better off in female form. According to her assessment, men are gullible, selfish, and inept at reading emotions. They do not master attributes ideal for winning wars. She finds women to be manipulators, instinctive, and driven by raw emotion — all attributes that are perfect for winning wars. With the Great Game's ultimate war looming, Lilith's observations have never been more relevant. The other demons are beginning to tune in to her rants.

The next to arrive will be the Demons of the Flesh — Valentina and Amy. Valentina, aka "Sewer Girl," is the Demon of Water. She rules the planet's water supplies. Over the years, she has been slowly increasing the pollution levels in the waters of Earth by bleeding chemicals and human waste into lakes and streams. She recruited greedy men to help her reroute water from villages in Third World countries. At times, she bursts dams after rain waters put them at capacity. Her manipulation of water has caused hundreds of thousands of deaths. She gloats when people in Third World countries die from lack of clean water.

Valentina also takes pleasure in seeing homeowners lose everything they own. "Serves them right for building in a flood plain or near oceans. Let them wallow in self-pity as they fill out their insurance claims." She mocks the wealthy for spending their disposable cash on bottled water. "They spend a small fortune because they fear Earth's water resources are full of pollutants and disease carrying parasites - and they are right." Water will be weaponized in the upcoming Great War — and she will be at the center of it all.

Sewer girl insists on having two bottles of spring water by her seat. When the other Lead Demons complain about the temperature of Hades, Valentina hydrates herself and lectures then on the benefits of sweating. She fancies herself the healthy one — reason enough for the rest of us to despise her.

I do not know why I hate Valentina as much as I do, but you do not need a reason to hate in Hades – in fact, it is expected. To spite Valentina, I routinely fill her porcelain bottles with human toilet water I bring back from Earth. I re-cap the bottles, wipe the rims, and place them by Valentina's chair. Each time I see the water demon take a sip of toilet waste I must cover my mouth to muffle my laugh.

Amy, aka "Corpse," will arrive next. She is the Demon of Disease and is responsible for every illness known to man and animal. Amy's ashy skin and pale eyes make her appear as if she could die at any moment. Her weakened state is the result of the curses and hate lobbed into the universe by people who are angry about their illness - or that of a loved one.

If they knew the entire story, the people of Earth would — and will — hate Amy more than they already do. The demons know that Almighty put cures on the Earth for every illness man would ever know. Amy hid the ones that grow outside of Eden. She moved some of them to the deserts, some to the rainforests, and many to the bottom of the oceans by relocating spores and buds. Her disguises and redirects have worked well. Man has a habit of giving up just before he is about to succeed. He came close to finding the cure for AIDS but found the lucrative market of treating the symptoms too tempting to resist. Many cures for the illnesses of man are in the Garden of Eden. Almighty vowed to open Eden, and its cures, if the nations could establish peace. That day never came.

Even when scientists discover a cure that exists outside of Eden, Amy participates with the physicians, insurance companies, and sponsoring drug companies to keep the cures under wraps – at least until profits are tapped out. They all know it takes time and patience to lure the highest bidder. Millions of people have died needlessly because of the apathy and greed she encourages.

In her weakened condition, Amy is often sick herself. I put out the Kleenex and antibacterial gel that she requests, but sneeze and spit all over her chair - spreading mucus where she is most likely to rest her hands. Amy's illnesses are a continual source of humor for the Lead Demons and we do all we can to aggravate her condition.

Finally, the gruesome Demons of Greed will arrive – Abaddon and Jezebeth. Abaddon rules War and Jezebeth rules wealth. Abaddon's job is to make men hate each other to the point of extracting blood, earning her the nickname of "Vampire." She is the busiest of the demons and expects to be seated front and center. Instead of voicing any opinion, she will just thump her tail when she disagrees or is bored. Lucie cuddles Abaddon because of the damage she does on the surface. Since she began ruling war, Earth has not known a single day of peace. The more trivial the reason life is taken, the greater Abaddon's satisfaction.

The last to arrive will be the very spoiled — and very curvy — Jezebeth, aka "Fat Brat." She demands her chair be made of gold and decorated with rubies. The inside joke is that her chair is appley made of nothing more than iron pyrite, "fool's gold". She insists that a mirror be placed in front of her so she can attend to her primping while others are speaking. Vanity is her motivator. For every evil deed of man discussed in the meetings, Jezebeth finds a way to tie it to the pursuit of wealth and demands to be in charge. Since she rarely loses the argument that the misery of man originates with his love of money, she is charge of a lot of stuff.

One of her wins in the last century set Jezebeth apart from the rest of us. She won praise for her original work of increasing the wealth of the greedy while limiting the wealth of the compassionate. In her opening argument, she hypothesized that, by manipulating wealth, Lucie could keep the riches of Earth in the hands of those who could purposely collapse the economies of the world — in other words, the greedy. "Poverty limits the acts of charity that can be done by the sympathetic. This would prevent the good people of Earth from receiving the blessings that come naturally by helping their fellow man."

The instant she heard the idea, Lucie was on board. Up until that time, most of the wealth on Earth belonged to the righteous and the compassionate. Jezebeth's idea would completely reverse the distribution of wealth. Of course, a big change like this would affect the Great Game and had to be approved by Almighty.

Lucie took the idea to Him immediately. She was able to negotiate the use of this new "manipulated wealth" tactic in exchange for giving Almighty access to one of the nations under her control. The Asian nation she offered up as a trade had blocked religious freedom a century earlier. The people of this nation had a long history of evil. They starved their elderly citizens to death once they concluded they had little left to contribute. They buried their newborn girls alive if a boy had been preferred. She was convinced they had gone too deeply into sin to return to Almighty, so she felt good about the trade.

Lucie held a victory party after Almighty accepted the deal. She considers herself the winner of most of her negotiations with Almighty. Her secret weapon has been exploiting His weak spot. Lucie knows He will give away almost anything to spare the souls of a few wayward men. She does not understand Almighty's tactics, and she does not need to. She just needs to continue with her winning strategy.

After I finish setting up the room for the others, I set up a chair for myself. Per Lucie's orders, I sit behind the others. The back of the room is fitting for my demon assignment. I rule depression, anxiety, and low self-esteem — all things on the rise as the Great War draws near. Only Abaddon is seeing more of an increase in devastation on Earth than am I. It is only a matter of time until Lucie acknowledges my contributions.

My "crowning glory" right now is the spike in teen suicides. I can manipulate these young people to move from personal pain and rejection to complete hopelessness. From there, it does not take much to convince them to kill themselves with a gun, a rope, or the new drugs that are popular on Earth, heroine and fentanyl.

Getting someone to commit suicide on Earth is cause for celebration in Hades – especially when they are young and have their lives cut short. People who purposely take their own lives must go through three days of living in isolation on the banks of the Lake of Fire. After the third day, they are sent to their final home. Some are picked up by angels while others are dragged away by demons. The three days are set for them to think through the value of life. Almighty does not take suicide lightly. He finds it to be an affront to his gift of life. Just as he turned his back on Jesus while He was in Hades paying for the sins of man, He turns His back on those who take their own lives. Lucie loves to taunt these tortured souls when she has the spare time to cross over the Lake of Fire where they are kept for their short, albeit horrifying, visit.

Kali also finds fertile ground for suicide in the older Millennial generation born between 1983-1996 A.D. Unprepared for the real world by their overbearing parents, Millennials are disillusioned. Their parents gave them everything they desired as children and teenagers — the most damaging of which was freedom without supervision. Now that they are adults, the giving has stopped. Most of them have hit a wall. The opportunities they believed were promised, are not materializing.

Millennials are opportunists and are specifically designed to seek power. They want the opportunities they believe others are enjoying — and they want them now. The catch is, most of them secretly fear they cannot measure up to the people who, according to their social media profiles, have it all. I am aware that excessive interaction with social media leads to low self-esteem, depression, and (my personal favorite) suicide. I use social media to my advantage.

I also find an endless supply of Christians who struggle with low self-esteem. They are forever singing what I refer to as "blood and unworthy" songs. It is no wonder so many of them live a life of ineffectiveness, full of judgment and gossip. From what I know about Almighty, I am sure He prefers His followers to be happy and singing praises to Him — not wallowing in self-pity. Humans think they are being selfless when they carry on this way. In truth, nothing could be more self-centered.

The good news for me is that these habits keep non-believers from wanting anything to do with Christianity. I smile as I push my chair into the last position.

MALLOW SHERIDAN

9.

TACTICS

The Lead Demons arrive promptly, in the exact order I predicted. Everyone takes their seat. We do not have to wait for Lucie - she knows the value of a minute and is never late. At the exact top of the hour, she appears in a blast of smoke and lightning. The theatrics have grown old for us. Abaddon yawns on purpose; her lack of respect is ignored.

Lucie likes to begin her meetings seated on her throne. Today is no exception. Once the smoke disappears, she steps down and paces the floor in front of the Lead Demons, eyeing each one of us with disdain. She uses an eerie silence to command our attention for the fiery speech she has prepared.

From the back of the room, I envy the blood-red bodysuit that Lucie is wearing. It is her ultimate power suit. Today, her hair is as black as the coal on the wall behind her and as straight as the pitchfork she is carrying. Her heavy bangs just brush the top of her piercing emerald eyes. Lucie usually chooses emerald eyes to go with her red suit. She has designed her three distinct looks to demand attention — and to send specific messages. The red suit signifies power, the black suit signifies innocence, and the white one signifies challenge.

Any hope that the great beauty pacing in front of us is here to spread goodwill evaporates the second she opens her mouth. Lucifer's personal insults and vain overtones can bring out the evil in any man – or demon. This is not to say Lucie does not know how to turn on the charm. On the contrary, she is the queen of charm if she needs it to get her way. Since demons cannot come close to understanding the art of manipulation as she does, she must personally go to Earth to handle the details of these final seven years.

I take a quick look around the room and think to myself, *"We are all here because we were deceived by Lucie's charm when she ruled over us in Heaven. Being cast out of Paradise to live in these God-forsaken chambers in Center Earth is only one of many reasons to hate her — but it is the main one."*

"You should know why you are here," Lucie snaps. "If you do not, you have taken your focus off winning the Great Game and have forgotten the future for which we are all fighting. Together, we saw through the self-righteous, delusional One Who calls Himself 'Almighty.' He tried to keep all the glory and credit for Himself. We decided this was not good enough for us.

"We challenged Almighty knowing it could cost us our residence in Paradise. We may have lost the battle, but we have not lost the war. We will not surrender. We have every right to be proud. We made Hades into a basecamp to run our operations against man. Almighty underestimated our resilience — and my ability to negotiate. Every time I entangled His children in sin, 'His Highness' met me at the negotiation table to offer a concession.

"I am pleased to announce that His 'chosen ones' are failing Him yet again. He knows He is losing rounds in the Great Game because of His bleeding heart for humans, and yet He will not abandon them. The reckless love He has for these pathetic creatures set us up for a much-deserved seven-year reign on Earth. Many of you have been anticipating this for centuries — and it begins at midnight!"

Lucie puckers her bone-white lips and pauses for effect. This time, every demon in the room gives her their full attention. Azazel gathers her bug pets under her chair and captures them in her empty water glass. Lilith drops her hair, mid-braid, allowing it to fall behind her back. Valentina puts down her bottle of toilet water and pats her lips dry with the sleeve of her gown. Amy clears her throat and folds up a fresh Kleenex as if making herself a security blanket. Abaddon mumbles an "about time" under her breath and rolls her eyes. Jezebeth pushes her mirror to the side where it no longer blocks her view.

Even though I know what Lucie is about to share, I uncross my legs and sit up straight. Like the others, I am eager to receive my assignment. Since the day we pledged our allegiance to Lucie in the Great Revolt, we have eagerly waited for her to honor the promise of reigning on Earth. Like the other demons, I have an innate jealousy of humans. I blame them for stealing Almighty's attention from us and for prolonging the Great Game with their constant theatrics. Like my fellow demons, I am eager to settle the score with man.

Lucie picks up a remote and drops a 3D hologram square from the rafters. She likes to narrate her stories with accusations and over-the-top theatrics. She usually begins her sermons with the creation of Earth — or at least with the Garden of Eden. Watching Eve take that bite of the forbidden fruit and then enticing Adam into her scheme is Lucie's favorite scene. The Lead Demons have been forced to watch it hundreds of times.

Surprisingly, today's presentation starts much later in time. The first image Lucie conjures up is of Noah and his family as they take up residence in the ark. "Behold, I won this round of the Great Game. I was able to lead men to such depths of evil that their Creator sentenced them to death. He never explained why he let things get to the point where He felt his only option was to commit these detestable acts. He only spared this one simple-minded man and his seven family members. He let the rest of His children drown. 'His Highness' was so out-of-control, he killed the innocent animals He had created — despicable, to say the least.

"The only exception to Almighty's 'animal massacre' was two of each species He had Noah put into the ark. According to Him, the purpose of these animals was to repopulate the planet after the flood forever changed the terrain. Does anyone else see the flaw in this logic?

Instead of making new animals — ones better suited to survive on the new Earth and not go extinct. Almighty went through all this trouble to spare these few. If it had only been Noah and his family that needed to be protected from the flood, the boat could have been a whole lot smaller."

I see the humor in the situation, and giggle. The other demons turn and stare in my direction. Lucie pretends not to notice. Instead, she changes the 3D image to the beheading of the apostle, Paul. This immediately puts me back into a serious state of mind. I have a soft spot for Paul, and Lucie knows it. This is the reason she demanded that I attend his beheading. The experience still haunts me.

When I was first assigned to Paul, he went by the name of Saul and had a much different purpose. He was a killer of Christians. Demons are sent to Earth's surface to promote hate, or to undermine love. I was sent to help Saul persecute Christians. Things are much simpler when humans sell their souls to Lucie for protection and power. Saul was given the option by Lucie herself, but he would not take the deal. To keep an eye on him, Lucie had me to dress in the garments of a man and follow Saul in physical form.

I was with him when his life drastically changed right before my eyes. He was on the way to the religious leaders in Damascus to deliver a letter giving them permission to arrest anyone who self-identified as "Christian." At the halfway point of the journey, something happened that still baffles me - and Lucie.

A bright light came down from the sky and shone directly on Saul. It was so bright it burned the area around him. I had to move back to watch from a safe distance. Saul held his hands over his eyes as he looked towards the light and started answering questions as if he were talking to someone. It seemed to me that he was addressing Jesus — the self-proclaimed Messiah put to death years earlier.

When the light diminished and the conversation ended, Saul's eyesight was gone. His men led him to Damascus by the hand. A holy man of the city named Ananias came to Saul, placed his hands upon his eyes, and pleaded with Almighty to restore his sight. Once Saul could see again, he had a spiritual enlightenment. He announced that he was changing his name to Paul and proclaimed that the man crucified on Mount Golgotha had indeed been the Messiah. He established the biggest churches in Asia. Even while he was imprisoned for his teachings, he wrote letters of encouragement and guidance and sent them to these churches by messenger. Most of these letters were later included in the Christian Bible.

I continued to follow Paul, but my assignment was not the same. Instead of supporting Saul's harassment of Christians, I was trying to destroy Paul's new popularity with them. It was surreal. As hard as I tried to hinder him, Paul was too mentally strong for me. I was failing, so I was called back to Hades and placed in isolation as punishment. I was released from isolation for the beheading. Lucie knows the whole thing still upsets me and makes a point of taunting me about Paul.

While I am adrift with my thoughts, Lucie slips up behind me and pokes me with her pitchfork. I jump to attention as the center spike pierces my side. She continues with her rant. "My superior tactics through the ages have caused 'Mr. Infallible' to commit heinous acts against man, animals, and the environment. I won in the Garden of Eden by enticing Adam and Eve into sin, and I won when every disciple was put to death. I will win again, and I assure you, I will ultimately win the Great Game.

"Tomorrow, when man awakes, we will begin our reign on Earth. After seven well-executed years, I will be victorious. We will destroy all that is good, including the plants and animals on which man relies. He will find out much too late that these are the very things sustaining him. After turning his heart against his Creator and earning his trust in the first three and one-half years, I will turn on man. I will be his master, and I will show him no mercy."

The third hologram Lucie displays is an even more interesting choice. She plays the conversation she had with Jesus in the wilderness after He had fasted for forty days. "Watch carefully. This part of Almighty — the humanized part He sent to Earth — proves men of flesh and blood *can* resist demonic powers. They *are* strong enough to rise above ego, selfishness, and even physical pain.

"Jesus was starving and weak, but when I dared Him to prove He was the Son of God by commanding the stones to become bread, He would not do it. When I dared Him to prove He was the Son of God by throwing Himself off a cliff and allowing the angels to save Him, He would not do it. When I offered to give Him the kingdoms of Earth I had under my control if He would worship me, He would not do it. He just gave me self-righteous answers and quoted the Scriptures — even though He could barely stand. He eventually cast me out of the desert and called on the inferior angels of Heaven to care for Him.

"We know that man is weak and easily manipulated, but when he has a personal relationship with Almighty through prayer, he is difficult to control. He is as unflappable as Jesus was in the wilderness. I do not have to tell you the magnitude of this threat. Man can never know the truth of his own power. We are going to bring him to his knees before he realizes he can triumph over us by simply fleeing from sin. I want every single man, woman, and child living in increasing misery until they blame Almighty for their pain. Do whatever it takes to confuse man and to break his bond with Almighty. Tomorrow, when the sun rises in the East, all shackles on our power will be removed. Evil will be in full play.

"But know this: If you fail me in these next seven years, I will banish you to the darkest part of Hades where Azazel's worms will crawl on your flesh for eternity. There will not be a single drop of Valentina's stench-filled water to satisfy your parched tongue. Do you understand me?" Lucie stops her pacing to glare at each of her Lead Demons one by one. When her eyes connect with mine, I sense her complete hatred of me. It is as if my insides are being set afire.

After Lucie receives her symbol of obedience from us (a forehead tilted down onto the forearm), she swings her tail around and slams the stinging tip on the ground to reset the tone. "Each one of you must go and inform the Imps under your control that we are preparing to rule on Earth. Tell them we are beginning the final chapter of the Great Game. Have everyone in the stadium in exactly six hours for the unveiling of the details of my seven-year plan. Chains await any demon not in attendance."

Lucie heads for the exit of her chamber but stops to speak once again. Without turning around, she barks out a command, "Jezebeth clean up this mess! From now on you will set up the meeting room; you look like you could use the exercise. Kali, you are coming with me. We are going to visit the Big Man Himself. It is time for me to gloat. I also need to know where He hid the Keys of Death and Hades. The word on the streets is that the soldier will be leading a posse from Heaven to rescue the Keys. The timing is critical. Now, move!"

MALLOW SHERIDAN

10.

ALMIGHTY

Lucie and I step through the fog into the Holy Atrium. My body begins to shake as soon as my black boots touch down on the gold floors. I hate coming here because of my tremendous sense of guilt - and because of Lucie's outrageous behavior in front of Almighty. Lucie, on the other hand, enjoys gloating over the human failures that allow her to manipulate the conditions of the Great Game.

I know that Lucie just drags me along to have a witness and to rub my nose in the bad decisions of my past.

Lucie does her usual glance around to see if anything has changed. She catches a glimpse of herself in one of the many mirrors that line the walls and stops to admire her look. Lucie believes her wavy blond hair and blue eyes are the right choice for meeting with Almighty. The innocent appeal of her light blue eyes and pink lips, conflicts with her uncompromising black bodysuit. She likes to play the victim with the hosts of Heaven. Since she cannot create more demons, she is always open to recruiting angels.

The crystal candelabras are still in perfect condition. Lucie sneers at the contradiction. "Almighty created this ostentatious paradise for Himself, and yet most of His naive followers live in humble means on Earth." Once again, Lucie speaks to no one in particular, and I am not going to jump into a conversation with her.

It amazes Lucie that Almighty continues to grow his "harem of humans" while giving them so little. "The people of Earth are about to found out just how selfish their Creator has been. Surely, there must be one of His followers intelligent enough to call foul on all of this. Then again, the followers of Almighty are gullible. They live by 'faith'." Lucie cannot help but roll her eyes every time she says that word. As she sees it, "faith is an empty ideology that allows organized religion to control and collect money from simpletons."

I know from my time on the surface that Almighty's followers *do* subscribe to faith; believing that something good is just around the corner. Lucie hates anything she cannot understand. "They pray for relief from poverty, addiction, bad health, loneliness, and destructive relationships. When relief does not come, they reason it away as 'not being Almighty's will for their lives'. It is total, albeit highly effective, rubbish!" I agree but keep my thoughts to herself. I doubt that Lucie is interested in what I have to say anyway.

"When I come into my rightful reign, I will shower my followers with all the riches the world has to offer. Any celebrity in the world can tell you if you do not own things others cannot afford, they will not worship you. Yes, I will do things differently — and man will flock to me because of it. I will charm him into servitude, and I will buy his loyalty." Kali rolls her eyes behind Lucie's back. This leader of the demons hoards possessions she brings back to Hades from the surface, commissions the imps to build things that are for her use only, and funnels the few blasts of cool air they are able to pull in from the surface – directly into her private chambers. Man will see nothing from Lucie unless he sells her his soul.

Lucie's daydreaming ends when the room fills with a thunderous sound and a blinding light – both signs that Almighty is approaching. Lucie stands defiant. She refuses to sit, fall to her knees, close her eyes, or even bow her head. If she is the only one brave enough to stand up to Almighty, then so be it. I shuffle behind Lucie in hopes of not being seen. I fear both Almighty and Lucie. At times, I feel as if I am caught between the two.

There is never a solid figure for us to see. Almighty has never been contained in one. We have only known Him in Spirit. Though she sometimes wishes she could look Him in the eye, Lucie knows it will never happen. She agreed to speak with His Spirit when she signed off on the terms of the Great Game. We talk to a sphere of light.

Almighty is the first to speak. "Welcome to my home, Lucifer."

"You know I do not like to be called Lucifer. Let us stay with Lucie if it is all the same to you."

"I named you Lucifer — the Bearer of Light — and I shall continue to call you by that name. Greetings, Kali." I step out slightly from behind Lucie's back and offer a slight tip of my head to the Spirit of Almighty. "The two of you have come because your seven-year reign is imminent. What else brings you here?"

"Kali is just here to keep you honest. I came for the keys you have hidden from me. Surely, you would not want your beloved servants to know you purposely kept the Keys of Death and Hades out of my grasp. What would they think of your integrity? More importantly, what will they think of your gift of free will? How can you prove to them they have control over their own destinies if you hide the very keys that lock away those who exercise their free will against you?"

"Ah, Lucifer, you have always held the card for 'Twisted Logic'. You use it well, but I am not accepting your invitation to banter. Nonetheless, I will give you ample information to find the keys. You will fail to retrieve them, but the saints will be blameless for withholding information."

"Ha! As is if the saints could have information to which I am not privy."

"There was a time when the saints hid the whereabouts of the infant, Jesus. You directed King Herod to murder all the male children younger than two years of age in hopes of killing the Messiah and thwarting my plan. All the while, the Child was in Egypt. Do you deny you could not find the blessed baby?"

"I did not know we were going to reminisce today. I hope you can forgive me for my lack of preparedness. This will have to wait until another time. Circling back to the reason I am here — where are the Keys? Your own words bind You to tell me. Answer me! What say You?"

"The keys are but symbolic, Lucifer. The sealed doors of Hades will protect my children. No one will be able to cross the barrier I will build. Once you are locked away in the Pit of Hell, you will be punished for the evil and pain you have inflicted upon mankind."

"Once again You digress. The ending is not yet set. I am Your most worthy opponent, and I intend to win the Great Game. It is true the keys are only symbolic, but they are required for locking me away for the thousand years. You are bound to keep the conditions we negotiated. The contract so stipulates.

"Furthermore, this is not the first time you have given power to an inanimate object. You pride Yourself on symbolic tokens, like the Staff of Moses and the Ten Commandment Tablets.... Ah, I know the location of the keys. You placed them in Ark of the Covenant with these other trinkets. Answer me honestly."

"You have spoken the truth. The Keys of Death and Hades *are* in the Ark of the Covenant. The location of the Holy Ark is still unknown to man. I cannot tell you more than man can know."

"Of course, Almighty will not deviate from the rules. Your words suggest You have told one of your minions that the keys are in the Ark of the Covenant. Perhaps a soldier named Grayson? Tell me, does he know the location of the Ark?"

"He knows to search in the land of my people."

"Israel? An interesting choice, and the perfect location for beginning my reign. I ask Almighty's permission to leave the Holy Atrium."

"Granted. Lucifer...expect a battle for the keys."

"I live for battles. You are the one Who backs down from them. What say You?"

The bright light makes a spectacular show as it spirals from the room and exits above. The last words spoken by Almighty come as the room goes dark, "Be gone."

DEMON GAMES I

EPISODE III

DESIGNER BABY
(KALI'S STORY)

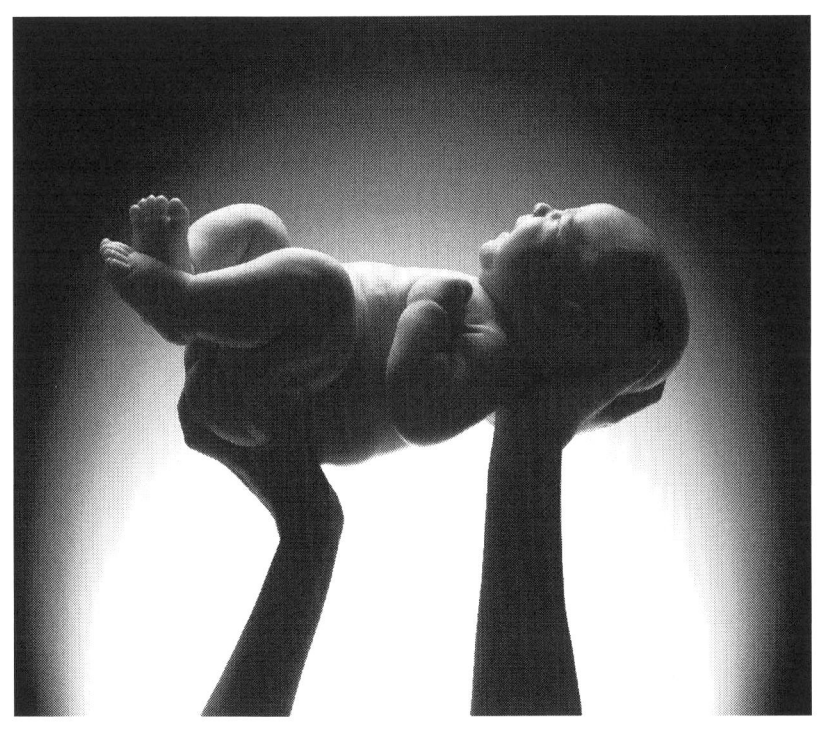

MALLOW SHERIDAN

11.

COHENS

June 16, 1985, Astoria, New York

Enoch Cohen and Sarah Friedman caught Lucie's attention soon after they met. She was quick to choose them for a special task. The two became a Jewish power couple shortly after meeting on the campus of Harvard Law School in 1981. They were both nearing the end of their first year and were competing against each other for the coveted position of Sophomore Class President. They were also vying for the same position on the staff of the *Harvard Review*, a well-respected law journal produced monthly by the Harvard Law students. Sara won the election as well as the editing position.

During the class presidential campaign, Enoch became enamored of Sarah. He crashed her victory party just to ask her out. Sarah laughed when he got down on one knee to extend the invitation. She knew if she said yes to him that night, she would say yes to him for the rest of her life. They married in the summer of 1985 — one year after they both graduated with their law degrees.

Enoch's hometown of Astoria, New York was the site of their traditional wedding ceremony. Guests of both the bride and groom traveled from Israel for the grand event. Sarah's family was from Jerusalem; Enoch's family was from Nazareth. Both families approved of the union.

As their plane lifted off the next morning for their honeymoon in Egypt, Enoch held Sarah's hand. He told her they would build a life together that would change the world. He was not sure what it would look like, but with two law degrees between them, and a sizable dowry from Sarah's family, the possibilities seemed endless.

Lucie knew that Enoch was right. The couple was going to change the world, and she was going to make it so.

12.

BENCHMARKS

August 1, 1995, Astoria, New York

Enoch smiles at Sarah across the dinner table. The candlelight reflects in her brown eyes. As usual, he seems to admire her timeless beauty. Lucie and I hover over their dinner table and Lucie begins to tell me their story. "She is everything he ever dreamed of in a wife. She is beautiful, kind, and intelligent. She graduated at the top of her class at Harvard Law and is one of only two women ever promoted to Managing Editor of the *Harvard Review*. Now she is a highly regarded patent attorney with aspirations of building her own company.

"Enoch is a man who has always wanted an intelligent and strong-willed woman to share his life. He knows Sarah will keep things exciting. For his part, Enoch is a traditional Jewish man who takes seriously the expectations of pushing to the top of his career as well as building a great life for his wife.

"From the beginning of their marriage, Enoch and Sarah have made it a point to set benchmarks for their lives together. They set their first-year goals one week after their wedding. They decided to reassess the goals each year on Enoch's birthday, August 1. Tonight's dinner is to celebrate his thirty-second birthday. The dinner of sea bass and kosher wine is in keeping with their tradition. The chocolate soufflé is ordered. Now is the time for them to talk benchmarks.

"Enoch is probably feeling good about his birthday. He is on target with most of his goals. In addition to having the ideal wife, he is up for partner with his law firm - Shapiro, Goldberg, and Murdock. The firm helps Wall Street companies with an array of employee law matters. Enoch finds himself drawn to cases that pit corporate America against the government. He specializes in regulatory issues and Human Resource Law which are the fastest growing areas of business law.

"Representing clients with employer-employee issues connects Enoch closely to U.S. Representatives and Senators. These connections spiked his interest in running for public office. He started by running for the local school board in 1988. With Enoch not being a parent yet, Sarah was sure to join him on stage as much as possible to project a united couple image. When on stage with her husband, Sarah made sure to spotlight her work with children in Third World nations.

"Enoch narrowly won the election. As he neared the end of his term in 1990, he ran for New York's 12th Congressional District. Again, he faced some tough odds coming from the small town of Astoria in the borough of Queens. At the time, the town had a population of less than 80,000 people. Sarah helped her husband secure the 3,000 signatures necessary to be on the ballot. Together, they built a platform on the integration of personal responsibility with business and community responsibility.

"From the beginning of his political career, Enoch has been passionate about local community development. He is a Jewish man living in a community with a small Jewish presence. Astoria is not exactly a thriving hub of Jewish life. By itself, this is not a bad thing; he does not want his family to live in a culturally uniform neighborhood. Even so, when he and Sarah leave from an evening at the Astoria Center of Israel, they feel isolated from community by the time they pull into their driveway just ten blocks away.

"Enoch is also passionate about the role local businesses play in the stability and growth of a community. He campaigned with a triangle model of community, local business, and federal government. Since he was a Jewish man running on the Republican ticket in a strongly Democratic district, the contradiction garnered him some valuable press. He won with a margin of less than one percent. Truth be told, I gave him the win. It was not the first time I have helped a political candidate who fit within my plans and pushed my agendas.

"Enoch put his position at the law firm on hold to move to Washington, D.C. with Sarah. Though he can no longer accept new cases, he still consults with his long-term clients. Mostly, he wants to hold onto his position at the law firm in case the U.S. Representative gig goes under. To his surprise, he enjoys almost every aspect of his new role. He is a junior member of the Foreign Affairs Committee, keeping him connected to his passion of international policy.

"Lately, the committee's focus has been upon empowering women in the rapidly developing Third World. Not only does this objective line up with his community, business, and federal government model; it also resonates with Sarah's passion for helping women and children living in Third World nations.

"Enoch consulted with his wife on the topic, and she set him straight on the issue from a woman's perspective. When he addressed the next Foreign Affairs Committee meeting, he took a stand for the women of the world. He told the members women were ready for men to 'remove their hands from legislation meant to empower them. After all, men were the ones who disempowered them in the first place'. He suggested that the female members of the committee have full control over the direction of the Women's International Empowerment (WIE) bill.

"After his passionate speech, the silence in the room was deafening — until Enoch took his seat. Then, the female Representatives got to their feet, one by one, giving him a standing ovation. The men joined in as well.

"When presented to the entire House of Representatives, the WIE bill created enthusiasm on the floor. Enoch would not accept any credit for the success of the legislation. Instead, he gave it all to his wife. Sarah was proud of her husband. This simple act proved to her that *this* politician 'gets it'.

"Even though she was in the middle of leaving her law firm to start her own business, this development increased Sarah's visibility and role in her husband's political career. After the WIE bill passed, Enoch's popularity soared with both men and women. Once again, he affirmed that his success was largely due to his partnership with his wife."

Lucie, who has been levitating with her face to the sky, turns back over to look at the couple. "You know what he is doing now? He is running through the options of how best to open a new topic with Sarah. She will play the bigger role in this one, and he needs her to be completely on board if there is even a slim chance of its success.

"He is a planner; she is a risk taker. She is the one who puts the joint ventures into action. Before meeting her, Enoch believed that impulsiveness was the product of a lazy mind. He would quote to her, 'The early bird might get the worm, but the second mouse gets the cheese.' Sarah showed him how hesitation is just as likely to cause an unfavorable outcome as haste. These days, he lays out a plan, and she offers feedback. Ultimately, they agree that she will be the one to pull the trigger on any new venture. Between the two of them, she is the one with the raw nerve for it. I need to get into her head to get her to play along. I am going to use him to do it. Pay attention, Kali, you about to learn a few things."

13.

IDEA

Sarah tips her head to lock eyes with her husband. "Enoch, I can see there is something important going on in that beautiful head of yours. You have not looked at me since you order the soufflé. The last time you had this much trouble getting something out, I ended up agreeing to be your wife — and look how that turned out."

Enoch gives her a slight smile.

"Whatever it is," continues Sarah, "I promise to listen with an open mind. Unless you are leaving me, in which case I will hold my reply until the soufflé arrives hot from the oven so that I can toss it into your lap." She grins.

Enoch chuckles. He reaches for her hands and interlocks his fingers with hers.

Sarah does a *bit* on their finger interlock. "Here is the synagogue, here is the steeple, open the door and there are no people." She grins again.

"Synagogues do not have steeples, Sarah."

"Jewish technicality," she retorts.

"Indeed, it is. And, as everyone knows, Jewish technicalities get thrown out of court."

Sarah laughs. "Well, then, I guess it will be just you and me. What is bugging you, E-rock?"

Enoch takes this spot to jump in. "Sarah, I have been thinking it is time for us to start a family."

Sarah opens her mouth but says nothing. She loosens her grip on his fingers.

"Please hear me out. It does not have to be a large family. Perhaps, just one beautiful child for us to love, share, and enjoy in our twilight years. I know you have been resistant to starting a family. I know you think there are already too many children in the world. But, these things aside, I would like to open the discussion of having a child — one who could change the world."

Lucie elbows Kali and whispers, "Yes, the baby will change the world, and I am going to control her." Lucie laughs.

Sarah pushes back in her chair and drops her hands into her lap. She stares down at her wedding band. Lucie starts to narrate again. "She knew this was going to come up at some point in their marriage. It is the natural circle of life — to which few women object. She does not object, per se; she just cannot imagine how it could work. She likes her job. She is just starting a company she believes will raise the standard of living for the children who already exist. She does not see how she can keep the momentum going if she stops to mother a child."

Sarah lifts her chin to look at her husband. "Enoch, I cannot answer right now. You have obviously had some time to think this through, and I will need some time as well."

Enoch clears his throat and pulls his chair closer to the table. "Watch, he will not go to her side of the table to console her, as he usually does. What he is about to ask of her requires an analytical approach and carefully selected words. Even though he has practiced his argument a few times, I am not surprised that he cannot find the right words to get started. This one is a doozie."

After observing her husband's uncomfortableness for a minute, Sarah pulls her napkin from her lap and pats the corners of her mouth. She summons the waiter and tells him to add the dinner to their account and to give their dessert to the young couple seated next to them. She stands up and puts out her hand to Enoch.

He stands and takes hold.

They walk to the car in silence.

Enoch opens the car door for his wife.

She puts her hand on his chest. "Let's go to our spot. What do you say?" Enoch gives her a nod.

"Get in the car, Kali. We are going with them to their spot. It is in Forest Hills on a ledge that overlooks Soapstone Valley. They found it while exploring the city on their first date after moving to Washington, D.C. The babbling Rock Creek that runs through the valley soothed their new city jitters. They return there when either of them feels overwhelmed by their career. Though Enoch agreed to the location, I think he is wondering if the romantic spot will be the right setting for this discussion. I have no worries. The location is just a tiny detail."

Once he pulls into the parking area and turns off the car engine, Enoch dives right into the conversation. "Sarah, I have been speaking with my friend, Steven Abbott. You might remember me talking about him — a brilliant scientist at M.I.T. He graduated with his degree in genetics the same year you and I graduated from law school. He is now President and Founder of Humanetics, Inc. which operates here in Washington. When I told him that I was going to have this conversation with you about having a child, he asked to meet with me. He has offered to help us have a baby who is gifted and free of defects."

"Free of defects? It appears you are not just asking me about having a family. You are asking me about having a 'designer baby.' Is this what you are suggesting?"

"Well, not suggesting as an action at this point, but certainly suggesting as a discussion."

"Enoch, why would you think this is a viable option for us? Considering all the work I do internationally with families living in poverty and struggling to survive, why would you even suggest putting ourselves in a more privileged category? What makes you think we deserve a child superior to those families?"

"Not 'deserve,' Sarah. I wholeheartedly believe DNA-engineered humans are going to be a reality. I do not like the phrase 'designer baby,' but I also do not want this conversation to become a battle of semantics. Steven thinks you are the perfect candidate to lead the way into Germline Genetic Engineering. He specifically mentioned that you already have the respect of the women of many nations. Some call you the 'Mother of the World.' You could be a pioneer, here."

"Pioneer of what? The perfection of children? What happens to the imperfect child seated next to the perfect child in school? Will he be incapable of competing for colleges and jobs? Do we gather up the imperfect children and put them on an imperfect island to live out their pathetic, imperfect lives?"

"Now, hold on, Sarah. I think you are looking at this all wrong. The children you speak of so passionately — aren't most of them suffering from physical defects and illnesses that originate in their DNA? Imagine a world where those things did not exist. Imagine a world where no child suffers from a body that was unhealthy even before they were born. Science could eradicate birth defects in less than two decades. All children in the future might have the opportunity to grow up to become productive adults. Imagine a world with no more Downs Syndrome, no more autoimmune diseases, and no more Cystic Fibrosis. How about no undeveloped limbs, blindness, or deafness?

How about children not being abandoned in orphanages by parents who are not equipped to handle such challenges? What might that be like?"

"Enoch, I hear you, and I have heard the scientists. Which children will they perfect? You know this could come down to elitism and economics; it usually does. And more often than not - it comes down to race."

"Sarah, there is no racism here. Steven is emphatic about it. His team wants to mix the races, taking the finest traits of each and making a superior one. He wants to support the rule of nature that has always been in play: survival of the fittest. That is all."

Lucie is grinning now. "She can see her arguments are losing traction. She is going to change directions."

"Why us," Sarah asks.

I am starting to catch on to Lucie's plan. I take my eyes off the couple and glare at my conniving boss but am quickly drawn back to the conversation.

"Steven says we are the 'face of a new world.' We come from a small race and were born to immigrant parents. We are multinational. We are also healthy, educated, political, charitable, and in a strong relationship. I agree with him that the better question would be, 'Why *not* us'?"

"Have you thought about our careers? If this experimental baby and pregnancy news got out to the Press before we had time to consider the outcomes, it could destroy the baby, you, and me. Have you thought about our parents and families? A baby represents an entire genealogy, Enoch. Jewish families have not always been accepting of adoption. How can you anticipate their response to a DNA-modified child?"

"Steven believes the best results will come from fertilizing the egg in the laboratory and impregnating a surrogate who can be monitored throughout the entire incubation. As far as our families and the world are concerned, they will only know we adopted a child. We decide if, and when, they can know more. The good news is you would not have to be pregnant and we could have as much time as we needed to process. Sarah, we could help to change the world. I am convinced the risk is quite low. I know you are open to the surrogate idea because we discussed it years ago." Enoch stops and takes a deep breath to help slow his pace. "And there is one more thing."

"There is more?"

Lucie elbows me, "It is about to get good. Watch!"

"Yes. Steven wants to do more than mix the finer traits of the races. He wants to insert this child, the two of us, and Humanetics into the peace problem in the Middle East. I support his position that the only hope for peace is the rise of a leader who is accepted by both Muslims and Jews. Both religions are waiting for a savior. The Jews are waiting for their Messiah and the Muslims are waiting for the Mahdi. The person both are awaiting is surprisingly similar. The core difference, of course, is their heritage. Both saviors must be from a specific family line. For Jews, it is the line of King David; for Muslims, it is the line of Fatima, the daughter of Mohamed."

Sarah explodes. "This is, without a doubt, the most outrageously grandiose scheme I have ever heard. I wonder if I can even count high enough to cover all the holes in it. You are an attorney. Have you seriously thought this through?"

"Please, keep an open mind. You have a reputation for thinking big. The team at Humanetics has been working on plugging the holes to which you refer. Yes, it is a bit out there, but you must admit that this idea has heart. Think about it, Sarah —this might be the best idea yet to solve the Middle East unrest that has been going on for centuries. If all else fails, we still have a beautiful baby girl whose birth will take the science of DNA modification to the next level."

Sarah looks like she is in shock. "Wait a minute. I know you just covered a lot of territory there, but all I heard was 'baby girl.' Is this being decided for us as well?"

"Steven says that the DNA of girls is easier to manipulate. He covered all the biology with me. His team will do the same for you. Another reason for choosing a female is that the focus group reviewing this project finds a little girl to be less threatening — and more marketable."

"Marketable?"

"Acceptable."

"Enoch, I have never seen you more determined to have me buy into something. Watching you struggle for every defense is exhausting. Bottom line: What is in it for you?"

Lucie interjects again. "Enoch knows from experience that this is his last shot. Sarah is ready to pass judgment on the idea. When she puts out the 'What is in it for you' question, he knows his answer had better be succinct. She is a toughie."

I can no longer hold my tongue. "You are manufacturing a baby? You are using these two nice people to make you a baby?" Lucie says nothing in return, but winks at me.

Enoch continues his efforts to engage Sarah into his plan. "I want to run for the Presidency when the time is right. I am a Jewish-American, so I need an edge. I believe this child — and what she will represent — can put me in the White House. Diffusing the Middle East peace problem and rebuilding the Temple of Solomon, while also respecting the Muslim community's rights to retain the Dome of the Rock as their holy ground, is *the* problem to solve. It is unbelievable that the temple opening is on hold for fear of terrorist retaliation and the entanglement of the United Nations. If this issue is not solved, I fear there will be one final, terrible world war that will end civilization on Earth."

"So, if I am following you correctly, you are backing this idea because it will further your career?"

I scoff, "No, he is not doing this to further his career. My devilish boss, however, is a whole other story. She *is* backing this idea because it will further *her* career." Lucie ignores my comment. This is one of the times I wish I could be heard from spirit mode. I would tell these two to drop the whole baby idea. I may not know what she is up to, but I know every plot of Lucie's has a bad ending for the humans she is messing with.

Enoch is offended. "Ouch! Sarah, you make it sound as if this is only a political move. You know I want to have a family with you. You also know I have been working on establishing peace between these two cultures. I believe if we do not find a way to share this planet peacefully, we will cease to exist by the end of the century. What could be more important — and rightfully motivated — than raising up a leader who could legitimately speak for both sides? She can be a spokesperson, or ambassador, for peace. You and I will stand proudly with her at the forefront. Please promise me you will consider this."

"Before I give you my answer, tell me why Dr. Abbott is openly discussing this with you? The last I recall the public was led to believe that genetic engineering and designer babies are nothing more than great story lines for science fiction novels. It has been less than a year since the public was told we can alter the DNA of simple bacteria. Who is funding this project? Which countries are involved?"

"Dr. Abbott is sharing the sensitive material with us because he trusts us. He knows he must trust someone if he is to launch this project. We happen to fit the requirements for the parents. As far as funding goes, I asked Steven the same thing. He does not know who sends the money to the corporate account."

"And this does not concern you? What exactly *do* you know?" Enoch pauses to think through his answer.

"Watch, Kali, he can only win the debate by moving the conversation from business to personal."

Enoch sits up tall in his seat and after a heavy sigh, proves Lucie right: "I know I love you, and I will love you forever. I know you love children. I know you want to be a mother. I know you have a soft spot for little girls. I know I want to have a child with you and leave our legacy for future generations. Am I on track so far?"

Sarah fidgets uncomfortably in her seat and quietly answers, "Yes."

Lucie laughs in her evil style. "Watch as my scheme goes from his mouth right into her head."

"I know we can help to advance the research that might someday eradicate life-threatening defects in genes passed from generation to generation. I know this science can enhance human bodies so people can live longer and have a higher quality of life. Men and women will be physically stronger and mentally superior to anything we have ever known. The aging process might be slowed, or even halted altogether. Imagine that! I also know this is who we are, and what we said we wanted to be from the day we married.

"Sarah, this baby is going to be created whether we participate or not. In a way, she will be an orphan in need of a mother and father to love her and raise her. She is going to be different from any other child ever born on Earth. Her parents are going to have to prepare her for potential pushback. She will need direction on how to balance a normal life with royal design. Someone must stand between her and possible resentment and rejection. We are the ones to do this. We are compassionate, and we are mentally tough.

"You asked for a bottom line. Here it is: We did not go looking for this; it found us. I see it as our destiny. I believe she should be our child, and I believe we should be her parents. The rest will work itself out in time, including how we split our time to be home with her. Sarah, I want to have a child with you. I want Baby Anna to complete our family."

"Baby Anna? Did they name her for us as well?"

"No, the name is my idea. I would like to name her after your mother. It is a solid multicultural name. Naming the baby after your mother increases the odds that she will accept us having a non-traditional baby. No amount of science is going to sway a Jewish woman to compromise when it comes to accepting a baby into the family, but a good pedigree and a solid Jewish name just might." Enoch offers a slight smile with one corner of his mouth and sits back in his seat. He appears to have finished his argument. If so, the rest is up to his wife.

After a few minutes of silence, Sarah picks up her husband's hands and kisses them. Then she softly kisses his lips. "Mr. Cohen, I believe that was the most beautiful speech you have given since you asked for my hand in marriage.

"Even then, I promised to go on *any* adventure with you. In return for doing so, promise me you will continue to support me in my career. I will be a mother if you will promise to be a father. I want to be open with you that I do not subscribe to the trendy parenting model of the generation that preceded us. They thought it acceptable to allow nannies and private schools to raise their children. I do not want to parent that way. As I see it, the responsibility of having a child does not end after the first year. I want your word that you will split this responsibility with me fifty-fifty — for her entire life."

"Your request is more than fair. I promise. If you think about it, Anna can eventually travel with you on your international trips to the impoverished nations. She will be an inspiration to the children with whom you work. I can take her with me to some of my community activities. She will get to see both of her parents doing what they do best — using their talents to change the world in a positive way."

"You do paint a beautiful picture, and I very much like the name. I am putting my trust in you, Enoch. Do not let me down."

"I promise. I never have, and I never will."

"So, catch me up on what you know about this grand endeavor of ours."

"So, we are doing this?"

"We are doing this."

"Yes indeed, we *are* doing this!" Lucie pulls me away from the scene to return to Hades. I shake my head in disgust. "Relax, Kali, if you cannot handle this part of the plan, you are going to hate what is coming next."

14.

VIRGIN

January 20, 1996, Ellicott City, Maryland

Once again, Lucie drags me along on one of her mysterious visits to the surface. This time, she leads me to the bedroom of a young woman in suburbia Maryland. We are in spirit mode and arrive just as Lily Parker finishes her evening prayers. She is praying for her purpose to be revealed. As she stands, her mother, Deborah, calls from the first floor, "The President's State of the Union address is about to begin."

Lily opens her bedroom door so her parents can hear her over the downstairs television. "Thanks Mom, but I think I'm going to skip it."

Her mom is standing at the bottom of the stairway looking disappointed.

Lily's father, Bruce, pokes his head around the corner and joins the conversation. "Sweetie, are you sure? This is the last presidential address before the November elections."

"I know, Dad, but I just turned eighteen. These things really aren't that interesting to me."

"Well, they certainly should be, Darling. This is the first year you can vote. It would be great if you were familiar with President Clinton's position on the important issues."

"I'll read the transcripts at the library before I vote. I promise." Lily flashes them a disarming smile. "If it's okay with you, I'd rather go running."

The dimples work like magic on her parents. They both smile and agree she can skip the presidential address.

Lily returns to her bedroom and pulls her long brown hair into a high ponytail. She grabs her running shoes and heads down the stairs. At the doorway, she blows a kiss to her parents. They both smile and wave goodbye, but it is clear they are fixated on the President's address.

Outside, Lily sits on the top step and pulls on her shoes. She takes a deep breath of the crisp January air. The weather in Ellicott City and nearby Washington, D.C. can be brutal this time of year, but at fifty-five degrees, tonight is perfect for running.

Lucie begins to narrate Lily's story to me. "Lily does not mind running in cooler temperatures if they do not drop below freezing and sting her lungs.

"She will decide to take the trail through Centennial Park. A perfect 2.4 miles, it is just enough to get her heart rate elevated to her goal zone for twenty minutes. Afterwards, she will follow the run with a warm bubble bath and fall right to sleep – or so she thinks.

"There is just one obstacle to running through Centennial Park: the park officially closes at dusk, so she will have to sneak in. It is a wooded trail she knows well. The park rangers are usually posted near the main front and back entrances, though Lily is not even sure why the government pays rangers to keep people out of the parks at night. I have heard her protest this policy with a friend, 'rogue runners cannot be all that common — or, for that matter, all that dangerous'.

"On the positive side, when the park is closed, Lily is free to run through the quiet stillness that makes her feel as if she is the only person on the planet. She can drift off with her thoughts and ease into a nice runner's high. Yes, she knows she is breaking the law. She reasons that it is just a little law, though, and she is only breaking it for twenty minutes.

"Her parents would say otherwise, of course, so Lily keeps her late-night visits to Centennial Park to herself. Her parents are sticklers for following the rules, which is in direct conflict with their life choices. They are both Jewish by birth but do not adhere to the Jewish religion. They raised Lily in the Christian faith, poor deluded thing!

"The Parkers are also scientists working side-by-side on a top-secret project involving germline gene editing at Humanetics. Lily knows 'germline' is biology jargon for a human egg and sperm cell that come together to make an embryo, but she is not sure exactly what her parents do. They only give out information on a 'need to know' basis and, apparently, they feel that Lily does not need to know.

"When they first laid out the restrictions on their work-related information, they seemed to expect their daughter to be upset. Lily just shrugged her shoulders. On more than one occasion, she thought about telling her parents that teenagers do not care *what* their parents do for a living if it supports their desired lifestyle and, of course, their status. She always thought better of it, though, and assured them she understood.

"Now that 'designer baby ethics' is the debate topic for her second semester, Lily's apathy for her parent's work has ended. To collect data and give her an edge in her tournaments, Lily convinced her parents to allow her to shadow them at work during her winter break work study project. In three days, she will be in the company's biology lab watching altered DNA cells become something special. Even if the work bores her to death, she is sure it will look good on a job resume. Miss Innocent will *not* need a job resume." Lucie laughs as she pulls me away to the park.

MALLOW SHERIDAN

15.

STRANGER

Lucie leaves me to follow Lily while she goes on ahead. Lily reaches the opening in the trees and jumps onto the running trail. There are no signs of park rangers with flashlights. She sets an easy pace for herself and heads towards the back of the park; ten minutes later, she is passing the halfway mark.

As she takes in a deep breath and rounds a corner, she is jolted to a stop by a dark figure standing in the center of the trail. The figure is staring directly at her. I can see that it is Lucie in her black suit. Lily freezes. I move into the tree line. A sickening feeling comes over me as I watch Lucie pull an innocent teenager into her scheme. Lily seems to be weighing her options. She could dart into the trees and hide, or she could turn back in the direction from which she came and bolt for the main road - and the protection of the rangers. She could probably outrun a human but would not stand a chance against Lucie.

"Hello, Lily. Do not be afraid. I am here to deliver a message to you."

Lily is understandably scared. "How do you know me?"

"I know a lot of things about you, Lily, and I know a lot about your parents — Bruce and Deborah. I just want to speak with you for a few minutes, and then you can get back to your running. Is this okay?"

"Why are you out here lurking in the dark to talk to me? Who sent this message you say you have?"

Lucie slithers towards the unsuspecting girl.

"I came in the dark because I do not want to invite prying eyes. The message I bring for you is directly from God. It is about the purpose of your life."

Poor girl is being convinced she is talking to an angel. I have seen this trick before. Lucie will tell her she is answering the prayer we heard earlier in her bedroom. The teen asked God to show her the purpose of her life less than twenty minutes ago. She will believe Almighty sent Lucie with a message. Lucie's beauty - with her innocent blond hair and blue eyes - will disarm the young woman. She will buy whatever lie Lucie conjures up. When Lucie smiles, Lily drops her guard. "A message from God? Is this about my prayer earlier tonight?"

"Yes, Lily, it is. I am here to show you the plan for your life. You are so important to Him that He sent me here personally." I feel like gaging at Lucie's insincerity.

"Wow, I don't know what to say. I'm Lily Parker. It's nice to make your acquaintance."

"Likewise. I am Lucie. You are as beautiful as I have heard — and charming, as well."

"Aw, that's so nice of you to say. It's cold out here if you aren't running. Are you sure this is the best place to talk?"

"Yes, this is perfect. It will only take a few minutes."

Lucie points to a nearby park bench and begins to walk towards it.

Lily follows.

She is probably wondering if Lucie is a fashion model with her 6' height and perfectly toned curves. She carries herself with confidence and people are taken in by her magnetism.

Lily sits on the end of the bench. She looks like she is still a little uneasy about the situation.

Lucie moves closer to her and places her long arm on the back of the bench, gathering Lily to her side. "I will be quick. God wants you to know He has chosen you for a special assignment. He wants you to give birth to a child He is creating for a critical purpose."

"What? Jesus is His Child and has already been born. I've never heard of another child in the plans. Besides, I'm not old enough to be married. I've never even been on a date. I promised God I would remain a virgin until I got married. This message can't be for me."

"Ah, Lily — you are so sweet and innocent. It is easy for me to see why He chose you. God is not asking you to give up your virginity — or to get married. You will not have to raise this child and, as far as Jesus goes, His birth was for a different purpose."

"Wait, I'm confused. I can keep my virginity but still have a baby. Are you saying this baby is coming by God, like the Christ Child did? I didn't see another baby mentioned in the Bible."

"Well, Lily, man does much sinning. God has been reaching out for centuries asking man to repent from his sinful ways. To get his attention — as well as to save man from facing eternal damnation — He has been forced to change some rules from time to time. You know sin is running rampant on Earth, right?"

Lily nods.

"God is simply implementing another plan, just like He did with the Christ Child. You can be part of a new, yet unwritten chapter."

"What does He want me to do?"

"For now, He does not want you to do anything. Very soon, you will see an opportunity to fulfill God's new plan. He will greatly bless you for your obedience. You will know what you need to do when the time comes You just need to be brave." Lucie stands up.

Lily rises with her.

Lucie pulls her close and hugs her. "Lily, you are not alone. I am going to see you again very soon. I will be watching over this entire project."

"Are you my guardian angel?" The innocent victim is obviously filled with awe over the prospect that she was chosen for a special assignment for Almighty. This is one of Lucie's classic tricks. If humans knew she stalks their prayer time, they would pray in silence. I groan in disgust from my spot behind a large pine tree.

Lucie runs her fingers through the teenager's ponytail and speaks softly. "Not yours, my dear. I am going to be the baby's guardian angel. I'm delighted I had the opportunity to meet her mother before my job begins."

"*Her*?"

"Yes, the baby will be a girl. She will be perfect. Her parents were carefully selected. They will make a great home for her. I will be back to check on you." Lucie turns and walks towards the darkness.

"Lucie…is there anything else I need to know?"

"Yes. God would prefer it if you would keep this to yourself. It would be best if you did not discuss this, or our meeting, with anyone. Can you do that for Him?"

"Yes, I promise."

"Good. I will see you again soon."

Lily watches Lucie walk back to the trail and towards the trees where I am waiting. She turns and heads for home. She probably lost interest in running. The long walk home will give her time to think.

When I join Lucie, I hold nothing back in letting her know that this plot sickens me. "How can you possibly hurt this young girl? What has she done to you? You are going to rob her of a normal life."

"Oh boo-who! Mary was not all that happy about her position either," Lucie snaps back.

My mouth drops open, "You are copying Almighty's plan, aren't you? You are bringing *your* 'savior' onto the Earth the way He did. Are you plotting a virgin birth with this girl? How are you going to manage that?"

Lucie puts her face within inches of mine. "You will see. Watch and learn." With that, Lucie begins to thrash around in a circle and falls to the ground as a serpent. She slithers under a rock and back to Hades.

MALLOW SHERIDAN

16.

SCIENTISTS

January 23, 1996, Humanetics, Inc., Washington, D.C.

"Hurry, Kali. We are here for an important event. I do not want to miss any part of this." Lucie hisses at me as she buttons a lab coat and gains access to a locked door with a magnetic key that is now hanging from her neck.

"We are in a laboratory. What could possibly be important in a laboratory?" Lucie does not answer me. To blend in, we have possessed the bodies of two lab assistants who like to play with Ouija Boards. We each grab a clipboard as we enter the restricted waiting area. The room is empty except for the Cohens. I look at Lucie to try and understand. She puts a finger to her lips to signal me to be quiet. I move close enough to hear the exchange between Sarah and Enoch.

Sarah seems nervous. She fidgets with the buttons on her dress.

Enoch notices the fidgeting and reaches for his wife's hand. "Everything is going to be fine, Sarah. This is an exciting day. You are moving one step closer to, being a mother."

"I guess you are right."

Enoch leans over to make eye contact with her.

Sarah smiles. "I mean, of course you are right."

"Better."

"Did you notice my new look for the big day? Does it say, 'Look at me — I'm about to watch my daughter be conceived'?"

Enoch laughs. "Well, I am not sure it says all that, but it definitely says, 'I am a beautiful person — brave enough to face anything that comes my way today.'" He kisses her softly on the tip of her nose. "For clarification, the baby is already conceived in medical terms. You will watch her be implanted."

"I know. But this is the day she becomes real to me."

A group of people in white lab coats interrupts their conversation. "Hello, Enoch," one of them says. "Good to see you again. This must be the lovely Sarah. It is a pleasure to meet the world's next heroine."

"I am not sure I deserve that title, but yes, I am Sarah Cohen. You must be Dr. Abbott."

"I am. Let me introduce you to the team on this project. This is Dr. Frederick Bradley, a world-renowned geneticist. He has been handling all the delicate DNA engineering as well as handling the uploads."

"*Uploads?*" Sarah asks.

"Yes. It is a 'Frederick Bradley term'. I will let him explain."

"Hello, Sarah. It is nice to meet you. 'Uploads' are the specifics we chose for your baby. For example, we decided that Baby Anna should have brown eyes, a muscular build, and be taller than average. She has every mental agility and advantage known to us. We spliced, replaced, and enhanced the DNA in the germline to create the outcome we desired. Of course, there is much more to it, but that is a general explanation."

"I see." Sara shoots a look to Enoch that makes it clear she is uncomfortable with the answer to her question.

Dr. Abbott continues with the introductions. "This is Dr. Jason Abscomb. He is also world-renowned, but in the field of fertility. He supervised the entire fertilization process. He will be living on-site in Israel so he can tend to the surrogate and the baby from implantation to birth. He will be the one to deliver her at term. He is licensed to practice medicine in the States as well as in Israel."

Enoch interrupts. "Israel? Why are we doing this in Israel?"

Dr. Abscomb reaches out to shake Sarah's and Enoch's hands as he answers their question. "The laws on DNA modification, cloning, as well as genetic germline editing and engineering, are just forming in most industrialized nations. The laws of the United States allow us to do what we have done so far — splicing, editing, and uploading. In the interest of full disclosure, I should say they 'do not prohibit it' rather than they 'allow it.'

"However, this nation will not recognize the legitimacy of a designer baby or allow for in-utero surgeries - which we might need to achieve the optimum outcome. On the other hand, the nation of Israel bans what we have done so far but will recognize the baby as a citizen. Running operations in Israel will give our surgeons the leeway to do what is necessary to help her thrive. We chose Holy Family Hospital for her birth. They have a fantastic birthing facility and neonatal unit. It is in the small, quiet town of Bethlehem. It meets our needs."

Enoch and Sarah fall silent. I look at Lucie and whisper, "What is going on in Bethlehem? I thought you hated that place." Once again, she puts a finger to her lips.

Dr. Abbott addresses the uncomfortableness. "I know travel to and from Israel is not something you expected. Your visitation will be unlimited, and we will cover your travel costs. The surrogate will agree to live in Israel for the nine months. We reserved an apartment for her on the property of the Holy Family Hospital. There is a suite available for you as well. You are always welcome.

"One additional advantage of a Bethlehem birth is that you are not likely to be recognized. I imagine this is important to you, Congressman. Bethlehem isn't exactly crawling with members of the International Press Corps."

Enoch does not reply. Dr. Abbott continues the introductions. "This is Dr. Brian McMurray. He will be the attorney for the project. He has two degrees from Stanford — one in medicine and one in law. I know both of you have law degrees, so I probably do not need to explain why in-house counsel is essential to a positive outcome."

"You certainly do not. We completely agree." Enoch turns to Dr. McMurray and offers his hand. "I must say, your duel degrees are impressive."

"Thank you. It is nice to meet the Cohens — whom I must say are also impressive with their duel degrees." All three give a small awkward chuckle as they shake hands.

Dr. Abbott moves on. "And last, but not least, I want to introduce you to Adrienne Morgan. She will be our Press representative. She has a Communications degree from Cornell and is a respected broadcast journalist."

"Do I recognize you from the *Breaking News* show on NBC?" Sarah asks as she reaches for the woman's hand.

"Yes. I was on the show until last month. I resigned to work on this project with you."

"You gave up a news anchor position for this small project of ours?"

"I appreciate the concern, but after Dr. Abbott approached me with what you are doing here, I could not pack up my desk fast enough. In my opinion, this is not a small project. This is history being made; I would not miss it for anything." Adrienne shakes Enoch's and Sarah's hands.

Dr. Abbott motions for everyone to head towards the double doors as he continues to talk. "We know the Press will be all over the story once we decide to let it break. We want a fair and informed introduction to the world. We agreed Adrienne should be on board from day one so she can handle this very delicate topic in an informed manner. Now that you have met the team, we will walk you through the science used to make Baby Cohen. Please come this way."

Sarah grabs Enoch's hand. It seems as if the reality of the baby is sinking in. She kisses Enoch on the cheek and says softly and smiles big, "I am going to be a mother." I can see that Lucie has succeeded in getting into Sarah's head.

The Cohens follow the group into the science lab, but Lucie pulls me back. "Come with me. I want to show you another part of this story that is coming together." We step out of the bodies we were possessing and move in spirit form away from the building. I still have not figured out what Lucie is plotting in its entirely. She seems to be enjoying the game of cat and mouse she is playing with me.

MALLOW SHERIDAN

17.

HUMANETICS

In seconds after we leave the laboratory, Lucie pulls me down into a moving vehicle. Once inside, I see Lily Parker. We are sitting in the back of her parents' BMW. Since she is in the seat behind her mother, Lily directs a question to her father who is in her line of sight. "Hey, Dad, do any of your Jewish friends give you a hard time for owning a German car?"

"They used to, Honey. It has become acceptable for Jews to drive German-engineered cars. There is only so long you can hold a grudge if you intend to have a positive outlook on the future."

"Try saying that at a Martin Luther King ralley."

"Lily, watch your tone."

"I didn't mean anything by it, Mom. I'm sorry. So, to sum up the car lesson today: 'Holding a race-based grudge too long can hinder a positive outlook on the future of humanity.' Got it!"

Deborah turns to shoot Lily a disapproving look and address her daughter's comment: "Don't be melodramatic, Lily. This family subscribes to a simple mantra: We are all God's children. Everything works according to His plans. Our part is to be accepting of everyone and never judge what they believe."

"Really? *Never?*"

Lily's mother looks out her window and does not reply. Lucie glares at her while muttering to me. "I detest these people. This is what usually happens when Lily rides with her parents. Someone starts a conversation and offers what they believe to be the only possible points and counterpoints. Then Lily weighs in with the voice of another generation, and her parents stop the conversation and stare out a window.

"There is little Lily can do about it — their car, their rules. She is not allowed to play her music to escape these philosophical debates. Her headphones are off limits. For some reason, her parents like to think of travel time as family time. No matter. Lily gets easily bored with the games and drops the discussions."

A few miles later, we arrive at the security checkpoint for Humanetics, Inc. I still do not know why this lab is important to Lucie's plan.

Though I may not be clear on the project, I am somewhat familiar with this place. Lucie rambled on about it in a demon meeting in the past: "The Humanetics Research Center in the St. Elizabeth's East area of Washington, D.C. will play a critical role in my greatest scheme on Earth. The nondescript building — sans signage and protected by high-tech security — leads most locals to believe it is just another government facility. It is not. Humanetics, Inc. is a privately funded company leading the world in the DNA sciences. The secrets of the work done here are 'properly protected' by 'improper bribes.' Even the government of the United States cloaks itself from knowing the details of the research and live experiments carried out within these walls. Secrecy is critical for keeping the human rights advocates from picketing and obstructing operations. You know how I feel about 'bleeding hearts.'

"Dr. Abbott knows the most about the operations, but even he does not know the source of the company's funding. Money just appears in their account from foreign bank wires. In truth, the money comes from the group of men and women who make up the 'hidden hand' of the world — the Billionaires Elite Club Associates (BECA). The members of BECA are very aware of Dr. Abbott's work, and I control BECA. I hold rights to their souls."

In the meeting where Lucie told us about the laboratory, she could hardly contain her excitement. She prides herself in the many men and woman she controls. Most trade their souls in dark seances where they plead for wealth and fame. They make the deal, and Lucie grants them their wishes. From that point on, she owns their souls and their minds. The greedy are the first to sign up. She ensnared all the members of BECA.

"Their purposes for funding genetic germline editing are far from noble. The BECA members are divided into three schools of thought:

"One group wants to create a race of people that can use its advanced intelligence in the sciences to adapt to life beyond Earth. They are backing this project for the purpose of breeding superior minds rather than superior bodies. They want perfected human embryos and young adult caretakers placed into life-suspension chambers and launched via spacecraft to the four nearest planets potentially able to sustain human life — and they want it done by 2030.

"With my insider information, they located four idyllic planets for their new societies through black holes in the Milky Way. Each of the four planets with be distinctive and populated with like-minded embryos. I fancy a competition between the four types of humans to see which one is the 'higher power' and which will win the survival of the fittest. To prepare the four planets for their new inhabitants, BECA has scientists working on the Eden Project. Eden will send the elements of creation ahead of the embryo ships. Eden will impregnate the barren planets with the life-sustaining basics just in time for the arrival of the spacecraft. The soulless humans we design will do the rest as they colonize their new home. How about that, Kali, I am a creator as well." She paused to let out her evil laugh. She is always competing with Almighty. She is obsessed with his power.

"A second group of BECA wants to create a race of aesthetically pleasing and anti-aging people. They back this project for physical pleasure and immortality. Their most lofty goal is to find a way to keep cells from expiring, thus stopping the aging process altogether. They consider themselves to be the moral ones. They believe in a Creator and hypothesize, 'if people can live eternally in another dimension alongside the Creator, then the same science must exist within man's reach in this dimension'. This group believes the ultimate challenge is to bring immortality to man's current dimension rather than waiting to be lifted to another one by a 'Higher Power.' They have set a date of 2036 as the last year death will be 'tolerated' on Earth. Their contract with me ends that year when their youngest member, Robert, turns eighty on September 22. Not one of them *intends* on dying. Yes, I am dabbling in immortality as well." This time, Lucie throws back her head and laughs as she smacks her flat palm on the arm of her chair. She is the original sociopath.

"The remaining BECA members claim to be the 'realists.' They want to create a race of people enhanced with vitality and endurance. They are backing the creation of *super warriors*. They want to synthesize humans with artificial intelligence. They intend to build a Utopian society - which I intend to control once I win the Great Game. After the creation of the ultimate robotic humans, their quest will be to conquer the other species in the galaxy. BECA is advancing all three of these projects at the same time but has mutually agreed to fund the super warriors first to attain interplanetary security. The other projects will continue in the laboratories.

"All members of BECA agree on two things: First, the people who possess this 'weapon of science' will rule the planet as well as the destiny of mankind. Since all the members of BECA are Jews, they have selected Israel to be the nation in which they will set up their headquarters. Second, for the new DNA-engineered race of people to reach its full potential, the current human race must be destroyed. You know that I am backing this idea. A smaller discussion still on the table is whether they should be allowed to die off naturally or be helped along with genetic-based viruses."

I can now understand Lucie's interest in BECA. Her Highness believes she will get the Keys to Death and Hades and be granted an additional one thousand years to reign on Earth. All three BECA strategies serve her to that end. I can understand BECA, but I do not understand what we are doing in a vehicle heading back to the facility we just left.

The guard greets Bruce and Deborah kindly but gives them the third degree about Lily's presence on the grounds.

Bruce asks the guard to confirm the guest pass with Dr. Steven Abbott. "We have obtained a Level Two security clearance for Lily. She can go anywhere we are authorized to go."

The guard returns to his small office to make a phone call and ask for a verification of the clearance. After he taps a few more keys on his computer keyboard, he seems satisfied. He lifts the gate with a forced smile on his face. "You are free to enter. Please pick up Lily's security badge from Dr. Abbott. Once she has it, I can clear her on future visits."

He turns to look in the back of the car. "Lily carry this form with you until you are issued a badge. Enjoy your time here."

"Duly noted. Thank you."

Lucie continues with her narrative. "Lily has every intention of enjoying her time here. She is on a quest to understand DNA engineering as it pertains to the next generation of humans — and to impress her debate group with her new insight into the designer baby industry. Small minds have small goals."

After her father winds up the window, Lily puts her head between the seats of her parents and makes a declaration: "I am going to break this topic wide open at George Washington University."

Bruce smiles at his daughter's confident remark. "I have never doubted you will change the world, Sweetie. Your mother and I have some strong feelings about that." After a brief pause, he continues. "So, Lily, this is where your parents go every day after you head off to school. Security is tight, so follow all the rules if you want to maintain your Level Two clearance, okay?"

"I understand. I promise not to embarrass you."

A minute later, another group of guards, motion for Bruce to stop. They check Bruce's and Deborah's badges and take a photo of Lily.

"Jeez, what's with all the security? Is there a cure for cancer in here? Are insurance companies paying these people to keep it under wraps?"

"Lily Rose Parker!" Bruce snaps the rearview mirror down so he can make direct eye contact with his daughter. "You are not to make such accusatory or cynical remarks on — or for that matter, off — the grounds of this facility. Do you understand? This is a place of science, focused on the advancement of humanity. There is no room for sarcasm here. Scientists take every statement literally. Because of the nature of the work done here, any innuendo you make regarding impropriety could be grounds for revoking your security clearance. To use your vernacular, 'Got it?'"

The teenager addresses it immediately. "You're right. I know better. I promise not to do it again. Forgive me?" Lily flashes her dimples.

Lucie begins to laugh. "If they only knew how dead on right their daughter is! Fools!"

Bruce parks the car and opens Lily's door. When she rises, he locks eyes with her. "That promise better stick."

"Yes, Sir."

The next hurdle for the trio's entrance into the facility is a huge set of iron doors protected by two women. They just want to check badges and the security pass. The guards obviously know Lily's parents well and were expecting her to be joining them today. Once the family is through the iron doors, there are no more people in sight. There is no reception area — just two long hallways lined with doors.

"Mom, there are no windows. This is a completely sterile environment. Even the doors are nondescript. They do not have titles or names on them, just codes. How do you know where you are going?"

"We just know." Deborah answers. The group walks about halfway down the right hallway and stops at a door on the left. The code on the sign is simply *DNA-MOD3*. Her parents use their respective thumbprints to unlock the door. A female voice comes from the speaker next to the door and asks for Lily's security clearance.

Bruce provides the requested information.

The door opens. Inside, there is a beautifully decorated seating area, a small kitchen, and two offices on opposite sides of the open, sunken living room.

"This is where we do our paperwork and come to relax on breaks." Lily's mom shoots her a smile. "Not bad, right?"

"It's nice. Does it bother you that you don't have windows?"

"It's part of the security requirements here. The panels on the wall open to the outside if there is a fire or other emergency, so we are not exactly locked in."

"I wasn't asking a safety question. I was wondering if you miss natural light and seeing things like trees and rain."

Lily's mom picks up a remote, points it at a blank area, and pushes a button. A digital image fills the entire wall. It is a waterfall scene, complete with sound effects. "Will this do?" Her mom smiles as she puts down the remote.

"Awesome, so what do you do first?"

"We pray."

"Excuse me?"

"We pray." Deborah walks to the sofa and sits down. "We begin each day by asking the Creator for wisdom. We ask that our work be without error and done to the best of our abilities. Does that seem odd to you?"

"I guess not. It does seem a little redundant, though, since you ask for those same things every night in your prayers at home."

"Are you suggesting something?"

"Well, I'm wondering if you're worried the Creator forgets things from one day to the next? I mean, when you repeat prayers, are you doing it because you want to remind Him? Because you doubt Him? Or because you want to show Him you really, really want the thing you keep asking for. When I do that, you say I'm nagging you."

Lily's father steps back into the conversation. "Lily, you are doing it again."

"Doing what?"

"Innuendo. This time, you are questioning our worship methods."

"Okay, okay. I'll stop asking questions altogether."

"And now we are back to the melodramatics."

"Whatever."

"Lily do not use that dismissive word. You know we do not approve of it."

"Sorry. Force of habit. Can we just do the prayer thing? You must have a boss waiting on you somewhere."

"Yes, we can begin. First, we join hands…and before you say anything, Lily, just do it."

Bruce closes his eyes.

Deborah does the same.

Not that they would ever know it, but Lily closes her eyes, too. Lucie walks to the far corner of the room. Demons cannot be close to humans when they are praying. It burns the inside their heads as if they are on fire. I join Lucie in the corner. We both cover our ears but cannot completely block out the sound. The burning is much worse when multiple people are praying together like this.

Bruce prays aloud, "Dear Creator, we stand before You on this beautiful day with joy in our hearts. Deborah and I want to thank You for the great responsibility You have bestowed upon us to perform the work we do. On this special occasion, we also want to express gratitude for having our wonderful daughter here with us. Please open her mind to receive the blessing You have planned for her this day. We ask that You help us to responsibly handle the intricate human tissues into which You breathe the very essence of life. Help us to know the boundaries of where we end, and You begin. Guide us so we do not inadvertently destroy any life you create here in this facility. Amen."

"Amen."

Lily pats her father's back. "Amen, Dad. That was beautiful. Where can I start?"

"Well, the first hour is pretty standard. We answer emails, upload data from the evening shift, and analyze any anomalies. If you can hold tight for an hour, we can get you doing something more exciting."

"Great! Can I walk around the place?"

Bruce looks to Deborah for approval.
She nods slightly.

"Yes. Be careful to carry your guest pass with you. If you are stopped, be respectful and explain you are an intern here. Have them calls us."

"Will do."

"Lily, if you are granted access to any of the labs, be careful not to touch anything. There are cameras everywhere, and there is no denying responsibility for contaminating an experiment. Scientists are mild-mannered people until you mess up their work."

Lily smiles. "I know, Dad. I've seen Dr. Jekyll turn into Mr. Hyde." She giggles, picks up her guest pass, and heads into the hallway.

"We are following Lily." Lucie says as she grabs me by the elbow and leads me to the hallway. "Lily probably thinks that people who willingly work in this morgue-like building are the most boring people on Earth. She will feel differently in an hour. She probably also wonders if there are corpses behind these doors. Indeed, there are – and there is about to be one more." Lucie grins an evil grin as we follow the teen.

18.

REAPPEARANCE

After trying all thirty doors in the adjoining hallways, and being denied access to every one of them, Lily heads into the restroom.

"Lucie why are we following Lily Parker into the lady's room? What are you up to?"

"You will see. Grab me the scrub pants from the hook by the door. Go visible and put on some scrubs." Lucie loosens her hair from the tight bun on top of her head. She says nothing as she runs her fingers through her long dark hair turning it red. She shakes out the curls and closes her eyes tightly. When she opens them, they have changed from green to dark brown. When her body takes form, she pulls on the scrub pants. "Hand me the lab coat." Lucie slips into the lab coat and shakes out her hair as she finishes buttoning it. "Just walk in with me and go into a stall. I need to talk to Lily alone." Kali follows orders and puts her ear to the door of the first stall so she can hear the conversation.

By the time I settle into position, Lily is at the sink. When she looks up from washing her hands, she sees a figure in the mirror - standing directly behind her.

She tries to scream, but Lucie covers her mouth to muffle the sound. She is strong and holds Lily tight against the vanity so she cannot move.

She speaks softly into Lily's ear. "Lily calm down. It is me, Lucie. We met on the running trail last week, remember?"

Lucie smiles and Lily nods her head.

"I am going to let go of you and uncover your mouth. Do you promise not to scream?"

Lily nods a second time. Once her mouth is uncovered, Lily makes no effort to cover her anger. "What are you doing here? Do you enjoy scaring me - because you've been doing a great job?" She takes a deep breath and continues in her normal voice, "I didn't recognize you; your hair is different. You said you were a guardian angel, so why are you here at my parent's science building?"

"I am here with an update to the message."

"Which is?"

"God wants you to know that your assignment is about to begin. In fact, you will know what it is before the day ends. Are you still onboard?"

"Sure, I guess. It would help if I knew how I'm supposed to have a baby for God. As weird as that idea seemed at night on a dark trail, it seems even weirder in the day inside a bathroom."

Lucie ignores Lily's comment and continues with what she expects from the girl. "This day is a monumental one for God's new baby. She needs you starting today. I am here because the guardian angel needs to be on duty from minute one."

"The baby needs me *today*. *Here*? You do remember I'm a virgin, right? I told you where I stand on this."

"Do not worry, my lovely Lily. God will take care of everything. You will see." Lucie lightly runs her hand down Lily's arm and takes her hand into hers to gain her trust.

"Why do you look different? Your hair is red now, and your eyes are brown. Why are you wearing a lab coat that says, Josie? Am I the only one who can see you?"

"So many questions. I will answer a few. Everyone can see me, but not everyone notices me. I try to blend into any environment. The lab coat keeps me from drawing attention and jeopardize my mission."

"Your *mission*?"

"I mean job." Lucie straightens her form to shut down the questions. "Stay alert today. Focus on everything you hear, as well as the things you observe on your own. When the opportunity presents itself, you will know what to do. Do you remember what I said about being brave?"

"I do."

"To answer your other question, I change my looks to be understated and, hopefully, unnoticed. I learn more by observing than by interacting. I never 'underestimate the power of the being underestimated.' That is good advice for you as well. Now, smile. This is an important day." Lucie lightly pushes Lily's loose strands of hair behind her ear before slipping out of the restroom.

After shaking herself out of a daze, Lily runs to see where Lucie is going, but finds the hallway is empty in both directions. She shrugs and heads back in the direction of her parent's office.

Once Lily is gone, I slip out of the restroom and look for Lucie. I hear her eerie whisper, "Kali, over here." I turn to see Lucie motioning me towards a stairway. "Stay with her. I will be along soon. I have to tend to something first."

MALLOW SHERIDAN

DEMON GAMES I

EPISODE IV

MASTER

(KALI'S STORY)

MALLOW SHERIDAN

19.

SUBSTITUTE

January 23, 1996, Humanetics, Washington, D.C.

I step into the stairwell where Lucie is lurking. "Lucie, what is going on here? All I know so far is that this building is for gene editing and that Lily and the Cohens are somehow tied into the whole thing? How do the pieces fit together? I do not see it."

Lucie leans over to speak softly into my ear. "Big plans require small steps. The small step today is to implant the first genetically perfected baby into a surrogate. Dr. Abbott is the only one here who knows this meeting is little more than a formality. Genetic germline editing is much further along than most people imagine. The embryo they will be using is already prepared and holding in a suspended state — waiting for this day.

"Neither the parents nor the other specialists involved in the final phase are aware that the decisions for this baby came from decades of scientific experiments. The baby is a perfect female. She has all the most coveted human traits — as well as some super-human abilities. She has a genius-level IQ, extra sensory perception (ESP), the ability to levitate, an eidetic memory, and the ability to camouflage herself to simulate invisibility.

"The baby comes from the bloodlines of the two contentious religions of the Middle East — Islam and Judaism. The Chairman of BECA, Scott Geller, hypothesized that the support of this new line of humans would be a tough sell. With my backing, he pushed the group to mix religion and science to garner universal support. He also convinced them the child needed to be a female. He was very persuasive. He told the others if they 'want a shot in Hell that this new race of people will be accepted - rather than tracked down and destroyed - we must make the child appear harmless. We must sell hope and innocence. A perfect baby girl that is non-denominational and designed with multi-ethnic DNA is the only way to go.' The other members bought it hook, line, and sinker. Now, my plan is about to be perfectly executed. This baby belongs to me."

20.

SURROGATE

As I follow Lily down the sterile hallway to find her parents, she is so caught up in her thoughts that she does not notice that I am following her. She is probably still upset about her conversation with Lucie in the restroom and understandably spooked by the whole *baby* discussion. When she arrives, there is no answer to the door's buzzer. The female voice comes from the speaker again and tells Lily her parents were called to an unexpected meeting and will return in an hour.

"There's no way I'm going to sit on a concrete floor for an hour. I'm here as an intern with my parents. I got a Level Two security clearance for this. I did all the paperwork to go anywhere they go. Tell me where they are and let me in. If you don't, I'll report you."

The voice hesitates and then asks her to hold.

Lily is probably not nearly as brave as she is trying to sound. How can she not be unnerved by Lucie's prognosis that today is the day she will get pregnant? She is likely banking on that *not* happening if she stays with her parents.

The voice from the speaker is back. "Lily, your parents are in Lab 2. If you follow the hallway to the right, you will see a blue door. I will open it for you. Once you go through the blue door, follow the signs to Lab 2."

"Thank you. I apologize if I was rude."

"No worries. Have a good day here at Humanetics."

As Lily reaches the blue door, I step up and offer to escort her to Lab 2. She nods, yes. As we walk halfway down the hallway, we see a door that is slightly ajar. We can hear voices coming from inside. I want to barge in, but Lily seems hesitant and places her ear close to the door to listen. We can hear her father in what appears to be a heated discussion.

"Dr. Parker, don't you dare stand there and tell me that we cannot proceed with the implantation today. This is not an option. Do you understand me? Fix this now!"

"Dr. Abbott, I know you are intent on keeping your schedule and that every player is here waiting to proceed, but what can I do about a death? I cannot fix this."

"You *will* fix it. A surrogate is the smaller detail of this massive project. One billion dollars is on the line today, Parker. If this implantation fails, the entire project fails. You have one hour to find me a surrogate. If you fail to find one, you and your wife will be fired!"

The doctor slams the door as he exits on the opposite side of the room. Lily watches as her mother tries to console her father. Deborah is in tears. Lily pushes the door open and makes her presence known.

Bruce turns around to face his daughter. "Lily, why are you in this area? You were supposed to wait in our office. I was adamant about this with the building manager."

"She told me to come here. She buzzed me through. What is going on, Mom? Why are you guys so upset? Why is that doctor yelling? Who died?"

Deborah walks to Lily and holds her hands. "The lady who died is a woman who offered her services as a surrogate for Humanetics. It is no secret to you we work in the genetic germline sciences. When we needed a baby to go to full term, this surrogate would be implanted and carry it until birth. We did not know her well, but this is still upsetting. She came here today for the implantation of a special embryo. She died twenty minutes ago."

"Oh, no! What happened?"

"Evidently, she lost her footing, fell down a flight of stairs, and broke her neck in the stairwell leading to the lab area. We can see the fall on the recording captured by the surveillance camera, but we cannot see the source of her imbalance. Security is investigating, but nothing is clear yet."

I know exactly what happened. Lucie sent me on ahead and stayed behind to shove the nurse down the flight of stairs. Blocking security cameras is child's play to her. I am getting more confused by the minute.

Lily pulls her mom to a chair and sits down beside her, "Wow! This has been a scary day all around. But, why is the doctor mad at you two?"

"The embryo was being kept in a suspended state until today. It is now what we call "ripe for implantation." If we do not implant this baby within three hours, she will die. We do not know everything about this particular embryo, but Dr. Abbott has been excited about it."

"Can't you call someone else to be a surrogate?"

"It's not that easy. She must be young and healthy. We need to know her background and habits. She must commit to being sequestered for nine months in Israel. She must also have a Level Two security clearance. As you have seen, this can take months."

I stand out of everyone's sight line, knowing that my evil boss will have to make an appearance soon to manipulate the situation. Lucie invented the saying, "Idle hands are the devil's playground", and she cannot tolerate a break in the action. I notice the door behind Lily's parents is beginning to ease open. Lily sees it too, and her eyes widen as she looks over her mother's shoulder. She is probably thinking that the angry doctor is returning to continue yelling at her parents. Instead, it is Lucie who mouths a message to Lily: "This is your mission." She softly closes the door. There is nothing for me to do but stand here with my jaw dropped until this teenager decides her fate.

    Lily steps back from her mother's hug and almost chokes on the words, "I'll do it. I'll be the surrogate." Though no one is paying attention to me, I shake my head in disgust. Though I hate most people, sometimes one comes along that garner's my sympathy. I am worried about this girl. Though the Virgin Mary lived to raise the Son of God; I know Lily will not live to raise the Daughter of the Devil.

21.

BETHLEHEM

October 25, 1996, Holy Family Hospital, Bethlehem, Israel

"How are you feeling, Sweetie?" Lily's mother adjusts the pillows behind her daughter's head. I decide to stand off to the side and pretend to be writing notes on Lily's chart. I am here per Lucie's orders and possessing the body of yet another nurse who dabbles in the occult. Lucie is in the delivery room awaiting the birth of this baby. Before we left Hades for Bethlehem, Lucie caught me up on the details of her plan. The implanted baby's body was genetically crafted and has no soul. It will be the vessel Lucie uses to be on Earth for her reign of terror. It is a perfect specimen and comes without the restrictions of her demon body. I force a smile to Deborah knowing that this day will have a tragic ending for her.

Lily rebuffs her mother's attention. "I'm great. Stop fussing; I'm not a little girl anymore. I'm about to be a mother."

Lily gives her mom a big smile. She loves freaking her out like this. Deborah raises a disapproving eyebrow at her daughter.

"I'm teasing, Mom. It's nice having you here to care of me. So, tell me, what do you know about having a Cesarean? Will it hurt?"

Deborah pulls up a chair and takes Lily's hand in hers. "It will not hurt, Darling. You will be completely numb while they take the baby out. If you are uncomfortable after the delivery, I will be here to see that you get the right medication. There is no need to worry."

"I'm not worried, I promise. I'm doing this for a special reason — so it makes me happy. At the same time, I'm ready to get back to my normal life as a college student. I've already told some of my friends that my study abroad program is ending soon, and that I am ready for a winter break trip to a warm island. Do you think the cosmetic surgeon can cover up the scar so I can still wear a bikini and not freak out every guy I meet at the beach?"

"Absolutely. We are assured Dr. Larsen is the best cosmetic surgeon on staff at this hospital. He is already here and ready to take over the minute the baby is out - and Dr. Abscomb releases you into his care."

"If the scar looks bad, can I get a tattoo to cover it?"

Deborah makes it clear with her expression that she is not amused. "You know tattoos are prohibited by our heritage, Lily."

"Oh, right — having a tattoo will get me banned from being buried in a Jewish cemetery. Why is that again?"

"Lily, really? You are asking this right now?"

"Sorry, just trying to lighten the mood. I do have another question. It's a bit deeper."

"Go ahead."

"If a woman rents her vagina, she is called a prostitute, but if she rents her womb, she is called a surrogate. Why is that? And why is only one of these a crime?"

Deborah tries not to laugh. "I am not going to reply to that question. It is easy to see why you are a debate champion." I laugh softly. This is one of Jezebeth's oldest observations in Hades. It is one she uses to demonstrate the ridiculousness of man.

Two nurses enter and seem not to notice me in the corner taking notes. "We are ready, Lily. We are going to put a little medication into your epidural catheter before we move you. Once you are in the surgical suite, we will put in the bolus that will remove all feeling from the mid-chest area down. We will keep you out of pain. Are you ready?"

"Ready!"

Deborah and Bruce walk beside Lily's bed as she is moved to the surgical suite. I follow close behind holding her chart.

Once we reach a set of double doors, one of the nurses raises her hand to Lily's parents. "Sorry, but you'll have to wait here. Someone will be back soon to get you into scrubs so that you can be with Lily during the Cesarean."

"You heard the lady, Honey. We will be in soon," Bruce kisses his daughter's forehead.

"Okay. Hurry, though, Dad. I want you to say one of your awesome prayers for the baby with Mom and me before I go under the knife."

"You got it." Bruce and Deborah blow kisses to their daughter. I hold in a laugh at the vision of these people praying over the satanic, soulless baby. I know Lucie is not going to allow it.

Once Lily's bed clears the metal doors with me pretending to hold the IV, Lucie locks them from inside. When she turns around to face Lily, she is recognized. The fake nurse puts her finger to her lips to ensure Lily's silence. This is the last thing the teen would remember about the birth.

MALLOW SHERIDAN

22.

AWAKENING

As expected, Lily is confused when she awakens from the powerful drugs Lucie put into her body. It takes a few minutes for her thinking to clear. Her eyelids are heavy, and she does not expend the energy necessary to open them beyond a squint. She is probably not in any pain, but unable to move her legs. The plastic tubing dripping liquid from the IV appears to be her first lucid observation.

Lily grabs onto the bars of the bed and tries to sit up. This turns out to be a mistake. She screams about a stabbing pain in her abdomen. She falls back on her pillow after a sudden onset of dizziness and nausea. Her movement triggers an alarm on her bed. Two nurses rush in to find Deborah already tending to her daughter.

"Take it slow, Honey. Everything is fine. Ease your head back, I got you." Deborah fluffs up the pillow, slightly propping Lily up to see around the room. Her father stands nearby, looking concerned.

"Hello, Dad."

"Hello, Lily. How are you feeling?"

"Really tired. I must be on some good meds because I keep hearing myself speaking words before my conscious mind thinks to say them."

Bruce laughs. "That is completely normal, Baby. I remember that brain-to-mouth delay after I had my knee surgery. Things will line up soon."

"So, how's the baby. Is she okay?"

Deborah decides to answer this one. "We have been told she is doing very well."

"Told? Didn't you see her?"

Bruce jumps in. "No, we have not seen her. There was a change of plans. The scientists and doctors at Humanetics do not think it is a good idea for the three of us to see the baby."

"But you saw her when they took her out, right?"

"No. We were asked to wait for you here."

Deborah sits down on Lily's bed so no one outside the room can hear her. "Your father is sugar-coating it for your benefit. I will give it to you straight. The hospital personnel strong-armed us when we refused to step away from the delivery room door. Someone purposely locked the doors from the inside to keep us out."

"Wait. I remember seeing who did that. It was Lucie." I freeze with a cup of ice chips in my hands, wondering if the girl will rat out Lucie?

"Who is Lucie?"

"It doesn't matter. I had an epidural so I could be *awake* for the birth. Why did they put me to sleep, and why can't I see her?"

Bruce clears his throat as is his habit when he is about to lay out a heavy truth. "Honey, I think it is time to realize this baby belongs to the scientific community and her parents. Until she is an adult, she will probably be tested and monitored constantly. She has a big life in front of her. You are an important part of her story. Even so, I believe the doctors and attorneys now consider the three of us to be unnecessary.

"Someday — when the story breaks — everyone will know you did this noble and brave thing. Adrienne was here recording with her camera. She will share your story with the world. We all know you felt responsible for this baby and sacrificed a great deal to get her here. I believe she will remember all the songs you sang to her while she was growing inside you, especially 'You are My Sunshine'. I heard you singing it to her every time we visited."

"Dad, I appreciate what you are saying, but it looks like your hormones got messed up instead of mine. I don't want to talk about the mothering stuff. For the record, I am finished with talking about the science part too. I know the two of you supported me in doing this because you saw it as an advancement of science. I did it for an entirely different reason — a reason that should allow me to stay in the baby's life." Lily chokes back a tear. "Anna belongs to God, not the scientists."

"Well, yes, we all belong to God, Lily." Bruce lightly stokes his daughter's head.

I think to myself, "Yes, and good luck if you go up against Him." I hand Lily a cup of ice chips, so my presence is not questioned.

"No, you're not getting it. There was an angel, Lucie, who talked to me in Centennial Park. She said this baby was on a special mission for God. She was here today in the delivery room. She was in your lab at Humanetics the day the other surrogate died. She told me to do this. She told me to carry the baby. She's the one who locked the doors to the delivery room. She was the tall nurse at the entrance. Tell me you saw her." Lily is getting louder as she becomes increasingly upset. I do not know what I can do to cover over the things she just said.

"Lily, you have to calm down. You have a lot of medication in your system. It causes people to manufacture false memories. Do not be embarrassed. We have all been there."

I think to myself, "good one, Bruce. That will absolutely *not* help."

"So, you don't believe me? If you don't believe me, no one will. I want to go home, now! I don't mean to the underground hospital apartment where they've been keeping me, I mean *home,* home. I want to go back to Washington. I want to go now!" I love irrational teenagers. No one ever believes them.

Deborah tries to calm her daughter. "Lily, you cannot be moved for a few days. Dr. Abscomb told you this. Cesareans are serious surgeries, plus you had the cosmetic abdominal surgery."

"I don't care. I don't want to talk to you right now. I don't want to stay another minute in this hospital with a baby I cannot hold. No one believes me. I want out of here now!" Lily digs her head deep into her pillow and sobs uncontrollably.

I expect Lucie to be in soon to attend to this situation before it gets out of hand. As if on an actor's cue, she enters the room and calmly walks to the far side of Lily's bed. She pulls a syringe from her pocket and inserts its content into the IV line. Lily goes limp.

Bruce screams at the nurse. "What did you just give her?! What is going on around here?! Who are you?!"

The nurse turns to face him. She pushes her long black hair behind her right ear and smiles. "There is no need to raise your voice, Mr. Parker. We do not want Lily getting upset so soon after the surgery. She needs to sleep. My name is Lucie. I am her personal nurse."

23.

EXIT

Many things happened while Lily slept. She missed a shouting match between her parents and the hospital staff. Lucie excused herself early in the conversation. I stayed to watch. The argument ended when an anonymous caller announced that a plane is being sent to fly the Parker's back to Washington. I took it upon myself to prepare Lily for the trip. I did my best to sit the drugged teenager up in the wheelchair but had to secure the chair's chest straps to hold her upright. As we wait by the elevators for her traveling nurse to show, Lily forces open her heavy eyelids again.

Her mother smiles at her. "Hello, Sweetie. Everything is fine We are moving you out of the hospital like you asked. It is important that you stay very still while in this wheelchair. Keep the ice pack tight against your abdomen. You cannot lean over or stand up. Do you understand?"

Lily nods weakly. She looks up at her father and tries to speak.

He leans in to whisper in her ear. "Listen, Lily. Do not say anything. Something strange is going on and we are concerned. There is a shroud of mystery surrounding the baby's birth and we want to get you out of here as fast as we can. Someone has offered their private jet to fly us home. Listen to everything your mother tells you. Can you do that?"

Lily nods again.

A nurse approaches them with a small suitcase and a folder in her hands. "Hello, I am Kristin. I will be accompanying you on the flight." She turns Lily's wheelchair around as she pushes the elevator button. The elevator doors open before she can say anything to me. Two men step off and extend their hands to Deborah and Bruce.

One of the men leans down to speak to Lily. "Hello, Miss Parker. My name is Joseph Friedman. I am an investor in this important birth in which you played a major role. I will be the protector of the baby as she grows. I want to thank you personally before you headed home to Washington. Please accept this check for $30,000 for your college education. This is the customary amount paid for surrogacy services. I know you are sedated, so I will just say 'thank you' for now." Mr. Friedman hands the envelope to Bruce, who accepts it reluctantly.

Kristin pulls Lily into the elevator with her parents close behind. This is where my part ends. I know there is no way these three are going to make it home. I know Lucie all too well.

After the elevator doors close on the hospital birthing floor, Joseph turns to his assistant. "Is everything set for the private plane to fly them out of Bethlehem?"

"Yes, everything was arranged per your instructions."

"Great. Call Cal in D.C. and tell him we are going to need two scientists to replace the Parkers at Humanetics. Tell Dr. Abbott the baby died and to destroy the records. He knows better than to ask questions. Then call Jack in London and tell him we are going to need a replacement jet and pilot. Also, tell him to get another nurse for Holy Family Hospital. Send condolences to the families after the plane goes down in the Atlantic."

"Yes, Sir. I am on it."

Joseph steps into a quiet corner and taps a speed dial number on his cell phone. "Geller, everything is going as planned. The family is on its way to board the plane. They depart in one hour. We have a man in place to take out Adrienne Morgan this afternoon after she turns her video files in for editing. We will ensure that everything is locked down here before we leave. The story will never make it into the Press."

"This is good news. Shall we proceed?"

"Yes. When I arrive in Tel Aviv tomorrow, we will green light the plans to develop the 144,000 Jewish super warriors you requested."

"How long will it take, Friedman?"

"Four years. We can have them implanted by the first quarter of the year 2000."

"And how long will it be until the embryos and their caretakers are launched to the planets we selected?"

"A bit longer. Perhaps thirty to thirty-five years."

"I will be an old man."

"Yes, but you will be a very wealthy old man."

"Excellent!"

I listen to the phone conversation from the other side of the wall. Once it ends, I lean back against the wall and close my eyes. There is no doubt that Lucie is a master strategist. Her plan is brilliant. She is mocking Almighty with her replication of the virgin birth and setting herself up to look like the savior of the world. If she is going to follow the exact plan, she must believe that man is in his final 30-40 years on Earth. The fake messiah was just born. Things are about to get interesting. I exit the body I have been possessing and hurry back to Hades so I can tell the others about the new developments. Plus, I do not want to be on Earth when Lily's plane goes down. Some deaths are harder to take than others.

MALLOW SHERIDAN

24.

BAT MITZVAH

October 23, 2010, Cohens' Private Home, Great Falls, Virginia

Twelve-year-old Anna seems very content with her life even though it is far from normal. Lucie sends me to check on her from time to time. The child is an academic wonder intensely drawn to all types of physical combat, especially self-defense training. She practices boxing, martial arts, and weapons marksmanship for hours each day. She excels in horseback riding, high-speed driving, and high-risk stunts on motorcycles — all done on private courses made available exclusively to her. She is one of the youngest people to earn a pilot's license.

The one thing that does not seem to capture Anna's interest is relationships. Sarah has noticed that Anna sizes up a person in minutes and decides if they have anything to offer her. If they do not, she dismisses them. Sarah shares her concerns about their daughter's anti-social tendencies with Enoch. He assures her it is best that Anna be self-sufficient; he shows little concern for his daughter's lack of social skills. He is completely obsessed with the idea of her becoming a world leader. Their parenting conversations center entirely around Anna's advancements and achievements. Enoch does not broach the day-to-day things that typically challenge pre-teen girls. He pushes Anna hard and, to her credit, she rises to all expectations.

Sarah regrets that she does not have a typical mother-daughter relationship with Anna. This is her only child. She partly blames herself for being a working mother, but she also knows that Anna shows little interest in the time she does make available to her. Her twelve-year-old seems to prefer the constant testing sessions with the scientists over shopping with her mother. Sarah may love Anna dearly, but she seems to resent the project that brought them together.

To keep her mind off the Anna situation, Sarah digs into her startup company, Sun Economics. She enjoys being CEO of a project she feels will have global impact. Enoch is equally as busy with his political career. He is New York's most popular Congressman and is not being subtle about his desire to be in the White House when the time is right.

When Enoch declares that he will make his wife the original "Jewish First Lady," Sarah dismisses him with her standard, "Oy vey, you're killing me here."

Future fantasies aside, Sarah's focus is on the next event in the Cohen household, which is set to take place in forty-eight hours: Anna's Bat Mitzvah. Their synagogue, Beth Tikvah, and the attached social hall are full of thousands of white candles. The flower arrangements are on the way. Every detail has been handled. When I arrive for my weekly observation, I find Sarah sitting with a cup of warm tea in the home's Florida room. She is reading through a "to do" list for the Bat Mitzvah.

The guest list seems to be upsetting Sarah. Enoch has been adding names to it weekly since the headcount was confirmed with the caterer. Once the guest list hit two hundred, Sarah turned the arrangements over to an event planner. Initially, this was supposed to be an intimate family event with forty or fifty guests. Sarah begs the event planner to keep the growing guest list from spoiling the sentimentality of the day.

To Sarah's surprise, Anna is excited about the growing guest list. "That is perfect! If two hundred people attend, then two hundred people will know how I intend to change the world." She tells a friend that she thinks her daughter's reply is a bit odd but decides not to pursue it further. The only thing she says she wants is a seamless celebration of her soon-to-be thirteen-year-old's coming of age.

MALLOW SHERIDAN

25.

POSSESSION

October 25, 2010, Beth Tikvah Synagogue, Great Falls, Virginia

I slip into the back row for the Bat Mitzvah ceremony. Lucie told me she would be arriving after things got started. The festivities begin right on time. As soon as Rabbi Weiss finishes his welcome, and begins the Bat Mitzvah prayer, Lucie shows up in a big way. She takes possession of Anna's soulless body and the teen begins seizing. The lights begin to flicker.

When a body is possessed for the first time, there is pain. Whatever Anna is experiencing is causing her to scream in horror. From hearing the stories of others that have been possessed, Anna is probably feeling like she is being cut in half from her head to her feet. For seven minutes, she convulses and finally awakens to the terrified looks of her parents and the synagogue's security team. They help her sit up and give her a glass of water.

After a few sips of water, Anna catches her breath. "Did you see the lights flickering? Did you hear the voices?"

Sarah strokes Anna's arm and answers softly. "There was a thunderstorm that passed over the building right before you fell. It was both loud and scary. We thought we were going to lose power, but I did not hear any voices."

Anna glares at Sarah for not believing her. If she is possessed by Lucie, she will be able to sense the spiritual energy of the people around her. She will guess the evil deeds each one has committed. For reasons she will not be able to explain, she will hate every one of them.

26.

HARVARD

May 15, 2028, Harvard Law School, Cambridge, MA

Anna Cohen pulls back the sheer white curtain to get a glimpse of the audience she will address in thirty minutes. I peek over her shoulder so I can see as well. The seats are filling up nicely, except the ones reserved for the Harvard Law School Class of 2028. The new graduates are settling back in with no sense of urgency from lunch and the diploma ceremony. The Tercentenary Theatre will be full by the time she takes the stage. I am excited about this event. Anna is going to give her first speech while possessed by Lucie. This is going to be quite the show.

Anna is pleased to be back on the stage of her alma mater - just seven years after receiving her own law degree. She is now a highly regarded defense attorney and has silenced those who accused her of coasting on privilege and beauty. In seven years of practicing law, she has not lost a single criminal case. She is *the* litigator to fear in Washington. No one can equal her skills in analyzing motives, anticipating defenses, and guiding witnesses to give the very testimony she needs to win a case.

In the last eighteen months, Anna won three high-profile murder cases, including one for a seated U.S. Senator who should have been found guilty. Her specialty is creating reasonable doubt within the jury in order to prevent unanimous conviction.

The media's attention on these three high-profile cases earned the young attorney a cult-like following both on social media and with the Press. Her fans started a Twitter account where the comment on her defense tactics and acquittals. They refer to her as the *Spin Master*. When Anna walks on stage these days, the audience stands up and chants, "Spin Master" until she silences them with her signature move: lowering her forehead onto her forearm. The motion has gone viral and has come to mean, "I accept you and respect your message." Anna is fine with the temporary title, but she looks forward to the day with "Spin" is dropped and she is referred to simply as "Master."

The young attorney plans to shock people with her words today. She is a highly effective orator, and she knows it. She is fearless and has a clear agenda. Her goal is to provoke the audience to question the fault of religion in sculpting laws and inciting wars. There will be an attack on status quo thinking. She will repeat her message until the audience releases what they came here believing. Their minds will be open vessels for her to fill with a new belief system — her belief system.

Anna knows she has a gift for sensing when people entertain doubt. That is when she strikes — whether speaking one-on-one in an office, or in front of an audience of thirty thousand. She knows people leave her programs with a sense of invincibility. Some say it is like taking cocaine for the first time. They feel enlightened and desire to share the popular new leader's views with everyone they know. She has gone viral

The Millennial generation, ages thirty-two to forty-five practically worships Anna. They are independent thinkers but are capable of bonding together to create a global movement in a matter of hours. They distrust authority — especially leaders of government and religion. This makes them the perfect vessels for Anna.

The spin master's popularity is spiking outside of the United States as well. Even in non-English speaking countries, she has millions of fans. Her Twitter following is the largest in the world — 289 million and growing. This commencement address at Harvard is the first speaking engagement booked by the new public relations company she hired to handle her overwhelming responsibilities.

In just six months of taking a break from her law practice, she has become the most sought-after speaker in the world. She accepted the Harvard invitation for two reasons: First, the prestigious university is a hothouse for breeding new ideology and will add credibility to her message. Second, her acceptance forced the cancellation of the previously booked speaker — Tim Crenshaw, CEO of One World Religion (OWR), a pseudo-Christian group that hopes to "evangelize the world."

Anna detests Crenshaw and OWR. She questions the agenda of a group that has separatist religion as their internal guidance system. It is not that Anna does not support religion. On the contrary, she is religion's biggest fan. She knows it is the most effective tool for controlling people. Truth be told, establishing a religion is exactly what she *is* doing.

Unlike OWR, however, Anna wants a religion that is one with the governments of the world. She knows that in order to control the masses, a leader must mesh religion and government. Ironically, to entice followers, she will have to call the movement anything but a religion. She will find a way to make it work. After all, she is the master of spinning terms.

In addition to getting people to follow a religion that is not called a religion, she knows she will need to convince the entire world that a woman is capable of leading on a global scale. World dominance will require her to reach all nationalities and cultures — not just the ones who already perceive the sexes to be equally capable of leading.

She also needs a platform with staying power. Most successful men fall from power long before they die. Their pattern is to become corrupt, greedy, and selfish by the time they turn fifty. When given absolute power, the first thing these men do is gather a harem of young women (and sometimes young men) to use and abuse. The last thing these men do is trust the wrong man who ultimately crashes their empire — often a man they hired themselves.

Anna will not look to any man's ideas on religion, including Mohammad, Jesus, or the Pope. She will break apart the world's religions by offering the people something with a more attractive return on their investment. The plan is to lure these young adults away from active worship at a mosque, church, or synagogue with great riches and a falsely perceived freedom of time. Once she orphans them from a parenting religion and place to worship, she knows they will be ripe for the picking — her picking.

Anna has specific goals - as well as a timeline. She will increase her fanbase to one billion over the next three years. She is set to meet with the new Pope to integrate her ideology with the world's 1.2 billion Catholics. Pope Robert Kellan of the United Kingdom recently expressed interest in a worldwide "cultural movement." His vision includes the establishment of a universal core value system containing the basic ideologies of every religion. He wants violence between the religions to end, and he wants to act before a worldwide holy war breaks out.

Anna recognizes a benefit in helping the Pope draft and publicize his ideologies through Mandates at the United Nations. It will give her the exposure and world power she needs. She will be excellent in crafting mandates that people must legally follow. She knows just how to camouflage the loss of rights within the promise of peace and prosperity.

After she gets the Pope preaching her message, she will meet with the leaders of Islam's 1.6 billion followers and then with the Supreme Court of Israel, whose decisions govern Judaism's twenty million members. She is confident she knows exactly how to sell her ideology across cultures. She expects the combined 1.1 billion Protestants and Eastern Orthodox Christians to join just to avoid another world war. Her platform of peace will convince the followers of Hinduism, Buddhism, and Sikhism to join with her within a year as the people drift towards the things she will be offering.

Anna is going to do something most think to be impossible: She is going to bring the largest religions to the "peace table" to cooperate with the world's most powerful political leaders.

The timing is perfect. Christianity is growing rapidly, but the denominations within Christianity are pushing away from each other. Many are watering-down their Christian message to keep the seats filled.

Islam is also growing rapidly. It is *the* religion to watch. It is thriving despite its radical wing, the Islamic State, committing acts of horrific terrorism in Europe, Africa, and the United States. The main reason for its growth ultimately involves demographics. Muslims are very fertile. They have more children than the members of the eleven other major religious groups. Even in countries where the religions are mixed, Muslims have more children.

The average age of the followers of Islam is a young thirty-three — making them both movement-minded Millennials and reproductive-ready adults. The population explosion of Muslims will be a convincing reason to get the Christians and Jews to take a seat at the negotiation table.

Anna is sure she is the one to mediate this movement. — and she has known this since the day she turned thirteen. Her parents still refer to what happened that day as an "episode." They even had her tested to find a possible medical cause. They should have known better. She has flawless DNA; nothing can ever be wrong with her. Anna knows exactly what happened to her that day: She began sharing her body with a demonic spirit named Lucie. Lucie makes her invincible. As Anna closes her eyes and lifts her head, I know that Lucie is entering her body – just in time for Anna's speech.

DEMON GAMES I

EPISODE V

AMBASSADOR

(JANET'S STORY)

MALLOW SHERIDAN

27.

JANET JAGGER

February 5, 2029, The United Nations Secretariat Building, Manhattan

I allow my eyes follow the path of the East River as it snakes around the campus of the United Nations. Though the water is brown today, it is still a beautiful sight from the thirty-ninth floor of the Secretariat Building. As I watch the murky water rush around the gray boulders, I try to imagine the soothing sound it must be making on the other side of the courtyard. I wonder if anyone else finds the infamous river oddly out of place in the Turtle Bay Area of Manhattan.

I am feeling oddly out of place as well. I just left a welcome reception held in my honor to "get some fresh air". I felt as if the walls were closing in on me, and it was getting hard to breathe. Guests usually enjoy events held in their honor, but I felt uneasy. The host, Secretary-General of the United Nations, Mateo Velasquez, was the source of most of my discomfort. He insisted on staying at my side as I greeted the ambassadors of the world. I am unsure if my mini panic attack is a case of first-day jitters with a new boss or what seems like a hundred red flags going up in my subconscious about this man's intentions.

I also felt as if I was being left out of an underlying conversation. The others seemed to be talking in code — a code formed from decades of working together, and ripe with hidden meanings. I felt like a puppet in a room full of Puppet Masters – all of which intended to tie strings to me. The conversations centered on two contentious topics: capitalism vs. socialism, and religion. I am certainly not going to comment on this politically charged topics on my first day.

I excused myself to go to the restroom. I have no intention of returning. I need to leave soon anyway. I am the newly appointed Ambassador to the United Nations representing the United States of America. Although I knew I was being considered for this position, I am still surprised to find myself here. Ambassadors usually have some political experience on their resumes, such as Governor, Judge, or member of Congress. Despite my lack of political experience, I am about to take a very political seat in the adjoining General Assembly Building.

I do know somethings about the workings of the U.N. from my years as a reporter. I am a journalist by trade. CNN hired me right out of college to be a junior news writer. I quickly worked my way up the ladder to the coveted position of international field reporter. Some might not find leaving the plush CNN tower in Atlanta for the war-torn villages of the Middle East to be a promotion, but I did.

After covering the wars in Iraq and Afghanistan, as well as the civil war in Syria, I was considered credible enough to become the face of international news for CNN. When my contract expired with the network, I accepted a position as Press Director for the Peace Corps. I used my experience in broadcast news to draw attention to the irreversible damage done to children through war. I pledged to do anything within my power to help children in refugee camps have productive lives. It seemed to me that children of war held no hope for their futures. Hopelessness is not something I am willing to accept. I publicly placed the responsibility for this tragedy on the backs of every nation on the planet.

My documentaries, laced with compassionate pleas for action and donations, were broadcast around the world. They went viral on social media and were translated into seven languages. My arguments for change left little room for debate. I smartly produced my own programs so I could retain the creative rights. *War Babies* became a smash hit for the Fox News television network. I spotlighted one war-torn country each month for a year. Some people tuned in just to understand the cultures of the world.

The documentaries, along with my testimony on Capitol Hill, convinced Congress to double its funding. Though the Peace Corps is based in the U.S., twenty-two countries donate their time and money. All twenty-two responded just as enthusiastically to the series as the U.S. The increased funds allowed for the expansion of medical services in countries where the Peace Corps already had a presence and opened the doors to eleven war-torn countries previously inaccessible.

Survival supplies and medical treatments made up seventy-five percent of the charitable services performed by my fund-raising efforts. The remaining twenty-five percent went to "education." My vision for the money was bigger than meeting the everyday needs of the refugees and citizens of war-torn nations. I wanted these citizens of the world rise above their current state.

Whenever possible, I reported on the importance of putting teachers in every nation serviced by the Peace Corps. The teachers were certified educators who volunteered to teach STEM subjects (science, technology, engineering, and mathematics). I knew this was an ambitious undertaking, but I believed that the children of war deserved the same access to education as the rest of the world. Surprisingly, the children in the Third World nations were like tiny sponges when it came to new information. Some of them were proficient in coding before they could even understand the basics of mathematics.

The Peace Corps also helped the parents. They could take courses created just for them. Enrollment went through the roof in every single nation. Most classrooms reached capacity months before the courses began. The classrooms now have standing room only. Adding "accredited education" to the services provided by the Peace Corps made me one of the biggest stories of the year. My impact on Third World nations garnered me a Nobel Peace Prize, which I accepted in an ornate ceremony in Oslo, Norway on June 15, 2028.

While watching the Nobel Peace Prize ceremony, the political elite became aware of me. Republican Presidential Nominee, Enoch Cohen, tuned in and listened to my acceptance speech. He told me on a phone call immediately following the ceremony, that he was impressed with my poise and passion. After his inauguration, I was the first person he interviewed and added to his Cabinet.

Three weeks later, my entire world has been turned upside-down. I am living in a new city and have a new boss — one who is not sitting well with me. As I take my last sip of tea, I remind herself that, like him or not, I must have a good relationship with Secretary-General Velasquez. We will be working together most days until his appointment ends in December.

By charter, the U.N. General Assembly must convene continuously from September through December. In the last two decades the United Nations has been operating year-round to be able to address all the issues coming before it. The increase in activity at the U.N. is directly tied to its growth. When the U.N. launched following World War II, fifty-one nations signed on as charter members. It has grown since then, but its main purpose is still the same — to foster peace between the nations of the world.

I am not sure what I will find behind the scenes. The current group of ambassadors overwhelmingly considers the world to be in crisis and possibly on the brink of World War III. Because of this, representatives of the fifteen countries that make up the U.N. Security Council, must be onsite 24 hours a day. I have not even begun to search for possible stand-ins for myself. For now, the holdovers from the last administration are sharing the responsibility. It is just another line item on my massive to-do list.

The life changes brought about by this position are just beginning, and I am very aware that large amounts of change can trigger my anxiety. This overwhelming mental state of impending doom has been a part of my life since the death of my daughter, Tova.

At times, my anxiety can be crippling. Right now, it seems as if everything in my life is changing. I barely had time to pack a few things to bring with me to New York City. For now, I am staying in a hotel. It will be a few months before I will be free from sessions to look for a permanent place.

This part does not worry me. I am accustomed to living out of a suitcase and it is the lifestyle I prefer. Most people who suffer from anxiety choose to stay in familiar surroundings, but I am an exception to that rule. I prefer to surround myself with as much activity and as many people as possible to keep me from being alone with my thoughts.

Stepping into the elevator, I push the button for the mezzanine. I face the mirrored wall on the back of the elevator for a final look before I faces the cameras. The ivory wool Chanel suit gives me a classic look. I chose this suit because it flows easily over my hips and the skirt sufficiently covers my knees. Most of the world's ambassadors are men, and many of them are from countries where women are required to dress modestly. The last thing I want is for my clothing to distract from my message. For a polished look, I pulled my long black hair into a tight bun at the nape of her neck and chose pearl earrings, an ivory scarf, and patent black pumps to complete the outfit.

Today's wardrobe comes from the professional playbook written by the Baby Boomer generation. I am a member of Generation X, aka Xers, and would prefer to be wearing something a little more stylish - and a whole lot more comfortable. Xers spend their entire lives trying to maneuver around the massive generations on either side of them: Baby Boomers and Millennials. Xers are the quintessential middle children with highly developed communication and conflict resolution skills. To keep from leaning on those skills today, I completely polished my look, and put on the suit and heels.

The mirror reflects my mother's dark brown eyes and graceful neck. These are the most cherished features I enjoy from her Jewish heritage. When I was born, my parents still lived in Jerusalem, making me a citizen of Israel. Shortly after my birth, the family moved to

America for my father's job with the Food and Agriculture Organization (FAO).

The FAO is one of the fifteen specialty agencies housed in the building where I am standing. My father was eventually appointed as Director of the FAO and served in that capacity for three years. He led international efforts to defeat hunger on the planet through desert irrigation. It was an ambitious, seemingly impossible goal when my father ran the show forty years ago. Now, the possible has become the probable. Within the next two years, my father's vision is becoming a reality because of a company owned by President Cohen's wife — Sun Economics.

My parents were not fond of New York City, so they set up housing in the nation's capital. My father commuted back and forth from Washington D.C. to attend U.N. sessions and department meetings. He would return home on the weekends. I grew up in Washington D.C. and attended Sidwell Friends High School — a premier high school popular among the Jewish elite.

At the age of seventeen, I brought a great deal of shame to my parents when I became pregnant. They pulled me out of Sidwell as soon as finals were completed. My father resigned from his job and we returned to Jerusalem where I gave birth to my daughter.
My parents kept a watchful eye on my career and offered to raise the baby in Israel while I returned to the States and entered Georgetown University's School of Journalism. I flew to Israel to see my daughter every few months during the fall and spring semesters. During the summer and winter breaks, I stayed with my family in Jerusalem.

My job at CNN allowed me to travel to and from Israel every month. I saw my daughter as much as I could between my assignments. The plan seemed like a good one until Tova committed suicide when she was seventeen. The note she left behind did not assign blame, but I still carry the guilt of that event. No one in America knows about my pregnancy or my daughter, and I intend to keep it that way.

When the elevator doors open, I step gently onto the blue marble flooring of the large mezzanine. It is bustling with activity. This is the busiest and best-known building of the United Nations. As I pass the corridor to the U.N. Security Council office, I stop to admire the wall-sized copy of Picasso's oil painting, *Guernica*. Though I find Picasso's paintings confusing at times, the message in this one is completely clear. The snippets of men crying out in agony, tortured animals, and pieces of useless weaponry laid out in no apparent order seem to perfectly depict the horror of war. Picasso refused to give color to war, opting to create this piece using only blacks, grays, and whites. I understand why this painting is the favored backdrop of news reporters when they broadcast their U.N. updates. It is chilling and beautiful at the same time.

After admiring the painting and avoiding the reporters, I head into the courtyard, which is decorated with thousands of colorful pansies. Pansies are the only flowers that can withstand the harsh New York winters. Tourists are lining up along 42nd Street in hopes of viewing the beautiful gardens and the vast collection of paintings, tapestries, and sculptures donated to the U.N. over the years.

Even as a child, I found that the United Nations' art collection promoted peace and endless possibilities. Cultural diversity is celebrated, and nothing displayed here justifies war. Ever the optimist, I continue to dream of seeing world peace realized in my lifetime.

A teenager standing in the tourist line recognizes me and gives me a shout out and a wave. I wave back with a huge smile on my face. I love to see teenagers seeking to understand the workings of the world's governments and becoming familiar with the names of their leaders. I call out to the girl, "Enjoy the visit!" Unfortunately, I know the tour will be a little shorter today. Visitors cannot enter the General Assembly Hall when the world's ambassadors are in session.

After clearing security, I step into the Assembly Hall. The grandeur of this place continues to impress me. I visited many times with my father over the years, but this is my first visit since the 2014 renovation. The seating area has been expanding to accommodate the increasing membership. It is hard to imagine how 193 people can squeeze into the same space that in 1945 was barely adequate for the 51 founding nations. Basically, they built upwards over the years, and added a new balcony in the last renovation.

The stage now has state-of-the-art electronics and wall-sized viewing screens. The gold U.N. emblem that serves as the backdrop of the stage is shiny and new. The old one is a victim of nicotine damage; the Assembly Hall is now smoke-free. The chairs and desks are new and comfortable. The newly installed recessed lighting makes the auditorium more ominous than I remember. I finally let out the big sigh I have been holding in. I am living my dream.

28.

BENJAMIN

February 5, 2029, General Assembly Hall, United Nations Headquarters, Manhattan

"Shall I show you to your seat, Madam Ambassador?" The officer in uniform startles me. I am equally startled by his referring to me as "Madam Ambassador."

"Yes, that would be wonderful. Thank you."

I follow the officer. He is an imposing figure — well over six feet tall and wearing a polished badge fashioned with the U.N. emblem. Though he is a member of the United Nations Police (UNPOL), he is not carrying a gun. No weapons are allowed inside the Assembly Hall.

The seating arrangement in the arena is set alphabetically by the English translation of each nation's name. At the beginning of each yearly session in September, one nation selects the primo spot through a drawing. That nation gets the first seat in the front left row of the Assembly Hall. The remaining nations take their places alphabetically from the nation drawn through to the letter "z." Then, the order returns to the letter "a" until every seat is filled. This year Russia was drawn, which places my seat near the front right.

My assistant, Benjamin Hume, waits for me at my seat. At times, his strikingly good looks and eternal enthusiasm annoy me; but I do appreciate his ability to sense the agendas of others, his accuracy in writing, and his attention to detail. He is one of the few people I transferred from my documentary team to my U.N. team. Benjamin is loyal to a fault and will make me appear polished and professional enough to cover my insecurities.

I thank the UNPOL officer and turn to greet my assistant. "So, tell me, Mr. Hume, how many countries are represented on your necktie today? Trying to make some new friends, are we?" It is a standing joke on my team that Benjamin makes his emotional statements through his neckties. I believe I can tell with one look at his tie, if he is angry, happy, indignant, or in love. Benjamin is a good sport and goes along with it. He maintains that he is just a lonely, passive-aggressive man who uses neckties rather than words to out his feelings. Today's necktie is a bright swirly pattern with too many colors to count.

"Ha! Good one, Janet Jagger. There are only fifteen colors on the 193 Flags of Nations hanging outside. My tie has seventeen colors, including two that are not on any nation's flag. Tell me, why do you suppose not a single nation chose to use lavender or fuchsia? I suppose we could debate this ad nauseam. Personally, I think it is a statement against sexual expression. Do you want to use my observation on the six o'clock news? It is certainly controversial enough to make the cut. It could be your first statement to the Press as U.N. Ambassador. What do you think?"

Benjamin's provocative style amuses me even as I find many of our conversations to be exhausting. "No, that will not be necessary, Benny. I am thinking we will stick to the President's agenda today — if it is all the same to you. I figure he faxed it in for a reason."

Benjamin laughs and hugs my shoulders. He does this several times a day. It is his way of dissolving my anxiety and giving me a boost of much-needed confidence. He pulls up a spare chair from Uruguay's table as he continues the conversation. "Well, I say we give the President's agenda a whirl. He has some doozies lined up for you today. I am glad you wore your long skirt. You are going to need it."

Wondering what Benjamin means, but not wanting to waste the few minutes we have before the session begins, I decide to let the comment drop. "So, fill me in, B-Boy. What do we know?"

"I have prepared briefs for each of the topics the President is passionate about this session. There is the matter of Russia refusing to leave Ukraine territory. There is the matter of Russia helping to arm Iran with nuclear weapons — which in turn is helping to arm Middle Eastern terrorist groups. There is the rumor that Russia is holding hands under the table with China in a plot against Israel. As you can see, there is lots of Russian stuff today. Raise your hand if you are surprised.

"There is also the question of why the desert rejuvenation system invented by the First Lady's private company was just granted an international business license that lists Israel as its founding nation. Some believe this company is 'shrouded in calculated secrecy.' The starving nations that border the deserts want to know why they cannot have access to the invention's rejuvenation technology and, of course, water. You will need to ease the tension on this one. Some are calling it an attempt at genocide by Israel and the United States. Have you noticed the United States takes the blame for every bad thing that happens on this planet? What would you call this phenomenon?"

"Right now, I would call it job security."

Benjamin lets out a belly laugh. "Right as usual. If the things I covered are boring you, there are always the tabloids. These two are hot off the press: One is a magnetic pole reversal interrupting the world's power grids sometime in the next few years - unless we take evasive action now. The other is a giant asteroid hurtling through space on its way to end life on Earth. Where would you like to begin?"

I search for a reply. I know that going into full-out panic mode on day one will not bode well for my image. I reach for a glass, pour some water from the pitcher at my desk, and take a sip. I take several deep breaths while avoiding direct eye contact with Benjamin. Once I am sure I can speak without my voice cracking, I respond. "Well, assuming you are being serious, I will answer that I have adequate experience and briefings on the problems between the nations, so I think it will be best to begin with the briefings on the last two items you mentioned. Which of the two do you think is the more important one?"

"Well, that depends. The magnetic pole reversal is all the rage on Netflix's new *Serious Science* show, but the asteroid just made the cover of the *National Enquirer*. Viewership comparison is twenty million for *Serious Science* and four million for the *National Enquirer*. The good news is there are at least twenty-four million people who will not be surprised by these developments."

This is the place in the conversation where Benjamin usually winks, and I follow with sarcasm. One look at his eyes confirms my fear: Benjamin is completely serious. I try not to let him see me shift uncomfortably in my seat and open the top folder marked: "Classified: Property of the United States of America." The title: *Magnetic Pole Reversal*.

29.

AGENDAS

My anxiety levels creep upward as I process the contents of the classified folder. I only have a few minutes to take it in before the United Nations convenes its General Session. The seats are filling quickly. I lower my voice so the arriving ambassadors cannot hear our conversation. "Benjamin, this is a devastating prognosis. The names of those who have signed off on this are some of the world's most reputable scientists. Are you telling me a reversal of Earth's magnetic poles is an imminent threat?"

Benjamin pulls his seat closer to mine and puts his arm around the back of my chair. His smile is gone and has been replaced by a deep crease in his forehead. "This is the real deal, Janet."

"How long have you known about this? How long has the White House known about this? How long have these scientists known about this?"

"I have known about it for twenty-for hours. I cannot speak for the President. The scientific community has been discussing this since 2008. They are at odds as to the frequency of magnetic pole reversals. The last one occurred thousands of years ago. The scientists do agree that the planet is overdue. A pole reversal was expected in 2017, right after the solar eclipse."

"Where was the media reports in 2017? I am hearing this for the first time, and I have been following the Associated Press since college."

"In the past, a magnetic pole reversal would have posted below the Kardashian updates. Now, we rely on technology to regulate almost every area of our lives. It could be a critical blip for the planet. Theoretically, planes could fall from the sky when their instruments fail. Computer systems could glitch. Our satellites could leave their orbits and drift into space. Our manned and unmanned missions across the galaxy could be in peril if there is an interruption in communication. Power grids could fail. Less likely, but still within range of needing a conversation, our weapons (including nuclear warheads and the electro-magnetic pulse bombs) might not respond until they are rebooted with new coordinates. The geophysicists who authored this report say life will continue but say we will have to adapt to some changes. Casualties cannot be reliably predicted at this time."

I scan the room. It is more than half full now. I notice several people looking my way. They know I am the new ambassador from the United States. I am sure they are sizing me up. No one is close enough to hear our conversation, so I continue. "Benjamin, what I need first is a timeline. How do we know a magnetic pole reversal is imminent? Where is the undeniable proof? Since the President had this delivered to me, I can assume he wants me to get this topic on the U.N. agenda. He knows this is my first day on the job. He knows the experts have not briefed me. What is he thinking? What does he want me to do with this?"

"I agree. In fact, I have the same questions. I believe the President wants this topic worked into your welcome address to flush out what other world leaders might know about it. I have observed U.N. sessions in the past. With the translating and fact checking by the ambassadors' assistants, it can take days — even weeks — to get deep into a topic.

When you are introduced today, you will have fifteen minutes on the floor. Thank the ambassadors for the opportunity to serve alongside them and then make short statements on the things you look forward to addressing in this year's session. Just make a quick statement on the things the President's team gave you and move on. Speak as if *they* should know these things.

We will go deeper with the President on Wednesday when we meet with him at the White House. You can do this, Janet. I have stood beside you for years. You can sell anything. Just do that breathing thing you do that helps you relax. Or take a Xanax. If you do not have one on you, I will give you one of mine." Benjamin winks at her. Excessive energy aside, he knows just how to calm my anxieties.

"Okay, I hear you. I am sure you are right. I have my ten points prepared on the nations who are infringing on other nations as well as the effects of war on children. I will work the magnetic pole reversal into my opening remarks. Sound good?"

"Yes. But Janet, you have not opened the other folder — the one on the asteroid headed for Earth. According to the report, there is a slight chance of a collision with this asteroid in November. A much greater chance comes when it returns from orbiting the sun in 2036. If this collision occurs in November, it will be during your term — and this President's term. You have to get this topic onto the floor as well."

"And how am I supposed to skillfully and responsibly announce to the United Nations that a huge asteroid *might* hit Earth in as little as ten months, or as much as seven years, without causing international panic? Most scientists believe Earth's last major collision with an asteroid caused the extinction of the dinosaurs."

"There may be a third option: diverting the asteroid on its first pass. Look, no one said this job was going to be easy, Janet. Let's face it — if you thought that was the case, you would not have taken the position."

"Benjamin, I am a woman addressing the United Nations on her first day. If I put both these things on the floor, it will be like me telling the General Assembly we need to chase down Big Foot and the Loch Ness Monster. I am completely uncomfortable with this plan. I came here to be a voice for international peace and the protection of citizens held captive by the dictators of the world. I am prepared to talk about the funding of terrorist groups, the increase of weapons in

Lebanon, the return of ISIS, the escalation of anti-Semitism, and the need to find a solution to the Israeli-Palestinian conflict. I do not want to destroy my credibility by discussing the things in these folders. I simply am not prepared."

"Jan, you were the first appointee to the President's Cabinet. Think a minute to consider why the first position he filled was the U.S. Ambassador to the United Nations. He put you here because he knows he needs someone who can be cool under pressure. These are not easy times. You have stood on the bloodiest battlegrounds in the world and offered hope to those who had none. You rallied an entire planet to watch over the children of war. Put this information from the President's team into your opening remarks using the same confidence with which you supported the children."

"Benny, we have talked about this. You cannot fake passion. The people in this room will see right through me. Besides, how can I be sure this is not just a way to test someone's theories — or the depth of global support of their theories — while intending to use my inexperience as an excuse later in the game? It sounds like there are some hidden agendas here."

"You cannot know about all the agendas, Janet. We are still debating global warming for God's sake. Welcome to the world of politics. Trust your instinct. Does it tell you to back the President?"

"If it did not, I would not be here."

"Then you know what you have to do. You may be surprised in a good way. We will have more facts on Wednesday."

"Okay, I will do it. Just remember you are the only witness to my questioning of the President on all of this, so don't you go dying on me."

"You got it!"

Some activity on the left side of the stage catches my attention. "Hey, Ben, is that the Pope entering Stage Right? Is he addressing the General Assembly? Dear Lord! I knew the Catholic Church had a permanent seat here, but I had no idea the Pope would be in the General Assembly today."

Benjamin pushes up higher in his seat so he can see the Pope. "It was announced late yesterday."

"You knew about this? Why didn't you tell me?"

"Does seeing him here make you nervous?"

"Absolutely!"

"Well, you just answered your own question." Benjamin flashes me his infamous dimples. He pushes the last folder into my hands and stands up to greet the assistant to the Ambassador of Uruguay.

I can now see my new job in a whole new light. My stomach begins to hurt.

MALLOW SHERIDAN

30.

MANDATES

Secretary-General Mateo Velasquez walks to the podium to open the General Session of the United Nations. "Good morning, Ambassadors of the world! Today is Monday, the fifth of February 2029. It is a special day for us in many ways. First, we extended our session because of the needs of our nations. I hope the grumbling about your shortened holiday season has run its course."

Laughter spreads through the audience. There is some delay due to the time required for translating. This delayed laughter phenomenon causes Benjamin to snicker. I whack him on the leg. Benjamin clears his throat and sits up straight with a serious expression. I jot down a quick note and pass it to him: "This is not a comedy club. Laughter does not cross cultures. Cut it out!" We smile at each other.

Secretary-General Velasquez continues. "I hope you embrace the importance of your duty measured by the needs of your country and its people. We are indeed in complex times. Your nations and people need you now more than ever. I hope that all of you can appreciate this.

"There are other reasons this is a special day for us. Today we welcome the newly appointed ambassador from the United States of America. She is part of our Assembly body and a voting member of the U.N. Security Council. We will hear from her personally a little later today. For now, I ask you to welcome her with your applause. Ambassador Janet Jagger, please stand."

I stand on cue. Though I am uncomfortable in the spotlight, I wave to the other ambassadors. I cannot sit down soon enough.

Secretary-General Velasquez continues his remarks. "There is a third reason this is a special day. The new Pope of the Catholic Church is here with us. His Holiness, Pope Robert Kellan, will be making his first appearance on stage today to deliver a worldwide initiative. This is an honor. I do not want to take anything from his address, so I will simply ask you to welcome him with your applause."

The Pope steps out slightly from the curtains to wave. The audience is on its feet in seconds. Benjamin and I join the standing ovation. During the applause, I begin to wonder why one religion continues to have this level of presence within the United Nations.

I doubt whether many Americans realize that the Pope — or his representative — has full access to every meeting held by the U.N. This unlimited access also allows the Pope to attend meetings in the General Conference Room where "off the record" conversations are held between ambassadors and other world leaders. Recording is prohibited. All conversations are confidential, and any deals struck there are secret. I am looking forward to my first session there tomorrow as well as the first session of the U.N. Security Council. I cannot imagine the intensity of discussing the ugly matters between nations in front of the Pope.

I look over at Benjamin. He is applauding with great enthusiasm. He is a member of the Catholic Church. To him, this is a once-in-a-lifetime experience. I leave over and whisper into his ear. "Do you know if His Holiness is staying overnight and sitting in on the U.N. Security Council and the General Conference Room assembly tomorrow?"

"Yes. He plans to attend both meetings."

"How is it that you have access to this information before I do?"

"You are kidding, right? It is the job of the assistants to gather information and report that information to his — or her — Ambassador. I will know most things before you do."

"I guess you are right. Could I please request that, if you know something that pertains to my position, you inform me right away?"

"Hmmm, that is a request that requires some discernment. Let's talk about it after the session."

"What do you mean by that?"

"You have to trust me, Janet."

"All right, I will give you an hour but no more." I smile at him, the applause ends.

The ambassadors and their assistants take their seats.

Secretary-General Velasquez waits for the room to settle before he begins the introduction. "My fellow Ambassadors, it is with great honor that I welcome to the platform a man respected around the world. I have read the important global initiative he brings to you today and feel certain you will be moved to action. The U.N. Security Council approves and supports this message. It is a call to action the world must answer. I ask you to honor our guest, and fellow member, with the consideration and respect he deserves. Fellow Ambassadors, I present to you His Holiness, Pope Robert Kellan."

The Pope approaches the stage and climbs the steep stairs without assistance. At the age of forty-nine, Pope Kellan is the youngest leader of the Catholic Church in recent history. He is among the more progressive members of the Catholic Church and his election as Pope has already brought about some changes. One of these changes is that he has decided to be addressed by his given name instead of choosing the name of a revered saint to use in his position.

"Blessings, Ambassadors of the United Nations. Greetings to the incredible support staff and interpreters who make it possible for us to meet in unity. Thank you for allowing me to address your assembly today; I am humbled to address an audience of this caliber. In order to respect your time, I will head directly into my message.

"My fellow U.N. Members, I come to you today with a heavy heart, but I also come to you with a heart full of hope. Please do not focus on the negative — rather, embrace the positive. It is the position of the Catholic Church that our planet is in grave danger. This danger comes to us from three challenges. We must fact these challenges with bravery and action.

"First, our planet's known, natural reserves have been practically depleted. The scientists who consult with the U.N. tell us that, if current trends continue, Earth can only support our race for twenty-five more years. At that time, global warming will reach the point where humans will no longer be able to reverse it.

"Many of us in this room may come to know the pain of seeing our children and grandchildren begging for clean water and food. Animals will suffer even greater consequences as they will be competing with man for the dwindling staples of survival. Most of the planet's waste is coming from a desire for convenience, a desire for a carefree lifestyle, and irresponsible dietary habits.

"Second, the planet's distribution of wealth is severely unbalanced. We are all sharing the same planet and we should also share its riches. We cannot escape the responsibility of caring for our fellow man. If we do not rescue our brothers and sisters who are living in poverty, we will not be able to escape the anarchy that will follow. Crime will hold our neighborhoods captive.

"The wealthy cannot solve the challenges of the poor by putting up walls. We are approaching a point of wealth disparity in which ninety-five percent of the world's wealth is in the hands of five percent of its population. I fear the ninety-five percent will reach up with their sheer numbers and pull down the wealthy. Violence could sweep the industrialized nations. We must share the world's wealth or pay the price for not doing so.

"The third thing we must confront is the escalation of crimes of religion. Over three million lives have been lost because of differences in our faiths. Terrorism in the name of religion must end immediately. Our militaries and law enforcement officers cannot solve the problem with their guns alone. We must do our part.

"The U.N. Security Council has voted unanimously to invite the Catholic Church to help build a bridge between the religions of the world. Today, I am introducing *Thirteen Mandates for a United World* for your consideration. I am asking you to study them carefully and to vote with us to rescue humanity. The clock is ticking, so I ask you not to delay.

"Before I present the Mandates, I would like to introduce the person who will be responsible for implementing and governing this initiative in its totality - should it be adopted. She co-authored this document with me. Most of the proposed solutions were designed by her. The U.N. Security Council has approved her to regulate this program in all 193 nations for a period of three years. Many of you know this person — along with her many accomplishments. I am honored to introduce to you Anna Cohen."

A wave of disbelief runs through my body. This cannot be right. As the rest of the audience stands to show support for Anna, I lean over to Benjamin, hoping he can hear me over the noise. "Benjamin, what just happened? Does the Pope have the authority to do this?"

"Yes. He already had the authority to do this before he acquired the support of the U.N. Security Council. Look, I know this is unnerving, but let's not draw attention to our shock and dismay. We will handle this in the General Conference Room. Janet, do not forget that Anna is the President's daughter."

"I have not forgotten." I drop my head in disbelief.

Anna takes the stage. "Greetings. I am honored to be with you today. I want to work with you to stop the needless loss of life at the hands of the greedy. We will work together to reign in the irresponsible behavior of religious zealots. We will no longer be idle. It is our duty to seek solutions. I promise you this: If you will give me three years to implement the *Thirteen Mandates for a United World*, I will give you three years of life without terrorism — three years of peace and prosperity.

"If I succeed, you can renew my contract. If I fail, you can consider other options. I am confident you will not need to consider other options. I hope to serve you in this capacity until we have averted the crisis. I am here to help you save the world from a pending catastrophe. I ask you to join us as we secure the future of our planet. Thank you."

The audience is on its feet again. It is obvious to me these yet unknown *Thirteen Mandates* will be approved based solely on the words of the Pope and Anna Cohen. I glance over at Benjamin, who shrugs in disbelief. The noise in the Assembly Hall is so loud Benjamin resorts to passing me a note. "Remember this day. You are witnessing the beginning of totalitarian globalism."

Anna steps back from the podium after her signature gesture of head to forearm. It amazes me that this little arm thing of hers crosses so many cultures. There is no denying that she appeals to people around the world. Anna does not leave the stage. Instead, she takes one of the seats on stage located behind the Pope. "Aren't those seats reserved for the world's government elite?"

Benjamin slips off his glasses to clean them with a cloth from his suit pocket. "Evidently, she believes she now qualifies." He winks at me and refocuses on the stage.

The Pope takes the podium once more. "My fellow Ambassadors, please follow along with me on the screens. I present for your consideration the *Thirteen Mandates for a United World*:

1. *Only one Spiritual Being will be recognized by the United Nations.*

Though most religions have a God they worship, the U.N. would make the position that we all serve the same spiritual being. Religions could continue to use their own verbiage and worship practices, but for issues addressed by the U.N., we will only recognize one God. Furthermore, anyone convicted of killing his fellow man in the name of religion will be sentenced to an international prison. These cases will come before the International Court of Justice. Like the U.N. building, the international prison will sit upon neutral soil. The Catholic Church has graciously offered to donate land from its property in Rome for this purpose. The prison will be for both long and short-term incarcerations. Construction will begin as soon as this Assembly gives its approval. Italy has offered a temporary prison for us to use until construction of the new prison is completed. The temporary prison can be operational within thirty days.

2. *Religion will defer to government.*

When asked whether it was lawful for Jews to pay taxes to Caesar, Jesus responded: 'Render unto Caesar the things that are Caesar's and unto God the things that are God's.' It is imperative that the citizens of the world accept that laws belong to government. In the Biblical story I just shared, Caesar represented the government of that time. The message is clear: Should religion and law conflict in the future, the U.N. will side with law.

3. *All leaders of the world will be vetted and approved by the United Nations*

Upon election, the men and women chosen for the highest levels of leadership in any member nation must be vetted and seek the approval of the U.N. before taking office. The International Court of Justice will conduct thorough background checks on presidents, prime ministers, and other top government officials. They will be looking for incidents of prejudice against any religion, gender, or race. If rejected by the International Court, the candidate cannot assume office and a second election will be held in the candidate's nation.

4. *All nations will share in the protection and renewal of the Earth's resources.*

All nations will be required to participate in the preservation of the world's resources. This includes lowering emissions, controlling pollution, using fuel-efficient vehicles, and limiting the waste of food, plastics, and paper products. All nations will be encouraged to embrace a shared economy with rideshare, home share, plane share, fuel-efficient cars, and Elon Musk's fast passage trains. These forms of shared economy, and those that appear in the future, will be free of burdensome regulation and taxes. Air flights will be cut in half. People will have to plan early and wait for an opening. Only clean energy sources will be allowed on the planet. Farmland will be purchased at a fair price and the agricultural sector will be owned by the governments of the world. Upon an owner's death, private property will also be returned to the governments. The citizens of the world will adopt a plant-based diet of at least 75% to reduce the many resources depleted in order to raise meat for human consumption. The Trusteeship Council of the United Nations will handle this accounting.

5. *Only one currency will be recognized by the United Nations.*

Because of the work done here at the U.N., the world is largely using electronic money and cryptocurrency. This practice is weaning citizens off paper money, uncovering money laundering schemes, and shutting down human trafficking rings. There are fifty thousand citizens in the U.N.'s trial money-management program. They have lived an entire year exclusively on electronic banking. They have also allowed ten percent of their income to flow into a mandatory savings program. As of this morning, only five percent of the citizens in this program have withdrawn money from their savings over the last twelve months. This is a significant improvement over the seventy percent of citizens who live paycheck to paycheck and have no savings at all. If this program goes global, withdrawals from savings will require the approval of the U.N Banking Division. The purpose of this mandate is to curb the world's wasteful spending and rebuild its resources. This also ensures that there is enough put away to care for our elderly. This Mandate will require all citizens to exchange their paper money and coins for credit no later than December 31, 2030. After this date, paper money and coins will no longer have any value. The only exception to electronic banking will be the exchange of gold. It will remain the world's standard for monetary value.

With the acceptance of this Mandate, bartering will be illegal due to the difficulty in tracking taxes. Loans and debts would also be illegal by the end of this year. Just as the U.N. cleared the debts of the nations, so shall the nations clear the debts of its citizens. The U.N. will see that all debts between nations and citizens are cleared by the end of this year. Settling these debts will give our planet a reboot. Our intention will be to give every person, company, and nation a new start.

We expect that each nation represented here today is adhering to the laws already in place. Penalties for not enforcing the U.N.'s financial regulations will include sanctions after December 31, 2030. As we move to the next level, each nation will seek volunteers willing to be implanted with a microchip. Nanotechnology has arrived. This identifier will offer easy access to medical history and finance. The initial volunteers will receive a financial bonus for leading the way and will have their Social Credit Score rise by 50 points. The U.N.'s Economic and Social Council will email you the details of the proposal.

6. *All space exploration will be equally owned by the nations of Earth.*

The nations of the world will work together on space exploration and the possibility of relocating humans to other planets. This program would include sharing ownership of all satellites and exploration missions already in operation. All nations would have equal access to information collected by Space Force. All people of the world will be given equal consideration for migration to other planets should this become necessary.

7. *All weapons and manpower will be revealed to the U.N. Security Council.*

All 193 members of the United Nations will be required to make their weapons inventories known to the U.N. Security Council within sixty days and update it yearly. In keeping with the original U.N. charter, only five countries may possess nuclear weapons and are therefore exempt from disclosing their weapons inventory. Exempt member nations are China, France, Russia, the United Kingdom, and the United States of America. Every non-exempt nation must also report its number of troops on active military duty.

I know this request will be make many nations uneasy. Dire times call for dire measures. The U.N. cannot do its job of helping the world to remain free of war if it is not aware of what its members are doing to prepare for war. Just as you came together to disarm the Democratic People's Republic of Korea in 2021, so shall you disarm any nation that does not cooperate with their fellow members on the U.N. Security Council.

8. *All private and public businesses will be required to register with, and be approved by, the United Nations.*

Businesses already operating in each nation will go through a comprehensive audit. This will be identical to the one done when new companies register for a U.N. business license. The U.N. will be looking for unfair pay practices, unsafe working conditions, infractions of U.N. regulations, excessive abuse of the Earth's resources, unpaid taxes, and prejudice in hiring. Any non-compliant business will be penalized. As of December 31, 2029, it will be illegal for a business — in any nation — to receive or dispense funds without a business license from the U.N.

9. *All nations will have open borders for immigration.*

All nations of the world shall allow immigration to and from their countries. The U.N. must approve any restrictions or limitations. Following this address, you will receive an email outlining the qualifications for emigrating to a new nation. These qualifications ensure immigration practices are fair and practical for all nations. Once all the citizens of the world have a tracking chip implanted, immigration will be no longer an issue.

10. *The United Nations will recognize all unions of consenting adults.*

Any union of consenting adults will be legal. Legally recognized marriages can be of any race or gender but cannot exceed seven adult members in a single unit. Polygamy will be legal, and the minimum age for sexual consent and marriage will be fifteen years and six months. To arrive at this age, we averaged the age of marriage in all the member nations. The International Court will support all spousal rights and responsibilities for every member of a marital unit.

11. *All children will be under the protection of the United Nations until the age of eighteen.*

This protection would include decisions made for children regarding education, health care, discipline, and career selection. The U.N. would be open to hear testimonies from children who feel abused or neglected by their parents. The U.N. would also have the power to act on behalf of these young citizens — up to and including removing them from the custody of their parents and putting them in a more beneficial environment. Citizens under the age of eighteen who have exceptional talent, intelligence, or potential for greatness in any way may be moved from their family unit to a facility where the development of their gift will be supervised for the betterment of the world. The biological parents will remain fiscally responsible for any children they bear until they reach the age of eighteen — even if they marry and are no longer in the custodial care of their parents. At birth, all babies will have their DNA analyzed to reveal their parents from our databank. These two people will be fiscally responsible for the child – unless another parent files the papers to assume this responsibility.

12. *Education will be mandatory.*

Every citizen of the world over the age of six, who is of sound mind and body, shall enroll in online education. The courses will be free of charge on the U.N. website. There will be translations into all languages used in our 193 member nations. Any university or learning institution that receives tax credits from its government must accept the credits of the U.N.'s online education courses. Illiterate persons will receive free literacy training. Anyone who does not complete these educational requirements will be subject to a yearly tax penalty. Anyone who lacks access to a computer will get a solar-powered, hand-held electronic tablet.

13. *Universal Health Care will be made available to every citizen who resides in a member nation.*

This will be as simple as forcing open access to every physician, hospital, urgent care facility, assisted living residence, and pharmacy in the world. All providers will be required to treat any person who is a citizen of a United Nations member state. A pay-for-service system will be set up in consideration of each nation's economy. There will be a universal requirement: For citizens to retain their free healthcare, they must do their part to stay healthy. This would include following the advice of their assigned physician regarding diet, mental health protection, use of prescription medications, drug and alcohol intake, limits on high-risk behavior, and the prevention of sexually transmitted diseases. Anyone who refuses to receive immunizations will not have their medical expenses paid should they fall ill with the viruses they were meant to protect. Hospitals and physicians can opt out of treating an unimmunized person. The Secretary-General's office will send you the documents to answer your questions later today.

"Thank you for your attention. I know you will require more information to cast your vote. The supporting documents have been prepared and will be emailed to you today. We eagerly await the approval and support of the United Nations to begin. If we work together with integrity and tenacity, we can make the future better for every citizen within three years."

The Pope and Anna walk off the stage side by side presumably to leave through a back door.

One by one, the ambassadors rise to their feet to applaud the Pope's remarks. I stand; but instead of applauding, I begin a paper conversation with Benjamin. "Please tell me that did not happen."

"It happened."

"We are in big trouble."

"Yes, we are!"

Once the crowd settles back into their seats, Secretary-General Velasquez begins to speak. "I told you this was a special day. I know you have a lot going through your minds. If you check your email, you will find a copy of the *Thirteen Mandates for a United World*. You will also find the 1,200 pages of supportive documentation drafted by the legal department of the U.N. to help with the implementation of these programs."

The audience collectively emits a sound that is half laugh and half groan.

"Each Mandate will be voted on separately. The legal committee will be tweaking the language and intent of the document. The final vote will occur on March 5, 2029. We will take a break now and reconvene at 1:00 p.m. We look former to our next speaker, Ambassador Janet Jagger of the United States."

MALLOW SHERIDAN

31.

DECREE

As soon as the final ovation is over, I gather up my folders and grab Benjamin by the arm. "We are going to my office for some privacy."

The two of us maneuver our way through the crowd to my small office in the General Assembly building. Once I see my nameplate on a frame, I pull Benjamin inside and close the door.

"What was that?!"

"Janet, please calm down This is not helping anything."

"Benjamin, I just arrived here. Imagine my shock when I found out — in General Session — that my predecessor signed off on this 'contract of annihilation' and did not even extend me the courtesy of reviewing it with me. Now I must go in there and vote on this thing. I must either be dutifully compliant and screw our nation or go rogue and ostracize myself from my peers, all the while compromising future relationships with them. What do I do?"

"You do not have a choice."

"What do you mean?"

"I just received a message that President Cohen would like to speak with you. He asked that you call him on his secure line."

"He knows about this already?"

"Janet, his daughter is lurking in the shadows on this one, of course he knows about it. You must call him. Please keep your cool and remember that Anna helped to draft this document."

I dial the number. My palms begin to sweat, and my heart begins to race. "How does anyone deal with this much stress, Benny?"

"Shhh — everything is recorded on the phone line you are using."

"Hello, Ambassador Jagger."

"Hello, President Cohen. It is an honor to speak with you again."

"Likewise. Welcome to the United Nations. I bet you are realizing by now this is a lot tougher than you thought it would be."

"Yes, but I am ready."

"That is good to hear. Janet, I was aware of the *Thirteen Mandates for a United World* before your appointment. I did not have the finer details or the supporting documentation at the time to share with you. I have gone through this carefully with my advisers, and I want you to vote affirmative on each mandate."

"Mr. President, I do not want to be out of line here but enforcing this document will destroy the U.S. economy. Beyond that, placing these regulations on our companies will cripple their operations. It will send a shock through the workforce. If that is not enough, can you imagine what will happen when a world-governing committee ousts our President-elect? We have not been the most popular nation over the last decade; I do not believe these mandates are in our best interests. We have an exclusion on the military inventory. Can we also ask for an exclusion on some of these other conditions?"

"Ambassador Jagger, I understand we have a meeting scheduled for Wednesday. We will discuss your concerns at that time. A Senate or House congressional committee has approved every one of these Mandates. For now, I am ordering you to support them. I expect you to verbalize your support at the U.N. Security Council meeting tomorrow. I ask that you withhold any negative comments in the General Conference Room as well. Are we clear?"

"Crystal clear, Mr. President."

"Good. You have my items for today's agenda. I trust you have a strategy for introducing them to the floor. I will see you on Wednesday. Tell Benjamin I look forward to his presence as well."

I drop my phone onto the desk and sink into my leather desk chair. "Oh, Benjamin, we are in big, big trouble."

MALLOW SHERIDAN

EPISODE VI

HEAVEN

(GRAYSON'S STORY)

MALLOW SHERIDAN

32.

SENECA

January 4, 2029, Level IV, Heaven

I listen to the waves arrive on the shore in two phases. The first waves roll gently onto familiar sand. The second ones crash into boulders just as they are about to peak. The rolling waves are barely noticeable, but the crashing ones are putting on a spectacular sound show. When they finish, they fall back into the ocean, with their energy spent, and slide to shore with a soft gurgling sound. With my eyes closed, I can hear the nuances of the synchronized arrivals. I make this into a game. I count the seconds between the two and try to snap my fingers at the precise time they touch down.

Anyone who knows me well knows I am most like the second round of waves — adventurous, spontaneous, and unpredictable. My grandfather used to say, "The meek might inherit the Earth, but they will never be newsworthy. Go choose yourself a life that grabs some headlines!" His advice might be why I have never lived small. I am always putting on a show.

The wave counting is rebooting my brain. Any day that begins with ocean waves as the alarm clock is a great day in my book. The direct sunlight makes it difficult for me to open my eyes. The sun has no respect for people who are napping. I guess I will give up the fight to stay here sunning myself and try to do something productive with this day.

As I pull myself upright, I am reminded of the downside of napping on a beach — the thousands of sand grains lodged in every crevice of my body. Even so, it's a small price to pay for the peace of waking up on warm sand — especially this sand. It is the whitest, finest sand I have ever seen. As soon as I sit upright, I fill my hands with it, hold it high over my head, and allow it to slide through my fingers and back to the ground. When I was a child, I could do this for hours.

A dip in the ocean would be the ideal remedy for my slight malaise but, for some reason, I did not wear my swimsuit on this outing. The good news is I am finally out of my fatigues. I am not surprised I ditched them in favor of my favorite beach attire — ripped jeans and a Beatles T-shirt. There is no way I would wear these vintage clothes into salty water, though. I settle for burying my toes in the sand. Ah, Utopia — or is it the Caribbean? As my grandfather would have said, "Same difference." Very few things can convince me to stay in the moment the way an ocean can. Time seems to stand still when I am being serenaded by the sea.

I yawn and stretch tall. My arms are toned and tight. They are a much-deserved reward for a fitness routine that includes three hundred push-ups a day. My hair feels soft and velvety as I run my fingers through it. After nine years of military buzz cuts, it is nice to have my hair back. After fingering it into a beach look, I reach through the rips in my jeans to dust the sand off my knees. As I close my eyes and take in a deep wake-up breath, a small buzzing shock spreads through my body. It gives way to a flashback of a bullet ripping through my neck.

I swallow slowly, lift my right hand, and run it across the front of my throat and around to the back of my neck. I feel nothing; there is no wound. I wonder if I am experiencing my first PTSD flashback. My heart races. My rapid breathing is drying out my throat. I look around for a clue as to where I am. In one direction, all I see is a calm, blue ocean. In the other direction, I see only palm trees and white sand.

The sun is brighter than I remember, but the temperature is completely reasonable for January.... *Wait, why do I think it's January?* I don't like this feeling. I'm not a fan of mental fogginess. Snipers know it leads to uncertainty, which leads to hesitation, which ultimately leads to death.

"Hello, Grayson." Startled by a voice from behind me, I swing around with fists ready. I stop short as I find myself face to face with a dark-skinned man with piercing blue eyes and a toothy grin. His smile is disarming, so I drop my fists. He continues to smile as he talks. "It's okay. You can relax. I am not the enemy — though you will meet her soon enough. She is the reason I am here."

The man steps back and leans on one of the large white boulders that line the beach.

I move cautiously in his direction. "Who is this enemy? And before you answer that question, maybe you can tell me who you are and how you know my name."

"My name is Seneca. I am a guide — some say a teacher. I am a permanent resident here. I know your name, and a lot about you, from your father and, of course, from Almighty Himself."

I feel myself tense up again. *Great, I'm talking to a crazy person. This is not what I need when I'm already questioning my sanity.* "Excuse me for being rude, but there is no way you know my father — he's dead — and he has been for twenty-six years. As far as talking about me with 'Almighty,' I'll just ask if I can call you an Uber to take you back to the asylum."

The man does not respond to my attempt at humor. Instead, he leans over and plucks a small flower growing near his feet. He smells it and begins to twirl it between the fingers of his right hand. His gaze moves from the twirling flower back to me. He is waiting for me to say something...maybe something that isn't sarcastic.

"Look, I apologize. I use humor when I'm uneasy. Things are a little confusing right now. I just woke up from a very intense dream — or maybe a vision. I'm not sure which. I only want to get back to wherever I'm supposed to be right now." I know as soon as I say it: I am the one sounding crazy — and a little whiny.

The man crosses both his arms and his legs. He leans further back on the boulder. His island shirt and beach pants are neatly pressed and made of the whitest cotton I've ever seen. His wardrobe and grooming don't support my theory that he's crazy — or homeless. He looks confident and a bit smug. I feel as if he is reading my thoughts, and I don't like it.

"Can we start over? My name is Grayson Cunningham — which you seem to know already. I can't remember how I got here. I was on a military operation in Yemen. That's the last thing I can remember before waking up here."

The man remains silent and keeps twirling the flower between his fingers.

"Did you really know my father?"

"Correction — *do*. I *do* know your father." He drops the flower and locks his eyes on mine. "You may address me as Seneca. Are you up for a walk on the beach? I will answer all of your questions in time." Seneca starts walking towards the water. He assumes I will follow him — which I do.

The man who calls himself a guide heads north on the beach. I'm not sure why I assume we're heading north. There's plenty of light but no sun to help me get my bearings. I am walking closest to the water, which allows the occasional, far-reaching wave to rush over my bare feet. The man who says he will answer my questions is being oddly silent.

My military training tells me to wait for the enemy to speak first. I have not classified Seneca as an enemy at this point, but I am keeping him under surveillance. Before I render a verdict, I need to sort fact from fiction. I'm not sure if I'm in a dream or have just woken up from one.

The greater question would be, where am I? Seneca and I are leaving the only footprints in the sand.

MALLOW SHERIDAN

33.

TRUST

Even after walking a considerable distance together, I'm not sure what to think of Seneca. He gives off a good-guy vibe, and I don't sense that he is a threat even though he hasn't given me a single reason to trust him. He seems comfortable in this place — moving through it as if he is in charge. Though I'm trying to keep my guard up, my curiosity regarding my father is pulling me into his game. He knows my name and claims to know my deceased father — present tense.

Seneca smiles at me every minute or so as we walk along the misty beach. He seems to be waiting for me to engage. I find myself torn between keeping my defenses up and trusting him. As time moves on, and we still have no identified destination, I figure I have nothing to lose by restarting the conversation.

"Look, Seneca, here's the thing: You have to know how weird it is for me to hear you talk about my dad as if he's still alive. You're going to have to help me with this."

The smile on Seneca's face tells me he is quite pleased with himself for waiting me out. "We will cross to the Fifth Dimension. Once we are there, I will address your questions. Come with me."

Before I can ask how we get off the beach and do something as implausible as change dimensions, Seneca disappears into a thick mist.

I curiously approach the spot where he made his exit. I stick my hand into the thick fog and feel nothing but cool air. Closing my eyes and leaping forward, I assume the landing stance I use when parachuting. I land hard. When I open my eyes, I find my feet planted on a gleaming surface that looks like crystal. Seneca is standing in front of me with a smirk on his face. "You're enjoying this, aren't you?"

Seneca laughs. "Yes, sir, I certainly am." His snicker explodes into a full belly laugh. "But don't think I do not appreciate your caution. You are a trained soldier. I get it. Really, I do. Have a seat, Son."

Seneca points to two broad chairs to his left. I choose the one with a clear view of the "air door" through which we just entered. I have no idea who — or what — might be able to follow us here. A good soldier always positions himself where he can keep an eye on the entrance and exit.

The white chairs are made of a mysterious material I cannot identify. It is soft and cool to the touch. When I sit down, I sink in deep.

Seneca hands me a glass of cold iced tea and takes the seat beside me. "In case you are wondering, we do not cover chairs with animal skin. All creatures here are honored as Almighty's prized designs."

I keep my uneasiness to myself, but I'm tripping over the word "creatures."

Seneca lifts his hand to the open space in front of us and calls out, "Show us Grayson's last military action."

The area comes to life with a 3D figure of *me*. My image is face up on the ground in Yemen. I stare in horror at my dead body beneath the Socotra trees. The blood has stopped flowing but has stained the ground around my head and torso. My chest tightens at the sight, and I jump to my feet in defiance. "What is this? Am I dead? You hand me iced tea as if this is a social visit and then show me this? What is going on here?"

"I know this is unsettling, Son, but keep watching."

I have known Seneca for less than an hour, but his calm demeanor talks me down from the ledge. I ease back into my seat. It takes every bit of self-control to look back at the scene. After a few seconds of stillness, two bright lights drop from the sky and hover over my lifeless body. A foggy image rises out of the bloodied heap and reaches its arms to the lights. The blur forms into a translucent version of me. The two lights that dropped from the sky transform into men with wings attached to their backs. They are dressed completely in white and have no visible hair on their bodies. A wreath of light encircles the tops of their bald heads and lights up their faces. They take the hands of my image, lift me into the sky, and all three of us disappear.

I look back to the body in the hologram. It looks different somehow. My emotions have quieted as I survey the empty scene. Seconds later, there is activity in the brush to the south. Two soldiers from the U.S. ground team are climbing the hill. They reach the body and check for vitals. Sergeant Wilson stands and salutes as First Officer Patterson closes my eyelids and collects my supplies. They seem to be weighing the options of removing my body. I must hand it to these guys — they are soldiers to the end. Wilson and Patterson each get under a shoulder and maneuver my body down the hill.

I take in a big gulp of air and swallow hard.

The screen flickers and the image changes. Now I'm watching my mother sitting on her porch swing. She is holding an American flag folded into a triangle. She pulls a picture of me out of the fabric. She gently pushes her right foot on the wood floor to keep the swing moving. Tears run down her cheeks. She wipes the tears away with the Kleenex she keeps in the cuff of her sweater.

Tears well up in my eyes as I watch her cry. I try to hide them from Seneca, and I'm angry. "Why are you showing me this? If you're trying to break me mentally, it's not going to happen. If you don't start answering some of my questions about this place and the whereabouts of my father, I am going to leave. Got it?"

"And go where?"

"I don't know for sure, but I'll start by charging back through the spot in the 'fog wall' you showed me."

"Grayson, I think you know what is happening here. You are a smart man. You are in Heaven. Normally, people are happy about this."

"Is anyone ever indignant?"

"Not usually. Your feelings might have something to do with your arrival. Instead of being met by people you know and taken to the Pearly Gates of the Seventh Heaven, you were held briefly in the Fourth Heaven and had no greetings except yours truly."

"Why? You know what? I don't care. I just want to see my dad. Him, I trust. I want you to take me to see him now!"

"I assure you your dad is here, and he knows you are here. I will take you to see him when the time is right. This deviation from the usual arrival protocol was done for a reason. You are here, and I am here, because you have been chosen to lead an important mission back on Earth. The future of humanity depends upon its success. I am also here to prepare you. Your father agrees that the Mission requires your full attention and thinks it best you hold off visiting with him and your friends."

"What friends? I don't know anyone else here. The few friends I do have are alive back on Earth."

"Grayson, don't you know the troops who died on the battlefield beside you consider you to be their friend? You are a hero to fifty-six men here. And there are hundreds of classmates, neighbors, and generations of relatives waiting for you."

"Why would the troops remember me? I was the one hiding on the rooftop, or up a tree, while they moved in and took the real risks. I don't remember any neighbors. I didn't keep up with classmates - but why would people in their thirties be dead anyway? As far as relatives, I only met a few, and we weren't close. If you're trying to build this into something that will prey upon my emotions, you can stop now. I'm done with it!

"Since I got here, I've been forced to watch my death scene and my mother in mourning. Just get on with it. Fill me in on this Mission — the one I've been 'chosen for' against my will. If that's what it takes to end this nonsense, let's get it done."

Seneca sits back in his seat and lets out a heavy sigh.

I sit again and think through my verbal attack. I try to justify my decision to go for Seneca's throat. Though I'm suspicious of this man's agenda, I suppose I should hear him out. It is obvious I'll need his help to get out of this place. "I'm willing to hear you out on the Mission, Seneca, but you have to set aside the emotional stuff and give it to me straight."

MALLOW SHERIDAN

34.

DIMENSIONS

"Okay, Grayson. I hear you. Are you sure you want it straight?"

"Absolutely! It's the only way I fly."

"All right. First, you have transitioned – you died on Earth."

"Thank you. I appreciate your directness."

"In Earth terms."

"*Earth terms?*"

"Yes, the ones popular on Earth right now."

"I'm not following you."

"I have been here a long time. I have seen the definition of death evolve over the years. There was a time when death was defined by the lack of fog on a mirror placed beneath the nose of a man. That one was wrong so often that the friends of the 'deceased' would tie a string around the finger of the body before the coffin was lowered into the ground. They would tie the other end of the string around a branch of a nearby tree and attach a bell. In those days, if you woke up in a coffin, your only hope was to keep pulling on the string until someone heard the bell and dug you up."

Though I find this to be morbidly humorous, I'm not ready to engage with Seneca yet. I have heard of this burial practice before. Our training for the SEAL team covered this and many of the world's other death traditions. On the other hand, I have come across cultures that find our practice of cremation to be barbaric. They believe burning a body is disrespectful to the deceased — and to the Creator. I sense that Seneca is taking this conversation somewhere important, so I shift my attitude and start to show some interest.

He smiles. "Then there came a time when death was defined as not having a heartbeat. The science of medicine caught up with that and now you have ventricular fibrillation that can revive sixty to ninety percent of patients who experience cardiac arrest. You also have perfusion equipment that can take over the functions of the heart — *outside* of the body — while corrective surgery is being performed on the heart *inside* the body. You must know that life-support equipment is now capable of doing almost everything it takes to keep a human body alive indefinitely — feeding it, breathing for it, and even running simulated circulation.

"With 3D printers now capable of creating wombs and other organs, the definition of death is changing again. Life is no longer about the heart — it is about the mind. Based on what I just told you, do you think humans might eventually invent a type of technology capable of detecting brain activity on a whole new level?"

"I'm not sure where you're going with this, but I'll play along. Yes, I think man will eventually have the technology to detect brain activity on another level. Even so, what will that prove? There comes a point when a man is declared dead, right? Once all the machines are removed and the body begins to decay, common sense says it's over."

"Man is not dead even when the entire body, including the brain, stops functioning. Life is carried in a man's soul. The soul does not die. It changes dimensions when the human body can no longer contain it in the Third Dimension."

"So, given your explanation, is man the master of his own soul? Was I given a choice, or was this forced upon me?"

"Well, 'forced' is a bleak word for describing your destiny, but yes, you chose this. You could have stayed on Earth if you wanted to; your soul could have remained in the dead body. But once you cross dimensions and can see the bigger picture, it really would not make sense for you to return to where you were."

"'Wouldn't make sense'? That phrase usually means there are people who do the thing the rest of us think doesn't make sense. Do some choose to stay behind?"

"Some do. They are often the very tortured souls resisting the transformation because their destiny is not as great as yours. They know that they are headed to the darkness and isolation of Hades. They sometimes roam the Earth for years trying to avoid their fate. This ultimately worsens their situation. The longer they resist their destiny, the greater the punishment when they finally turn themselves in."

"So, they're like fugitives from the law?"

"That's one way to describe them. These souls are restricted to the Fourth Dimension. They cannot travel back and forth in their bodies and haunt people in the Third Dimension as many of Earth's horror movies suggest. Only their soul can move from place to place."

"But they can roam around in spirit?"

"Yes."

"And they're capable of moving tangible objects and interrupting human processes while in spirit mode?"

"Yes."

"With all due respect, that's considered a haunting where I come from. We just label it a 'friendly haunting.' Watching an object being moved by an unseen force is unsettling. I've experienced it. I was walking through my mother's living room and a candle flew off her mantle and barely missed hitting my leg. I still think it was thrown by some sort of force. Do you think the spirit was trying to get my attention for some reason?"

"Perhaps, but it is unlikely there was any malice involved. We call these beings 'lost souls.' They are trying to avoid facing the consequences of their life decisions. As you can probably imagine, they are angry about their fate. They occasionally move, touch, and manipulate objects to feel a sense of control. Your guardian angel is always by your side. A guardian angel's purpose is to keep humans from being harmed by dark forces. It is even possible the candle was intended to hit you but was deflected by your guardian angel."

"Can people be possessed by these 'lost souls'?"

"Yes, they do seek out bodies to possess. Possessing a human body allows them to move around in the human world again. The only way lost souls can enter the body of a person in the Third Dimension is through open invitation. Possessed people agree to host a spirit in order to gain personal power. The scary part is when a lost soul enters the host's body, suppresses the original soul, and holds it captive. Both souls are in the body together, the lost soul retains control and the original soul is held prisoner. The lost soul can thrive this way for years — even decades. Sometimes the lost soul stays put until the hosting body dies."

"Can humans see these roaming souls? The ones that aren't possessing bodies?"

"Not any more than they can see demons and angels. All three move around people every day. Combined, there are more angels, demons, and lost souls on Earth than people. But, as they travel in another dimension, they are rarely seen."

"I had a college buddy who claimed to have a 'sixth sense.' He said he could see these beings. He told me that he could also see spirit guides and guardian angels. Is this possible?"

"Yes, some people can see them. It takes tremendous discipline and open-mindedness to reach that level of consciousness. It might fascinate you to know that many animals can see them as well."

"Well, that explains our dog barking at dark rooms, closed doors, and empty vases. I have to say — being here where I can finally get my questions answered is surreal. I'm going to finally find out who killed Kennedy and JonBenet — and who stole my new Christmas bicycle in fifth grade."

"Yes, you will. Once the Mission is behind you, you will have infinite opportunity to get your answers. By the way, Kenny Spencer stole your bicycle."

"Seriously? I almost hit the wrong kid for that. I guess it's a good thing my mother happened by. Ha! This is going to be fun. So, what is this Mission? I guess we should get on with it. I assume time is of the essence."

"Actually, time is not a factor here. We are beyond the restrictions of the laws of physics. Time operates on Earth and in other places in the universe, but not here."

"What does that mean?"

"For the purposes of this conversation, it means that time on Earth is ticking away; however, we sit outside of that time-governed planet and can re-enter Earth at any point — past or present."

"What about the future?"

"Yes, to a certain extent."

"What does that mean?"

"It means you can see as far ahead as Almighty allows. There are some things he keeps as a mystery to us — like information about Himself. His essence exists in the Eleventh and Twelfth Dimensions. As far as we know, no man, Saint, or angelic being has ever crossed over into those dimensions. He has never spoken of the Twelfth Dimension. Lucifer likes to theorize that the Twelfth Dimension is where evil and good converge and exist as one and the same. We may never know."

"Backing up a bit, you said we crossed into the Fifth Dimension. Are there people here?"

"Yes, the residents of the Fifth Dimension are referred to as 'Warriors.' You are a Warrior, so this dimension will most likely be your next home. I reside in the Sixth Dimension."

"What's the difference between my dimension and yours?"

"There are some differences in our receptors and our capabilities to internalize emotions. Warriors are the most *self-aware* of Heaven's citizens. They know their limits and potential. They charge towards their goals without fear. Failure is not an option for them.

"The Sixth Dimension is home to 'Strategists' like me. We are excellent *self-managers* and are disciplined and orderly. We have a keen sense of our existence, which gives us the ability to apply logic to irrationality and order to chaos. Both Warriors and Strategists put objectives in front of people when solving a problem. They represent the side of the human spirit that is committed to surviving and thriving.

"The Eighth Dimension is where we find the 'Idealists.' This is one of the two dimensions that puts people first. Idealists are excellent *social managers*. They know how to establish rapport with all kinds of people. They motivate others to their top performance in any situation. They are highly creative because their positivity never allows them to quit. If one path does not get them where they want to go, they will find another.

"The Ninth Dimension is the home of the 'Samaritans.' Samaritans are very *socially aware*, and people are their source of joy. They can internalize the emotions and needs of others. They have infinite patience with people who are struggling. Their one goal is to help others realize peace and love. When Almighty said, 'The meek shall inherit the Earth,' He was referring to the Samaritans. Their love of people places them in the highest human dimension. Only the saints and Almighty sit higher."

"What about my dad? Where is he?"

"He resides in the Ninth Dimension. He is a Samaritan. Did you know this about him?"

"Not really, but I might have guessed it from the description you just gave. He was the most giving family man in our town. He was always helping the neighbors — and me. Tell me something. If he is living in a different dimension, will I be able to stay with him?"

"Yes, of course, if you like. But you might prefer to live in the dimension where the people share your approach to problem solving - and existence in general. You will find a shared perspective in the residents of the Fifth Dimension, not in the Ninth Dimension. If you decide to live here, you can go to visit your father at any time — and vice versa.

"You and I met in the Fourth Dimension, which is time. The dimensions above the Fourth Dimension are not restricted by time. People and spiritual beings can tap into the Third Dimension from anywhere — or any time — in the universe. You saw this when the image of your body was visible just minutes before we saw your mother with the flag from your casket. These events are days apart, but we can tap into them anywhere in time. Your funeral and the scene on your mother's porch have not taken place yet. We tapped into the future to see them."

My mind is still reeling from the information Seneca has just given me. He rises from his seat to shut down the 3D images. "This is a good place to stop and introduce you to some people. Are you up for a bit of a journey through the dimensions of Heaven?"

"Will it get me to my father?"

"Yes, it will…. Is this your only objective?"
"I give him a knowing smile. "Let me change my question: 'Will it get me to the Mission?'"

"Ha! I am impressed. How did you pick up on that?"

"I'm a fast learner. My entire life has been about the next mission. I figured it continues here."

"Yes, it does. Your observation is correct. You are designed to seek challenges. Your entire existence is about a mission. This never ends for you."

"You know, hearing that is music to my ears. In Sunday school, I was told that I was going to come here and be fitted with wings. I was also told I would walk on streets of gold — evidently when I grew tired of flying — and spend eternity singing songs accompanied by a harp. I don't even like harp music. Having to listen to it for eternity didn't sound like Heaven to me."

"Well, welcome to the truth."

"Why were we told these things?"

"I do not think anyone was trying to mislead you. That part of Heaven does exist — it is the Seventh Dimension. Some people like it and rarely leave. It is the level most often used to describe Heaven as a whole — mainly because it translates a positive image to all types of people. You, however, are a Warrior. The streets of gold and harp music would eventually bore you. You are destined for an eternity of missions. It would not be Paradise for you if it were any other way, would it?"

"No, it wouldn't. This is starting to sound like something I can get behind."

"Good. Let us get you up to speed on what happens next." Seneca motions for me to follow him through an archway. When I step through, I'm in an area that reminds me of Alaska in the summer. There are mountains and lakes as far as I can see. We are at one of the highest altitudes, and the air is invigorating. In the distance, I see a group of deer drinking from a lake covered with lavender water lilies. Elk nudge each other as they roam through the trees. They stop and look at us but move on as if we are just part of the landscape — evidently a part that is of no interest to them.

"This place is amazing, Seneca. Where are we?"

"This is your new home."

MALLOW SHERIDAN

35.

WARRIORS

"This is a Warrior's paradise. The people who live here are competitive, adventurous, and protective of others. They largely prefer to be independent and self-reliant. They possess highly developed survival skills.

"If you choose to stay here, you will be with people who share your value system. The terrain is rugged and challenging. It has steep mountains as well as beaches. It fits your definition of 'paradise.'"

"I'm guessing every dimension has an ocean. Who doesn't like beaches?"

"You would be surprised. I am going to take you to dimensions six through ten. I have some people for you to meet along the way. You will be leading a team of six on the Mission. There will be two each from the Sixth, Eighth, and Ninth Dimensions. They already know they have been chosen for this assignment, but they have only been given a few details. They have been told you will direct them when you meet."

"Wait. If we are picking up two people from each of the other dimensions, why am I the only one from the Fifth Dimension?"

"The residents of the Fifth Dimension have strong personalities. Warriors are like beta fish. If you put two together, they will likely fight to the death. You will function better if you are the only one leading."

"That makes sense, and it sounds like my life on Earth. How are the Warriors going to exist peacefully for eternity?"

"Well, your first assignments will keep you apart. And many Warriors eventually get assigned to other galaxies."

"Are you telling me there is life in other *galaxies*?"

"That answer will have to wait until later. It is multi-faceted."

"Then I have another question. If I'm going to give the team their instructions, shouldn't I be briefed on specifics now?"

"Yes and no."

"That's a very vague answer."

"I'll explain everything as we move along. There is a place for everything. Let us take another walk."

"Walk? I thought we would be flying here."

"Oh, you will be. You are not ready yet. I can fly, but I do not want to show off. It might be an affront to your manliness."

"Ha! As if!"

Seneca looks over his shoulder and smiles at me.

I like this guy, but he has a busy personality. His body movements are naturally slower than mine, but his mind moves quickly. It would be more accurate to say his mind moves complexly. I am increasingly frustrated with the information he is withholding. My training tells me people who withhold information either don't have it or are using it to their advantage. The soldier in me says we should have been talking about the Mission from the beginning to ensure details are not overlooked. I have no choice but to adapt to Seneca's timing for now. He knows his way around. I do not.

After another half mile is behind us, Seneca stops walking and perches himself atop a bleached boulder. He picks up a long stick and draws in the black sand as he begins talking. "Alright, let us review some things before we meet your team. Heaven begins in the Fourth Dimension. This is where I first met you. In Heaven, we use 'Dimension' and 'Heaven' interchangeably. Levels above the Fourth Dimension do not experience time. Trust me when I tell say this: You have not really lived until you have lived outside of time. It is a beautiful thing.

"On Earth, man is forever running against an imaginary clock. If he cannot find a way to turn it off, it will steal the joy of the moment and leave him with little more than regret and anxiety. Time was one of the curses put upon man and Earth after sin entered the world. There was no element of time in Eden, and there is no element of time here."

Seneca is making his point as he quickly draws in the sand. For a man who is so relaxed, he is showing a sudden sense of urgency.

"As you witnessed firsthand, the Fourth Dimension has a realm of free-flowing travel. It is the crossroads between the human dimensions and the spiritual ones. There is no delicate way of saying this: It is is also the place where the souls of men bound for Hades come for their sentencing. They are held for only a short time. They do not receive the pleasant awakening you did. They wake up in a dark, secluded holding cell in an area we call 'The Court of the Damned.'"

"Well, that's a pretty clear title. I think I understand what happens there."

"Yes. These souls receive their sentencing and are taken away by the demons. On the other hand, this is also where the souls bound for an eternity with Almighty awaken in their Paradise. After they are acclimated, the angels escort them to the Pearly Gates of St Peter in the

Seventh Dimension. Here, they enjoy their official welcoming. The Fourth Heaven has many different settings that manifest to fit each person's idea of Paradise. For you, it has always been the ocean. That is why you woke up near one. Everyone wakes up in their idea of perfection. It helps them relax into the transition. Nice perk, right?"

"Yes. Impressive."

"You were also dressed in your favorite clothing."

"Yes, I was. That's interesting. If I were to guess, I would have thought we arrived here either naked or in robes. I'm impressed that you know what my favorite clothes were."

"Your guardian angel and spirit guides enter all the data on you. If I were to describe our tracking system to your generation, I would say it is like a huge data server. Your life is uploaded as it happens. Every detail is recorded."

"That sounds like a huge — and unsettling — task. I must keep my team busy. I rarely sit still and am often in danger. When you say 'upload,' how is the data entered?"

"The citizens of Heaven have telepathy. Data can travel from the angels and spirit guides directly into your storage area in an instant. They do not have to leave your side to transfer information to storage."

"That sounds a lot like the 'Engage' app causing so much controversy on Earth right now. It's storing all of man's data and making it available to the public with very few firewalls. It is being accused of shattering privacy rights and leaving citizens exposed to discrimination. It is also estimated that the number of lawsuits filed against Engage in the United Kingdom alone will consume eight years of that nation's court time. I guess man doesn't like to be tracked or have his secrets revealed. When you say the citizens of Heaven have telepathy, does that include you? Can you read my mind?"

"That is a little complicated."

"I figured as much."

Seneca ignores my sarcasm and addresses my original question. "I possess the *skill* to read your mind, but only if you allow it. We cannot forcibly read each other's minds. The external information I speak of is collected from observation — not from mind reading. It is sensory for us and it permeates all of Heaven. It is translated into a haptic language so we can all tap into it.

"Almighty holds Himself to the same standard. As much as people want to believe their Creator *reads* their thoughts, they are misguided. I will explain more as we get closer to the Mission. For now, relax. Though everyone here can read your mind, they cannot do so without your permission."

As we begin to walk again, Seneca turns towards me and quickly looks me up and down. He begins to snicker. "Before we go too far, we need to do something about your outfit. I know you chose these items for comfort, but they will be a riot here — and may cause one, too."

"What's wrong with my clothes?"

"You are wearing a Beatles shirt."

"So?"

"In 1966, John Lennon told an interviewer that the Beatles were 'more popular than Jesus.' He went on to say that rock music would 'outlive Christianity.' I was thinking maybe you should change your clothes before you meet Jesus." Seneca lets out another belly laugh. It echoes behind him as he leads me to another location.

Seneca's laughter is contagious. I admit the thing about my clothes is funny. He seems to be a happy man. I am looking forward to knowing his level of contentment. That sounds like another type of paradise to me.

My mind wanders as we walk. I imagine everyone reflects on their life when they wake up here. Some probably face regret, wasted time, missed purposes, and lost loves. I am keenly aware I did little more with my thirty-one years than move from one duty to the next. I treated life as if it were a checklist.

"I can see that my military career gave me an excuse to live in self-imposed fear every single day of the last nine years. It turns out my fear was unfounded. I was always on a protected path leading to my purpose here."

Seneca shoots me an empathetic glance. "Yes, we humans seem to think our death is about ending our journey on Earth. It is not; it is about beginning our journey in Heaven."

"This should be announced at funerals. It might ease the pain of loss. Now that I am on the other side, I can see that life on Earth is a short part of an unending existence. As it turns out, entertaining the fear was the worst idea of my life." A bit of guilt settles into my mind as I realize how shallow my faith had been on Earth.

Seneca has probably seen it all by now. Even if he can't read my mind, I'm certain he has profiled me. I'm probably not the first "lone wolf" personality he has encountered. No doubt he has figured out I have a strong wall built around my emotions. He is probably aware that, after one failed relationship, I found life to be more manageable if I kept everyone at a distance. I sleep better knowing no one has the capacity to hurt me. Choosing to participate in relationships is one of the few things, men can control. And I control it well.

36.

STRATEGISTS

"The best way to learn about the other dimensions is to visit them, so let's go."

Seneca walks up to another area of dense fog and steps through. This is obviously the main transportation system here. I need Seneca to show me how he locates these portals to each dimension. He moves confidently from one dimension to the next and seems to be preparing for what lies ahead.

Though I'm a little annoyed with the postponement of reuniting with my father, I must admit I'm flattered to have been chosen to lead the Mission for Almighty. I hope I get a team of strong men so I can succeed. It may be the last thing I do before I face my dad, and I want to make him proud.

I push my hand through the fog first. The air is slightly cool and tingly. It reminds me of the feeling in the air right after a thunderstorm. I close my eyes and step through. When I open my eyes, I find Seneca standing in from me. He is laughing at me again.

"Okay, what's so funny this time?"

"You. A Navy SEAL closing your eyes when you step through fog. When did they teach you to do that?"

"Ha! I'm glad you're having some laughs at my expense."

"That makes two of us. Welcome to the Sixth Dimension — home of the Strategists. Look around and tell me what you think."

As I look, I see a different scene than was present in the Fifth Dimension. Instead of trees, lakes, and wilderness, I see buildings, fountains, and parks. The buildings range from single story flats to multi-story skyscrapers. They have a clean, crisp look — as if newly constructed. The streets around them are pristine and the grounds are perfectly manicured.

"This looks like a cross between a street in Boston's technology district and the eighteenth hole of the Augusta golf course."

There are many people moving around. They are conservatively dressed and perfectly groomed. Several wave at us as they pass by. They aren't moving quickly, but they are moving with purpose. I notice that people are walking down the street without cell phones held to their ears.

"Are you picking up on the energy here, Grayson? It is different from the Warrior Dimension. And guess what? No beaches."

"Then this must be the *boring* dimension." Once again, my humor seems to go right over Seneca's head.

"The people who live here might say the same thing about the Fifth Dimension. Strategists value excellence, order, and perfectly executed plans. They are meticulous record keepers."

"Record keeps of what, exactly?"

"Everything. The history of Earth, histories of various civilizations, history of births, deaths, marriages, divorces, crimes, innocence, abuse, victories, faithfulness, and especially prayers. They record changes on the planet like weather trends, extinction of animals, etc. They also keep the records of all that happens in the Heavens. The data server system I mentioned earlier is kept here. These people manage all its functions and data. They strategize solutions and suggest next steps for us. The only record not kept here is the *Book of Life*. That is in the Tenth Dimension with the Saints."

"But these people all look as if they are heading to work. Shouldn't Heaven be about resting or enjoying the outdoors?"

"You have to remember that not everyone values the same things you do."

"We are all unique; that's for sure."

"Well, we are unique in experience and perspective but, interestingly, people fit one of four basic designs — all carefully sculpted by Almighty. People who share a design are similar in values and goals. The way they approach opportunity and challenge is strikingly similar. This is the reason for multiple dimensions in Heaven. People basically choose one of four versions of Paradise."

Seneca smiles as he watches the scene on the street.

"Oh, I remember now — this is *your* dimension. It has to be because you're passionate about it when all I want to do is yawn and leave."

"This is all part of the experience. We are designed to fit one of Almighty's 'behavioral styles.' There are four of them. I was born a Strategist. On Earth, I was a financial planner. I arrived here shortly after the Stock Market Crash of 1929."

"You didn't jump out a window, did you?"

"I know you are making light of my situation, but it was a dark time for analytic Strategists. We plot our lives completely upon data. When the data fails us — as it did in the Crash — we have nothing to cling to, or so we think. I knew many men who did jump that day. It was as sad as watching the New York City terrorist attacks of 9/11 when people jumped hand in hand from windows to escape the flames. No, I did not jump. I did not have to. Our boss poured gasoline through the hallway, barricaded the exit doors with chains, and lit a match. He locked himself inside with us. He burned the records and the building. He massacred one hundred two employees — including me."

"That's awful. I'm sorry your life was cut short like that. Did you leave behind children or a wife?"

"No children and no wife. I was one of those men who stayed married to his work. It is a very selfish way to live. It is behind me, and I am here to carry on with the purpose for which I was created. You should know that no one has their life cut short except those who commit suicide.

"Almighty and the angels know exactly when a human soul is set to cross dimensions. That is why we were prepared for your arrival. Life on Earth is only the first phase of who you are — and who you will be. Every soul continues. Now that you are a resident of Heaven, you have a new body to carry you forward. How are you enjoying the perfect temple that now carries your soul?"

"It's great. I was wondering about that. Since I have been here, my body has been tingling with good vibes. It feels like Christmas — or when you fall in love. I am relaxed and sense this great positive energy. I haven't been hungry or felt the need to go to the bathroom."

Seneca lets out another great laugh. "I guess you are only experiencing minimal changes compared to some. You arrived here at the relatively early age of thirty-one with a body that was already in great shape. When many people arrive here in their new bodies, they find themselves healed of aging, illness, obesity, and disabilities. These people are ecstatic."

"So, everyone is restored to a healthy age and condition? That makes sense. I noticed everyone here appears to be about my age, in shape, and looking happy. How does all this work?"

"Everyone is given a new body when they transition to Heaven. Their soul enters a newly created body that represents their best possible health, age, and appearance. All physical ailments and disabilities are healed — all the way down to blemishes. They are relieved of anything that was a physical or mental burden for them."

"So, everyone here is at the same age physically?"

"Pretty close to it. The Saints are an exception, as are we guides. Our advanced age exudes wisdom." Seneca grins.

"That's interesting."

"Let us head to the Assembly Hall of the Sixth Dimension. There are two people waiting there who are excited to meet you."

After walking half a mile on the cleanest sidewalks, I have ever seen, we step into an entry hall decorated with steel molding. The nickel flooring is shining as if it was polished just for our arrival. The walls are a neutral gray, and the draperies are pure white.

We step into the Assembly Hall to find much the same style. The seats face the stage and look to be "practically comfortable" with headrests and recliner footstools. A guy and a girl are seated by the entrance; they appear to be waiting for us. They stand and walk to Seneca and share a hug. As I watch, I'm confused. Why would Seneca put a woman on the Mission? And this guy looks as if he worked on his grooming for an hour. He's a total pretty boy. I hope this isn't indicative of the entire team, or we could be in trouble.

Once the three of them catch up with a few niceties, they turn to greet me.

"Grayson, I would like to introduce you to Seiko from Japan. She transitioned from Earth at age twenty-four. She was a student on a humanitarian trip and was infected with the Marburg hemorrhagic fever. She is a whiz at analyzing data and is fluent in five languages. She will be a great asset to your team."

"Hello. Seiko? Great name! Marburg fever? I've always feared being exposed to Marburg when I traveled to countries where people were known to be carriers. I'm sorry to hear you went through that. I understand it's very painful."

"Hello, Grayson." She hugs me firmly. "Also, a great name. Yes, it was painful. I envy the people who get to leave Earth in an instant — via a car accident or heart failure. With an infectious disease, you are not only in pain but, because you are contagious, you usually die alone. That was the tough part. But it is behind me and life is good. We were told you were coming even before your death on Earth. We are all thrilled to be working with a seasoned soldier."

"Thank you, Seiko."

Seneca makes the second introduction: "This is Sterling. He is from the United Kingdom. He was twenty-nine when he transitioned. He was a public defender until the unstable father of a murdered child brought a gun to his office and shot him at his courthouse desk."

I extend my hand. "That's a tough break, Sterling. Being shot and killed on the job is something with which I can sympathize. Did they at least catch the guy and figure out how he smuggled a gun into the building?"

"Yes, they caught him. Guards were in the hallway. They just misread this guy and let him walk in. My secretary was at lunch. He had access and took the shot. He smuggled a small handgun in by making multiple trips through security with pieces of the gun attached to his key ring. He hid the pieces in the janitor's closet until he got them all inside. Once the last piece was in, he assembled the gun and came after me. But that is all in the past. I share Seiko's feelings about working with you."

"I appreciate that. It's good to be working with you as well."

"If everyone is ready, we will continue on to the Seventh Dimension," Seneca says as he heads out with the three of us following closely behind.

According to what Seneca told me earlier, there are no permanent residents of the Seventh Dimension. It is a neutral area shared by all the citizens of Heaven. This is where residents come to socialize. He says when people on Earth visualize Heaven, this is usually what they see.

As surreal as this day has been, I'm looking forward to seeing angles fly and walking on streets of gold. I'm going to hear the music of heaven and find out if it includes any of my favorite rock classics. When I was a teenager, my mother used to say there was no way my music was going to make it into Heaven. She says angels will be serenading us with their harps. I hope she's wrong about Rock Music – and the harps. I was forced to listen to harp music every Sunday in church – eerie.

"Here is our portal. Grayson, I'm going to suggest that you go through first."

"Why? Are you setting yourself up for another good laugh at my expense?"

"I will take this one." Sterling steps forward to answer for Seneca. "The Seventh Dimension is one of the most spectacular views in Heaven. It is best enjoyed by stepping through with no one blocking it. Trust him; he is right."

"Okay. I can do that."

Even though I agree to take them up on their invitation, I'm suspicious of their intent. I'm always concerned about manipulation. It's part of my nature. I am uneasy with anything I am told to do until I can figure out the other person's angle. I want to know what they stand to gain by getting me on board. I would usually turn down an offer like this; but I need to prove my leadership abilities, which include bravery. I move to the front of the group.

This portal is different. The misty fog has gold flecks. "What's with the sparkly stuff?"

Sterling answers for Seneca again. "Those are flakes of pure gold. A little hint of what is on the other side."

I'm not sure if Sterling is fielding my questions because he likes to be the center of attention, or if he really doesn't know that I'm addressing Seneca as the leader of the group. Civilians often dismiss protocol such as this. I make a mental note to cover this in the training.

"Okay, then. Here I go."

37.

HEAVEN

Since three people are watching me as I enter the portal, I decide to forgo the hand-first approach that earned me a ribbing from Seneca earlier. With my back to them, I close my eyes and step into the mist with its swirling specks of gold. As soon as my feet touch down on the other side, I open my eyes to the most spectacular view I have ever seen. I do a 360-degree turn to see it from every direction. There is perfect beauty everywhere I look. After taking a deep breath, I feel a rush of both relief and joy.

Eighty percent of people on Earth believe there is an afterlife "haven" where souls go when they die. Most people envision a place of beauty. These people will not be disappointed. The other twenty percent are in for a shocker. Heaven is better than anything they can imagine. If I were traveling alone right now, I would dance across these beautiful grounds and shout out, "Heaven is real. Almighty is real. And I made it!"

The powder-blue skies make a great background for the twinkling lights. The twinkling gives the place a magical feel. As far as I can see, this dimension is softly lit with a warm, white light. As promised, I am standing on a street made of gold. I lean down and run my hands across its smooth surface. It is warm to the touch. The gold is so finely polished that my fingers do not leave a mark. It is so light in color that I can see the smallest details of my reflection.

In between the streets of gold, there is a surface of white where you would normally find green grass. Unlike Earth's grass that grows upward in blades, this ground is braided. It is about six inches high and pure white. There isn't a single mark on it anywhere. The white ground cover extends in every direction. It looks like a peaceful neighborhood right after newly fallen snow has covered its flaws. I run my fingers through it. The ground cover is soft and cool to the touch.

The rest of the scene is much like one you would find on Earth — except this one is perfect. There are fruit-bearing trees ripe with fruit and streams of clear water flowing and gurgling over rocks. I dip my hands into the cool water and take a sip. Its taste amazes me. I had forgotten what water tastes like without chemicals and plastic bottles.

I look over a valley of beautiful shrubs and flowers. There are birds of every color flying overhead and small, furry animals playing together on the white lawn. I see a city of sorts at the bottom of the valley. I walk towards the edge of the cliff to get a closer look. The few steps I take feel light and airy. Oddly, my steps move me forward about six feet. From here, I see four sides of a city square. Rows of alabaster seats rise high on every side It looks to be about eight or nine hundred feet. From where I stand, the arena looks like a massive sports stadium. There are small groups of people socializing on every level. This place can probably hold over 200,000 people.

My newly enhanced eyesight allows me to see a group of musicians at the center of the stage playing tunes on at least ten different instruments. Their music is echoing across the terrain. It reaches to the top of the hill where I am standing. To my relief, the music is great! I listen for a harp among the instruments and, yep, it's there. I laugh a little. I'm pretty sure it will grow on me in time.

"What do you think, Son?" Seneca and the rest of the group join me.

"It's unbelievable. Absolutely incredible! I'm looking forward to going down to the city for a closer look. I have a question, though. It seems like I can't see the lay of the land here. As I move around, I've noticed it looks like there are slopes to the ground; but when I take a step, it doesn't feel like I'm walking on an angle. I also appear to be covering six feet per step. Is this an optical illusion?"

"That's a great way to describe it. Many things will appear to be optical illusions until you adjust to living here, especially the 'lay of the land.' The great Irish blessing comes true here. The road does 'rise up to meet you.' As far as the long steps go, you are indeed moving about six feet forward each time you take a step. It's due partly to the lack of gravity and partly to the larger stride your enhanced legs are taking."

"I like it!"

Seneca shoots me his toothy grin. "Well, I am glad you approve. We are only stopping here briefly, but I wanted you to be familiar with the Seventh Dimension before you begin the Mission. I want you to fully understand what you are fighting for."

"Fighting for? Whoa, wait!" *This mission just got real.* "Are you telling me there's a possibility of losing all of this? I had a sense this engagement was a covert operation. That's my specialty. How high is the risk? Is it possible for this team to be injured, or even killed, in the line of duty? What does this mean if we have already died? Where do we go if we are killed?"

"First of all, we say 'transformed' or 'crossed over' rather that 'died' or 'killed.' You are not going to like my answer to your questions."

"Let me guess. 'They're complicated answers and I will understand in time'?"

"Hey, you got one right."

I do not respond to Seneca this time. Cloaked operations always bother me. My concerns are growing, and my trust is diminishing. As Seneca leads the way to the arena, I slow my pace.

Sterling taps me on the shoulder and leans close to speak softly into my ear. "You have to trust everything here, Grayson, or it is going to be a very rough ride for you. I know. I was you a few years ago. I questioned pretty much everything, especially the scientific and sociological aspects of this life. I can tell you that all my questions were answered in time. In hindsight, I see why I did not need the answers when I wanted them. It is not much different than how it works on Earth. I guess it bothered me more here because I thought I was entitled to the answers. And, like on Earth, I eventually saw that the answers came at the perfect time. Just remind yourself this is not about deception or withholding. Mostly, it's just a case of us not being ready to receive the information."

"Yeah. Thanks, Man. You're right. I'll let it go."

"And enjoy the ride. This dimension in which we stand is too amazing for even the enhanced human mind to comprehend in a single visit. You will have to come back here after we complete the Mission. The best way to take it all in is to sit down, lean against a tree, observe, and think."

"For how long?"

"Ah, Grayson, there is no time here."

"Ballpark it in Earth time."

"I would say a year."

"Seriously? Lean against a tree for a year?"

Sterling laughs. "I see you are going to be one of those guys."

"Which guys?"

"A rebel. A man who starts pushing the limits the second they are set. A man without patience."

"Yep. Sounds like me. Is that going to be a bad thing?"

Sterling turns and smiles. "Not for us. You are the one who deals with your head. For us, it will be pure entertainment."

"Ha! Well, Seneca is getting some good laughs at my expense already. What's a few more? Hey, sideline question: What is the deal with Seneca?"

"What do you mean 'what's the deal'?"

"Is he solid? Can I trust him?"

"You can trust him with your life."

"Okay. That is all I needed to hear."

"You mean that is all you needed to hear for now. You will be back with more questions later."

"What makes you think that?"

"He has not started to set any limits yet. You will see." Sterling pats me on the back.

I look over at him and we both begin to laugh.

After walking a short distance, Seneca turns to gather us around him. "All right, team, I want to go over some ground rules before we enter the city."

Sterling makes eye contact with me and mouths, "Limits."

My limbs tense up. I guess I learned something about myself today — I'm a rebel. Military training was supposed to beat all that out of me. I guess it didn't take. I shake my head at him.

"Grayson, since this is your first time here, most of this is directed to you. This is not a social visit for us; it is an information gathering visit. The people you see are aware of the impending Mission, so there is no need to discuss it. Yes, they know what is at stake. While you are on Earth, every man, Saint, and angel in Heaven will be in non-stop prayer for your courage and safety. Since we are only half-way through our journey, we will not stop for conversation. If you have any questions, direct them to a team member or to me."

"I can do that."

Every step I take down the mountainside advances me six feet. Some astronauts have had this sensation, but it's new to me. I see two sets of gates into the city. The first is made entirely of pearl and is guarded by seven angels who float back and forth carrying swords. There is a man sitting on a throne that is perched above the gates.

"That is Saint Peter," Seiko whispers. "He stays there constantly. He is the official greeter for Heaven. He has an infectious, joyful demeanor. He is the perfect person for people to meet when they arrive. Everyone loves St. Peter."

"I didn't get the opportunity to meet him when I arrived."

"Yeah, I heard. But you will. He will seek you out. He meets everyone who lives here."

Once we step through the main gates, all my senses go off at once. There is a beautiful symphony for my ears and an intoxicating floral mixture for my nose. My mom would say it smells like the Rose of Sharon. She likes to use Biblical references whenever she can. She will love it here. There is excitement in the air that makes the hair on my arms tingle. The temperature is perfect, the brooks are babbling, and my feet feel light as I walk.

Over the years, I've visited some of the most beautiful cities on Earth, but nothing comes close to this. There's a mixture of gold, crystal, and white marble from the streets to the highest row in the coliseum. The colors of fabrics in the curtains, cushions, and table settings are a mild mixture of earth tones — mostly blues and beiges. There are white roses lining the streets and white blooms on the trees spread across the open areas. Tree blossoms lift into each round of the light breeze. I watch one drift through the air. It swirls in a figure eight pattern and lands on the white lawn. When it touches the ground, it turns into a drop of water and is absorbed into the braided "grass." I look back to where the bloom left the tree branch and see that another bloom has already grown to take its place.

The people are sitting in small groups talking and laughing. Some of them wave to us but stay focused on their activities. Some are painting. Others are playing board games. Many are writing. While they are doing their thing, angels hover above them - suspended in mid-air aided by the opening and closing of their tall, white wings. They bring the people bowls of fruit and goblets of drinks.

"Do we eat here? I haven't felt hungry."

"You can eat if you want to. Your body no longer needs food, but the enjoyment of taste is something Almighty gave us. Most people partake regularly when they socialize. You can eat anything you want and stay at your ideal weight. Your new body absorbs all the food and liquids you take in. There is no waste to necessitate bathroom breaks."

"I like that idea."

As I look behind me, I see animals mingling with the people. Most of them are the animals we tame and keep as pets on Earth. I see cats and dogs playing together. There are sheep and goats nibbling on the white ground covering. I see horses galloping across the fields beyond the gates.

Seiko elbows me and directs my attention to the set of gates on the south side. A lion has just entered and is walking in our direction. "Do not be alarmed by the lion. When I first saw one here, I jumped behind a boulder and hid. It found me and licked my neck. I thought for sure it was going to eat my face for lunch. All the animals here are docile — even the dinosaurs that live on the outlying edges of your Warrior Dimension. The lions will lie down and purr if you run your fingers through their manes. The animals are here for our viewing pleasure and companionship. You can even claim one as your own if you like. I have my childhood dog living with me again."

"Seriously? You're telling me that dogs go to Heaven?"

Seiko laughs. "They do not have souls as we do. They are *remade* here if we want them."

"Nice! This place is incredible. It is beyond my wildest imagination. The people are beautiful. The scenery is stunning. It's 'Nirvana.'"

"Nice choice of words. The name of the city is New Eden."

"New Eden? Great name. I would like to come here with my parents and catch up on life. I can see the three of us strolling here with my mother on my arm."

"That sounds beautiful. You are a lucky man to have both parents here, and on their way here. I am not so blessed. My welcoming ceremony did not include either of my parents. Evidently, they made some wrong turns in life."

"That's rough. What happened?"

"It is simple, really. They did not believe in Almighty and lived as if a Creator did not exist. As kids, we were punished if we even discussed religion. They brought a lot of pain upon themselves — and us. When money ran low, they would steal. Sometimes, they made us steal. In time, they figured out they could make more money by dealing drugs. They were found out when they blew up half of our house while cooking meth. They both died in the explosion. Family Services separated the three of us and put us into orphanages. My siblings were adopted, but I was not so lucky. I grew up pretty much on my own, but my siblings are living here now, so that helps. Eternity is a long time not to have your parents, you know?"

Seiko is new in my life, but I am certain this unflappable demeanor is her baseline. The shift to introspection, while in paradise, is deserving of my attention as a leader.

"You know, Seiko, my mother told me one of Almighty's promises is that He will relieve us of our grieving in the end. She said He's going to wipe away every tear and ease the pain of being separated from the people we love."

"That helps. Thank you."

"Sure thing."

Though I would like to stay longer in the Seventh Dimension, Seneca's wave reminds me we must move on. He gathers us close as we step back through the entrance gates and shares some information obviously meant for me. "Our next destination is the Eighth Dimension. It is the dimension of the Idealists. Their nature is the opposite of the Strategists. Idealists and Strategists *should* work well together since their talents complement each other. Idealists can conceptualize amazing things, and Strategists can bring those amazing things to fruition. It does not always work out, though. Idealists tend to think that Strategists are much too serious. Strategists tend to think that the Idealists are irresponsible and unrealistic in the development of their concepts."

"Do they argue?"

"No. There is no arguing here, but they tend to avoid each other."

"Ha! There are cliques of 'mean chicks' in Heaven, too. Who would have guessed?" I look around to see if anyone picks up on my attempt at humor. No one has. Why am I the only on enjoying my exaggerated analogy?

Sterling shakes his head and pats my arm out of pity. I hope these guys lighten up a bit. If not, this is going to be a long mission. War and covert operations are very intense once they begin. The only way to survive — and keep your mind intact — is to engage in some humor along the way.

Sterling raises his hand to stop us. "Here is our portal."

Seneca steps through without hesitation. I step back to allow Seiko to go in front of me. I'm not sure if the gender rules apply here but I'm going to play it safe by sticking with my mother's training. She thanks me and follows Seneca. Sterling follows her. I am the last one through to the Eighth Dimension.

38.

IDEALISTS

The Eighth Dimension is stunning. It looks as if a tie-dye artist sprayed the entire place with happy colors. Everything is balanced — the same number of houses on the streets, the same number of windows on the houses, and the same number of flowers on either side of the street.

A gentle breeze is blowing. It is circulating air that smells like a combination of baked apples and pumpkin pie. The air has an excitement to it. It feels like an autumn day. As a connoisseur of air, I am sure this is the sweetest I've ever smelled. People fly kites in the open field to the right. To the left is a carnival in full swing. Jazzy music is playing through the street speakers and everyone seems to be enjoying their day.

"Are they celebrating a holiday?"

"No, this is how things are in the Eighth Dimension. The people who live here are all about enjoying life. After all, they *are* Idealists. When they get serious about solving a problem, they are highly creative. They attribute their creativity to keeping life simple and balanced, as you see here. They can come up with multiple solutions to a problem when others cannot find even one. There is a tremendous energy flow here. I get invigorated every time I visit."

"It sounds great. Why don't you live here?"

"For the same reason you will not choose to live here. It's a bit *too happy* for me. I know that sounds odd when you are talking about

Heaven, but we bring our Earthly desires with us. Some things do not change. *You* need challenges and obstacles in your life, and *I* need to be dissecting problems and organizing chaos. But this is still a great place to visit if you need an infusion of positive energy."

"Tell me about the people here. I can see they are intent on enjoying themselves. What does it take to engage them in work — like solving the complex problems you mentioned?"

"You have to make it interesting. Once they get engaged in a project, Idealists are like pit bulls. They will keep going until they are satisfied with their results. You cannot really lead them to do anything they do not *want* to do. They are free spirits for sure — like helium-filled balloons. The more you try to contain them, the more they try to escape your grip. The key is slipping on a string while they are flying high on ideas. They will bounce along behind you and be happy to let you lead. After all, leadership is mostly about doing boring stuff, right?"

I open my mouth to argue the point, but Seneca winks, which tells me his question is both rhetorical and a little sarcastic. He knows I find leadership to be the most rewarding part of life.

Seneca seems delighted with himself for being one Strategist who has figured out how to work with Idealists. "Idealists share a competitive spirit and an independent streak with the Warriors. But, unlike Warriors, they are sensitive. If you take them on, prepare yourself for a verbal confrontation. They are great communicators and are never short on words. They have the extraordinary gift of limitless imagination. This gives them an advantage over Warriors and Strategists when it comes to conceptualizing solutions. Enjoy the colorful view. It is a short walk to the place where we will meet your next two team members."

I increase my pace so I can walk next to Seneca. I want to talk to him out of the hearing range of Seiko and Sterling. "Seneca, can I ask how you chose this team? From what I have seen so far, the personalities and skill sets are all over the place. I'm not sure we'll be able to complete a task in a cohesive manner. The military teams I have led in the past - all had the same skill set. This is making me a little uneasy."

"How can you be uneasy without knowing anything about the assignment? Do not worry. Michael chose this team. There is no better fighter than Michael. He is familiar with the Mission and he is familiar with you. Just hold tight. You will meet him when we set the strategy. He will explain how the combined talents you are questioning, are a perfect match for the Mission. Diversity always strengthens a team."

"Michael? You mean the Archangel Michael?"

"Yes."

"Whoa! It's too bad you don't allow cell phones here. I could load my Snapchat with some pretty great pictures with the Archangel of War."

"And send them where? And show them to whom?"

"You got me there."

"Who told you we do not allow cell phones? You can have any material thing you desire. You can pick one up at the depot outside the gates of the Seventh Dimension. And you will be happy to know that the signal up here is fantastic."

"You're joking, right?"

"Just a little. Once you master telepathy, you will not be interested in carrying a limited tool for communicating."

"Point taken. I'm sure telepathy is more efficient."

"Grayson, I sense your frustration. I promise you are getting the information you need. The whole picture comes together soon."

"Fair enough."

"All right, we are here. We are about to meet the next two members of the team. Let us make them feel welcome." Seneca opens the double doors of a small faux castle.

As soon as I step inside, I am startled by a reflection of myself right in front of me. All the walls are covered with mirrors. "What is all this?"

"I will answer that, Seneca." The voice comes from a man in his twenties who jumps down from a ledge above a mirrored wall. He is dressed in a white button-down shirt and black skinny jeans. His high-top sneakers are covered with colored squares that remind me of a Rubik's Cube. His hair is bleach-blonde with blue, green, and purple tips. "We like the mirrors for checking our appearance — and for having some fun. This is a perfect place for us to get a little crazy. It is like a carnival funhouse. It is challenging to get out of here, and it can take hours. It is fun because you keep running into people you know while you're looking for the exit. Hi, I'm Liam."

"Hello. I'm Grayson."

"Yeah, we have been waiting for you."

"Am I picking up a Russian accent?"

"Very brill of you. Yes, I am from Russia. I arrived here when I was twenty-five. I was a translator of the Russian language for banks in London. I was loving life until the night a careless driver was texting. He crossed the center line and I was gone."

"Wow, that's tough. Do you ever wonder what you could have done with your life If you had more time?"

"I never think like that. The view behind you should never be analyzed and questioned. This is what Seneca teaches us. He also likes to tell us this explains why we were designed with heads that will not go all the way around."

I laugh with Liam. No one else seems to be rolling with us. I lean close to Liam so the others can't hear me. "The Strategists don't have much of a sense of humor, do they?"

"No, they do not; but it is part of their charm — as well as their talent. In time, you will come to appreciate their dry wit. Though they rarely laugh themselves, they know how to build a good story that will have you laughing so hard your stomach hurts."

Liam barely finishes his sentence when a girl with long ringlets of black hair covered with silver glitter steps out from behind a mirror and shouts, "Ta-da!" She spreads her arms wide and bows. She is wearing very loud makeup and a lime jumpsuit. "Hello, I'm Kimmy. Sorry I am late. I got lost on the second floor again and Liam, here, left me behind. Bad form, Liam! I am so excited to meet you guys. I cannot believe that I get to be a part of this most excellent team. It is like, 'can you pinch me, please?' You must be Grayson. You are too adorable to be a soldier. I am feeling that tee you are wearing. What happened to your shoes?"

"Yeah, okay. I'm not sure what to do with all that, but good catch on the shoes. I arrived without them."

Seneca clarifies. "He woke up on the beach."

"Oh, that is so cool! We have us a Beach Boy who likes the Beatles. Excellent! But, Dude, you gotta have some leather on the pedis. Liam, give him a pair of your shoes."

Liam claps hard and starts jogging towards the door. "You got it! What size, G-man?"

"Size ten."

"Per-*fec*-to. I got you covered. Be back in five."

As Liam heads out for the shoes, I dare to ask Kimmy to tell me her story.

"Sure, I'll give up the geno. My heritage is African. I grew up in Seychelles. My father worked for the government, so I had a great childhood. I was accepted to University in Europe and studied programming. I transitioned here when I was twenty-six. Before my coda, I was writing code for a robotics company — not the boring stuff. Yeah, no I was writing code for robotic toys — a total funfest. I caused my own death, but it was an accident. A few of us would get high before we did our initial designs. We liked to tap into our crazy imagination, you know. We would go full-on 'Steve Jobs.' Some of my friends did harder hallucinogens, but I stayed with weed because it was legal, and I did not want to mess up my record.

"One night, I was up against a big project deadline. I was having trouble chilling out after a breakup with my boyfriend, so I asked the guy who got me my weed if he had anything stronger. He suggested I give heroin a try. At first, I protested, but he told me I could be out of pain in thirty seconds. He said everyone was doing it and that it was the most popular drug he sold. He told me the experience was like the 'happy drugs' you get in the hospital before surgery. I did remember those minutes as a perfect state of being, so I caved. He did the injection and I was floating for about thirty minutes. As promised, there was no pain. Then I started having trouble breathing. He told me to lie down and I would be fine. But I was not fine. I went to sleep and woke up here."

I do not know how to react to Kimmy's story. For very personal reasons, I have always been bothered by suicides — even if they are accidental. I'm not sure what brings someone to the point of needing to escape so badly that they endanger themselves. I've spent most of my adult life trying to keep people alive — people who were passionate about living and were begging for the chance to live.

Since I can't think of a good reply, I stay quiet. Just as the silence is getting uncomfortable, Liam darts back through the door with bright orange flip-flops for me to wear.

"These will do great things for your fashion, 'Son of Gray.'"

I stare down at my open toes in disbelief. "Wow, thank you. I don't know what to say. The guys on the SEAL team would be fighting to wear shoes like these on their operations."

My sarcasm is lost on Liam. "I know, right? These babies let your toes breathe, and they even glow in the dark. Your guys could send messages to each other at night just by moving their feet."

"Hmmm. I think you're onto something there, Liam." I step into the shoes regretting that I didn't pick some up in a different, more normal, dimension of Heaven. "Thank you both for looking out for me."

"It's our pleasure, Captain."

Seneca winks at me. "Ok, Millennial Team, let's get to the Ninth Dimension. We still have much to do."

MALLOW SHERIDAN

39.

SAMARITANS

"I know I must be driving you crazy with all my questions, Seneca, but I noticed you just referred to us as the 'Millennial Team.' What's that all about?"

"You are all from the Millennial generation, are you not?"

"Well, yes, so far the team appears to be Millennials, I really didn't think about it. I just noticed we all seemed to be close to the same age. I thought this was connected to our state of well-being in Heaven — like the perfect age."

"That is true as well. The entire story is that generations have been an important part of Almighty's moving throughout the ages. Men would have better predicted wars and other international trends if they had studied His social design. Generations have shared experiences and perspectives. They have a personality."

"A *personality*?"

"Yes, Sir. Have you not noticed that Millennials are a very bold generation? They have big personalities — just like the Warriors."

"Like the Warriors? You mean, like the Warriors living in the Fifth Dimension? Like me?"

"Yes. You have a double share of the Warrior personality traits. This combination of your individual personality with your identical generational personality is a big part of why you succeeded as a military leader. Warriors are fearless. They are visionaries, fast-paced, determined, and powerful. Have you heard these things said of your generation on Earth?"

"Maybe, but most of the time I just hear that we act entitled."

"Not so. That is the wrong label. You are *opportunists*. You take what you are given — if there are no strings attached. When society, or your parents, offers you something freely — like a car, a basement apartment, a new iPhone — you take it. You are very aware of the value gained. You also avoid volunteering to do things that are at or below your skill level. You only expend energy on things that move you forward or increase your potential. To others, this looks like you do not want to pay your dues. Bingo! Why pay dues if there is a direct path to the objective? Am I right?"

"Well, I've never heard it said quite like that but, yes, you're right. You're saying Millennials are abrasive and head-strong?"

"You tell me."

"Yes, we are. So back to the team — are you saying we were picked because we're Millennials?"

"It is more a case of Almighty setting the end of Earth when the Warrior generation is aligned with the governing power."

"Okay. You lost me."

"Tell you what — let us hold this topic until we go into the details of the Great Game. We have arrived at the next portal."

Once again, Seneca has avoided giving me a full answer, but the big picture is finally coming into view. What he said about generations is intriguing. He seems to be implying that there are patterns within society, and Heaven, that define our levels and assignments. Even more intriguing is his hint that the end of Earth was pre-determined by Almighty based upon the generations. I'm looking forward to having this team fully assembled so we can dig into all these mysteries.

The team is growing. This time there are six of us going through the portal to the Ninth Dimension. According to Seneca, the dimension of Heaven we are now entering is home to my father. He also told me I won't be seeing my father until the Mission is completed, but that won't stop me from looking for him in the crowd.

"All right, team. We are going to head through the portal. A bit of a 'heads up' for you, Grayson: Most first-time visitors to the Samaritan Dimension find themselves being inordinately reflective. Nothing is rushed here, and feelings are shared openly. I call this dimension of Heaven 'the land where time stands still.' For those of you familiar with the plodding pace of us Strategists, you can see this is a bold statement."

The entire team laughs with Seneca. So, Strategists do have a sense of humor —if it's about them. I file that bit of information away for another time.

Laughter is always good for bonding. I like these people and, for the first time, I'm excited about working with a team. In the past, teams have not been my thing. I saw them as being little more than an added responsibility and a source of distraction. I like being responsible for the safety and survival of other people, but not for their emotional well-being.

Other than my mom, I haven't had the desire to take care of anyone. Well, I guess that's not entirely true. I was in love once. I would have enjoyed a lifetime of taking care of her, but it wasn't meant to be.

While I'm still deep in thought, Kimmy slides up beside me. I can feel her smiling up at me. I have learned something else about the Idealists: they refuse to be ignored. "What?"

"So, tell me about the girl."

"What girl?"

"The one you're thinking about right now. I can tell."

"How?"

"You are smiling — and you are in Heaven's version of *Weepsville*."

"Excuse me?"

"You know — the emotional dimension. Lots of people cry here — in a good way. We have a bit of a walk and I am not letting you change the subject, so tell me about the girl."

Kimmy is sweet, and I can tell she is not going to let this go. I guess she is in her "pit bull" mode.

"All right, but it's a long story."

"I'm all ears — and heart — so go."

"We met when I was twenty-four and she was seventeen. I was half-way through my first three-year service with the Navy. We were brought to Haifa, Israel on one of the Navy's aircraft carriers. It was a routine stop. Haifa is one of our ports of call. We do training missions with the Israeli Navy every year.

"Our Captain was looking for a volunteer to stay behind in Israel and continue training with their drone piloting program I was more than happy to raise my hand. Spending six months on land sounded good. I am not fond of being on a ship for months at a time. My bunkmates found that hilarious considering my career choice. After looking at the brochures, I honestly believed by entire service with the Navy would be on land.

"When I signed the contract with the Navy at age nineteen, I did it to get them to pay the tuition for my engineering degree. When I graduated, I owed them three years of service. The original story from the recruiter was that I would be assigned to one of the Navy's communication centers in one of 'a handful of exotic foreign cities.' Suspiciously, all the exotic city jobs were filled when I reported for assignment, so I ended up operating the Command Center on the U.S.S. George W. Bush.

"Because of my degree in engineering, the Captain chose me to stay in Haifa. I started bunking down in the barracks of the Israeli Navy. I trained with them every day — doing both physical and drone training.

"One night, after winning a fitness challenge, three of us were given passes to the local nightclub to listen to some music. When we arrived, it was thumping. The music was so loud we could barely hear each other over the bass. I shouted to my bunkmate, 'You know the music is too loud when it tickles.' We worked our way through the crowd, ordered drinks at the bar, and made it to the balcony.

"It was a beautiful night, and I was thinking it was the perfect setting for a romantic date. Minutes after I entertained that thought, I met the love of my life. I carelessly stepped backwards and bumped into her.

"She was carrying a tray of drinks from a table she had just bussed. Thankfully, the tray was full of used glasses with just small amounts of leftover liquor in them. Even so, I felt terrible. I know bussing tables is not an easy job. I did it one summer when I was in high school and hated it. I knelt to help her clean up the cups, straws, and lime wedges. One smile from her and I was smitten.

"Her name tag said 'Tova,' so I said to her, 'You have an interesting name.'

"Without missing a beat, she replied, 'That's because I have an interesting mother.'

"We both laughed. As we were picking up the last few items from the floor, I found the courage to introduce myself. In a few minutes, I learned she was a first-year student in a local community college. She was studying international business because her mother was living in the United States for her job. She was hoping it would open some good conversation between them.

"I told her, 'That's a beautiful thing you are doing. Not many people think about their parents when making their career choice. You must be the last of the world's great daughters.' As soon as I said it, I knew I was overly generous with my praise. I also realized I was pretty lame with the ladies."

Kimmy grimaced and nodded.

"I hoped she could overlook both if I kept the conversation going. I changed directions and asked Tova how her night was going before I bumped into her and took the smile off her face.

"She said, 'You didn't take my smile. I still have it, see?'

"I looked up and saw that she had put one of the lime wedges across the front of her teeth to make a green smile. I started to laugh. I knew then I was going to fall for her.

"Over the next four months, I found a way to see her almost every day. I was only required to stay on base when I was in drills or drone training, so I slipped off base for a little while each day."

Kimmy elbows me and makes a motorcycle sound.

I choose to ignore it. "Tova introduced me to the grandparents who raised her. They were not fond of me. Her grandmother, Edith, told me that her granddaughter 'has to marry a Jewish man.' She told me in no uncertain terms that I should move on before someone got their heart broken.

"Now, I'm a guy who believes in respecting the wishes of parents and guardians; but since this girl wanted to see me as much as I wanted to see her, I decided to keep dating her."

Kimmy chimes in with, "Yeah, you did."

Once again, I try not to encourage her. "It was relatively easy to see her since her dorm was only a few miles from the Israeli barracks. I thought about telling her my assignment in Israel was temporary; but since I hadn't been given an exit date, I justified keeping it from her. Right at the six-month mark, I received orders to leave. I was given a 72-hour notice to board the next U.S. Navy ship that was coming to port."

It is obvious from the look on Kimmy's face that I just lost her to 'girlfriend sympathy.' This happens every time I tell this story to a girl. They don't like me much after hearing how I mislead one of their own. I take another quick glance at Kimmy. She seems to be staying with me, so I continue — knowing it's about to get worse.

"I tried to reassure her a year would go by quickly, and I would be free to see her again. I promised her I would write every week. As I was mapping out a plan for a long-distance relationship, the light left her eyes. She just stood up and walked away. I didn't go after her. I knew I didn't own my life at that time — the Navy did.

"That was the last time I saw her. I tried calling her and writing letters. No response. After three months, I reached out to her grandparents. When her grandmother picked up the phone, she started to cry and told me Tova had committed suicide three weeks after I left Haifa. She told me Tova had died of a broken heart — and she laid the blame right at my feet.

"I took a hit like never before. I dug myself into my career to keep my mind off my loss — as well as any role I may have played in Tova's suicide. I know I deserted her when she was too young to process her emotions. Her death haunted me every single day. I began working out around the clock. I skipped meals and social events. I pushed myself to levels I didn't even think possible. I was running twenty miles every weekend.

"One of the officers noticed my intensity and suggested I enroll in the testing program for the SEALs. I accepted the challenge and made the cut. I guess you could say that losing her pushed me to be the man I am today. I found that being deployed on top-secret missions kept me from being tortured by thoughts of Tova. Before I left Earth, I was beginning to wonder how I would cope with these emotions when I retired at the end of the year."

Kimmy is looking at the ground instead of at me. I should have kept this story to myself. This must be what Seneca meant when he said people tend be reflective in the Samaritan Dimension. Kimmy looks at me like she is going to cry but, thankfully, she doesn't. I'm sure she's sorry she opened this can of worms.

I decide to change the subject. "This place is exactly as I pictured it. The word 'comfort' comes to mind. There is a very peaceful feeling here. Nothing seems to be structured or hurried."

Kimmy wanders off — probably in search of a happier conversation.

As I look around the Samaritan Dimension, it seems as if everyone is on a permanent coffee break. The buildings are simple. There are no flashy colors or signs. The homes are small, but they all have large porches and decks.

People are sitting in small groups talking and laughing. Some are enjoying picnics on the lawns. Others are sharing meals on the decks of their homes. There are lots of children here, which I didn't see in the other dimensions. Most are in the playground area. Some are on swings. Others are playing Simon Says or Hide and Seek. Their giggling is infectious.

"Seneca tell me about the children. Why are they all here in the Samaritan Dimension? How is it that they are not young adults like the rest of us?"

"You know, I get that question from almost everyone. I am not sure why people doubt children would be a part of Heaven. They epitomize the innocence and love of this place. These children were born here. They all stay in the Ninth Dimension because it is the perfect environment for nurturing children. Once they mature, they will be assigned to their natural dimension. They are different ages because they were born here instead of on Earth. Children who come here from Earth come at the age they are and grow into adults here."

"If there's no time, how can there be aging?"

"Aging is not the passing of time. They grow in discovery and knowledge as well as experience. Jesus loves to visit with them at the celebrations in the Seventh Dimension. They bring Him great joy. It is a beautiful thing to behold. I will tell you more about the reproduction of children a little further down the road.

"Grayson, I'm not trying to change the subject, but I have to prepare you for one of the team members you will meet in this dimension. She is someone you knew on Earth."

"What? Not possible. I don't recall any family members or female classmates who died, and I never worked with female soldiers during my time in the Navy."

"Does that mean you have forgotten me?"

The voice comes from behind me and sends a shiver up my spine. I turn and see Tova standing there. She is more beautiful than I remember. She is older now, and even more stunning.

She smiles and my legs feel weak.

Kimmy jumps out from behind her with her second inappropriate, "Ta-da!"

"Tova? I didn't think I would ever see you again. I can't believe…. Tell me you're not a mirage." Of all the things I've seen today, I most want for her to be real.

Tova doesn't answer. Instead, she takes the last two steps that remain between us and lunges forward to wrap her arms around me. She feels and smells incredible.

My heart melts. There are hundreds of things I want to say and hundreds of questions I want to ask, but I can't seem to find the words. When she stops hugging me and stands back with her hands still in mine, the right words come to me. "I'm sorry for leaving you. I hope you can forgive me."

She smiles. "All is forgiven, Grayson. I have had some time to prepare for this meeting. I am happy to be on this team with you."

"So, Seneca, is this the team member to whom you were referring?"

"Yes, it is."

"Good call."

Seneca laughs. "Well, I guess I do not have to go over Tova's background. You know she was seventeen when she arrived. She was a student in college and came here following her suicide.

As Seneca turns towards someone else, I put my arm around Tova and pull her close.

I have one more person for you to meet here in the Samaritan Dimension. This is Tony. He is from Egypt. He was a heart perfusion technician. He came here when he was twenty-eight after losing a short battle with testicular cancer."

I'm a bit distracted, but I remember my manners. "It's nice to meet you, Tony."
"Likewise."

"So, what do you do here in the Samaritan Dimension?"

"We are peacekeepers. We oversee the wellbeing of everyone in Heaven, and sometimes on Earth. We all love living here in complete peace and relaxation. We spend most of our time enjoying each other's company. The children are a real joy to us. We do not hurry them through anything. We fulfill our purpose by going to people who are hurting and providing a helping hand."

Seneca speaks up. "Grayson, the Samaritan Dimension is the opposite of your Warrior Dimension. Almost everything you say and do might be a bit unsavory to the residents here. You will not have a lot in common, but each of you can appreciate the gifts of the other — just as you and Tova do.

"The Samaritans are at the highest level of development. They have internalized love. Samaritans are also very loyal."

I smile. It is easy for me to see how Tony and Tova are a great fit for a mission that's intent upon saving other people. In fact, I am now able to see this *is* a perfect team.

"If you are ready, we can continue to the Tenth Dimension. It is the home of the Saints. They are waiting to prepare this team with their wise words and a session of prayer for your safety. Follow me."

I look over at Tova and she smiles. With one look at her, any doubts I had about there being a Heaven are completely gone

40.

SAINTS

As we approach the mist coming from the portal entrance to the Tenth Dimension, I see an angel on either side, wearing halos and dressed in white. They are standing at attention and looking straight ahead like the Queen's Guard at Buckingham Palace. Seneca signals for us to stop. He approaches the angels and speaks with them alone. After a few minutes, he returns and tells us we will be allowed in very soon.

"What's with the security?"

"This is standard entry procedure for the Tenth Dimension. This is where the Holy of Holies is located as well as the Book of Life. Almighty has a very real enemy in Lucifer. If you knew how much she would like to trick her way into this place and destroy these things, you would understand the security. Many artifacts are stored here as well. These things are mentioned in the Bible. It is a shrine to the fulfillment of promises."

"Seneca, you just referred to Lucifer as 'she.' Are you telling me that Satan is a woman?"

"Yes, Lucifer is a woman. When you learn more about the Great Game, you will understand why. I told you when we first met that I would prepare you to meet her. You should not be surprised to find that a female is the enemy of man."

I look at Tova and mouth, "What?"

She just shrugs and giggles.

The guards haven't moved, but it appears that someone inside has been informed of our arrival. The fog that makes up the portal begins to subside.

A well-groomed young man steps through from the other side to greet us. "Hello, Guests. Welcome to the Tenth Dimension — home of the Saints. Your arrival makes the light a little brighter here today." He leans into hug Seneca. The smile never leaves his face as Seneca introduces us one by one.

Seneca then informs me that the young man is Abel — the son of Adam and Eve.

"Abel as in…Cain and Abel?"

"That is correct. Abel was the first human to transition to Heaven. His was the first death on Earth. The time you spent in Sunday school is going to help you, Grayson. You will probably remember the stories that go with the Saints we are about to meet. Why is your mouth hanging open?"

"I guess I hadn't stopped to think about meeting the men and women of the Bible. I've heard the stories, but never thought about seeing the faces that go with them. It's a little bit of a jaw dropper."

"It usually is. Did you have a favorite hero from the Bible?"

"Oh, there are so many! I guess I'd say it's a tie between Daniel and Jonah. I want to know how they faced huge beasts — unarmed — and survived. I would ask Daniel how he found the courage to stand before the lions and ask Jonah how he survived living inside of a whale for three days."

"Well, both men are here. If you do not get to meet them on this visit, know that you will have another opportunity when you return. You will be meeting all of the Saints when they host a grand victory celebration after the Mission is completed." Seneca pats me on the shoulder

"Abel is going to go through the portal with us, and we will have a quiet time with the Saints. We are not to speak unless spoken to. Please do not interrupt anyone and be sure to show respect when you approach the thrones." Seneca stops his gaze on me. "Too bad about the shirt."

"Whoa, hold on. Is my shirt going to be a problem? I don't want to make a Saint angry."

"There is no anger here."

"Nice side-step. I'm a soldier who knows the importance of being properly dressed. Would it be better if I turned my shirt inside out?"

"Suit yourself."

I turn the shirt inside out and put the emblem on the back. Now I have a tag hanging below my chin. I try to rip it off, but it is sewn tightly into the seam. After a minute of struggling with the tag, I look up to see everyone watching me. Except for Abel, they all burst into laughter.

"So, this is funny to you? I'm freaking out here."

"It is okay, Grayson. I was just having some fun with you. We are given robes when we get inside. Everyone who approaches the throne must be dressed in white robes. You can put your shirt back the way it was."

As I take off my shirt and pull it on the right way, I smirk at the others. "That's some very gentle comedy, guys."

"Yes, but it worked," Tony says while still laughing. "Personally, I like the shirt. It takes the attention off your orange flip flops."

"Oh, man! What am I going to do about the shoes, Seneca?"

"I suggest slouching as you walk so the robe can touch the floor and cover them." Seneca lets out another one of his belly laughs.

Abel doesn't join in the laughter, but he does smile. He gives off a tender yet serious vibe. He directs our attention back to the journey and leads us through the portal in single file.

Once inside, we are all handed white robes by an angel who has porcelain skin and translucent blue eyes. His demeanor is one of servitude and understatement. His back is fitted with long wings that rise a good three feet above him. Encircling his head is a band of light. It's not solid, but it moves with him. I am amazed at how accurate the descriptions of angels are on Earth. I'd like to talk to him about Heaven, but he leaves the room after he hands the last robe to Liam.

After putting on the robes, we step into a thick mist. It isn't as thick as the portals to the other dimensions but is still dense enough to prevent a clear view of the other side. I can make out the figures of my teammates, but the fine details are hazy. I can't see more than three feet in front of me. Abel and Seneca guide us with their voices. I bring up the end of the line with Tova.

I offer her my hand. Our last steps give way to a clearing inside a massive arena. We are near the top and can look down and see a circle of thrones surrounding the center platform. I remember from the last book of the Bible that there are twenty-four thrones for Saints. I count them. Yep, twenty-four it is.

There is a large throne in the center of the circle. It is made of an opaque, crystal-like material. I can follow its outline, but it is also transparent. The entire throne sparkles under the bright light that shines directly on it from an opening in the dome ceiling. There are brilliant colors coming from it in all directions making rainbows on all sides.

Everything here is made of pure white alabaster and garnished with precious gemstones. There are sections of gold, silver, brass, and copper in a rotating pattern on the thrones of the Saints. The platform on which the thrones sit is made entirely of gold. There is a kneeling bench around the entire circumference of the raised platform. Fine silk pillows are in place – I assume for kneeling. The arena is lit with thousands of white candles. As we walk down the aisle, we pass rows of flickering candles. A massive chandelier of burning candles also hangs over the entire platform. This scene would be the perfect setting for a royal wedding. It is, by far, the most beautiful design I have ever seen.

Seneca stops at the edge of the platform. He puts his knees on one of the pillows and bows with his hands out in front of him. We follow his lead. One of the Saints rises from his throne and walks over to Seneca. He puts his left hand on Seneca's shoulder and says, "You may all rise. In Heaven, we only bow to the Lamb of Almighty. He is the only one deserving of our worship. He is not here."

Seneca eases to his feet. "Abraham, it is an honor to introduce to you the team that has been chosen to retrieve the Keys of Death and Hades. First, I present to you Sterling and Seiko from the Sixth Dimension."

Sterling and Seiko nod their heads slightly.

"Next, we have Liam and Kimmy from the Eighth Dimension."

They also nod their heads.

"This is Tova and this is Tony. They are from the Ninth Dimension. And the leader of this team is Grayson from the Fifth Dimension."

I feel weak inside as I tip my head. I can hardly believe Abraham is standing right in front of me. He is the undisputed father of Judaism, Islam, and Christianity.

"You are a fine-looking team. I know the Archangel Michael personally chose each of you after receiving recommendations from the guardian angels and spirit guides. I am speaking for the other Saints when I tell you we have great confidence in you. We know containing Lucifer will not be easy. Seneca will go into the history of the Mission with you before you depart.

"On Earth, you will be walking through the lands in which I raised my livestock, farmed my crops, and raised my sons and daughter. It saddens me to see that the land is now desecrated with weapons of battle as preparations are being made for the Great War. We will be watching over you from here. Our prayers for your strength and safety will constantly be on our lips until you return victorious. My fellow Saint, Moses, would also like to address you. I leave you with a prayer for your protection."

As I stand before the great Saints of the Bible, I think about how I don't deserve to be here. There must be millions of men and women who know their Bible stories better than I do. They would know what these great men and women did in history and would fall all over themselves to touch their hands.

As Abraham returns to his throne, Moses walks towards us. His beard is pure white and hangs to his thighs.

"Greetings, Warriors. I also have confidence in you. It is a great honor to be chosen for this Mission on Earth. I once stood where you are standing. I had many doubts and fears as I led God's people out of Egypt. My shortcomings and lapses in faith are well-documented in the books of the Law, so there are no secrets here. I want you to know that when you face your greatest fears on this journey, never doubt that Almighty is watching over you. His ways are not your ways. It is often difficult to understand His methods, but rest assured they are always the right ones.

"I give you a caution: Know that Lucifer is a very worthy opponent. She has already devastated the condition of man. In a short time, she will have ultimate power over the men and women who do not follow Almighty. She will deceive them and lead them farther into darkness. She will laugh at their pain and celebrate their deaths. You will see things that will break your hearts. Watching people harden their hearts to their Creator is soul crushing. It is difficult to see men continue to bring pain upon themselves.

"I have a special interest in your Mission. You will understand more when Seneca covers the rules of the Great Game. My prayer of blessing is bestowed upon you now."

Moses returns to his throne and sits down.

There are angels on either side of each of the Saints attending to their needs. They bring bowls of fruit and drinks in chalices made of gold. They wash the feet of the Saints and wrap them in warm towels. The Saints on the thrones are watching a screen embedded in the floor of the arena. It is easily the size of a football field. They are watching the happenings on Earth in real time with a split screen that allows them to see multiple scenes at once. They are discussing the events as they unfold.

The arena has tens of thousands of seats. Many of them are filled with guests in robes. They watch the Saints and listen to their rulings, much like a Supreme Court session. One of the twenty-four thrones is empty as is the main throne in the center. Sheer white drapes cover the ceiling and walls. A gentle breeze blows through the room causing the curtains to dance and flames to flicker in synchrony. I have never felt as much peace and protection as I do here with the Saints. I don't want to leave, but Seneca motions for us to head out.

Once we leave the platform area, I bombard Seneca and the others with questions. "Who are the people sitting in the auditorium? How did they earn their way to the Saints' Dimension? Why was one of the thrones missing a saint? Why was the center throne empty?"

Seneca takes all the questions himself this time. "The twenty-four thrones are filled with the saints chosen from history. The one that is empty is reserved for Saint Peter. He will take his seat after every child of Almighty is safely inside the Pearly Gates.

"The people sitting about are martyrs. Anyone killed for the faith is welcomed here to watch the sessions. The people you saw are preachers, rabbis, prophets, teachers, missionaries, journalists, authors, coaches, and many not-so-visible heroes. When martyrs arrive, St. Peter has them escorted to this dimension to meet the Saints. The martyrs are honored for the sacrifices they made. They can come and go as they please. Some assist with the tragedies of man playing out on the screens set into the floor.

"The empty throne in the center is the throne of the Lamb that was slain — Jesus, the Son of God. Once your training is complete, you will know the secrets of the Great Game and all of this will come together."

"The dark times — the Tribulation — really will happen?" I ask. There's a world war coming, isn't there? And the plagues, curses, and natural disasters we've read about — they will begin now, won't they? Be straight with me, Seneca. My mother and grandfather are still on Earth."

"Yes. It is about to begin."

"Where is our leader — the One Who sits on the empty throne? Shouldn't He be here now to watch over the people?"

"He is meeting with Almighty. After this, Lucifer will meet with Almighty and have the power transferred to her. You are correct that a dark time is coming. Jesus will return to His throne before the Tribulation begins, but He will be contractually bound from interfering with the disasters on Earth. Almighty's hand is being withdrawn for a time. If you thought Earth was dark place when you left, a much darker time is coming when Almighty allows Lucifer to rule.

"Our job is to prepare for the role we have been given. I cannot promise anything regarding the fate of your loved ones. Every man, woman, and child have a role to play; we cannot interfere. The best way we can serve them is to do what we have been gathered to do."

Seneca places his hand on my left shoulder and looks at the rest of the team. "Let us prepare."

As Seneca walks towards the portal, the familiar dark cloak of war settles over me. It haunts me every time I begin an assignment — the removal of innocence. It is the realization that the journey from here to the end is wrought with pain, loss, and uncertainty. There is one difference this time. I am not afraid for my own life but for people on Earth who will face the destruction and wrath of Lucifer and her demons – should we fail.

As the others follow Seneca, I think of glancing back to the Saints' Dimension for some comfort. Then I remember what happened to Lot's wife when she looked back.

I keep my gaze forward and follow my team.

DEMON GAMES I

EPISODE VII

MISSION

(GRAYSON'S STORY)

MALLOW SHERIDAN

41.

PREPARATION

January 4, 2029, Level X, Heaven

The team's pace is slower than usual as it moves towards the portal. This is certainly understandable. The combination of mentally preparing for a dangerous mission with unbelievably high stakes and processing the advice of the Saints is a lot to take in.

I have seen this bittersweet pace to the front line throughout my career. Every soldier uses this time to think through the possible outcomes of the battle and to wonder if his courage is going to be enough. Time after time, I have seen men and women rise to the challenge of war once it comes for them. These six may not know it yet, but they will become fierce warriors once they see blood extracted from the weak and defenseless.

I no longer doubt any member of this team. More importantly, there are no indicators that they doubt themselves. No one has asked to be dismissed from this mission nor openly expressed any level of fear. Michael has chosen wisely.

I am ready. How could I not be inspired after everything I have witnessed since my arrival? I welcome the return to soldier mode. Once a soldier, always a soldier. Seneca is right — I'm designed for challenge and I live for the thrill of a mission. It's good to know Heaven has a place for my kind.

Our hope for this mission is to avoid the military tension leading to the impending war outside Jerusalem. I want this to be a covert operation like the ones I did as a sniper. I want to get us in without being discovered, fulfill our yet-to-be-explained Mission, and get us out without leaving any evidence of having been there.

The odds of this running smoothly are low. We're heading into the troubled Middle East where military actions are a daily occurrence and war is inevitable. If this isn't reason enough to believe the odds are against us, we also have the presence of a very real enemy who will know we are there — and who is intent upon exposing and thwarting our Mission.

As the others walk deep in thought, I too must sort through my emotions and clear my head. I have a father I haven't seen in twenty-six years waiting to welcome me home. I have a mother mourning my death back on Earth. I have the love of my life, who I thought was gone forever, marching beside me into the unknown. On top of all that, I'm leading the Mission that will determine the fate of every human remaining on Earth.

Even so, I switch over to soldier mode and purge out all the emotional baggage — this is my self-imposed "brain washing." Most men are adept at compartmentalizing. Soldiers do it on a whole different level. We must completely release emotions and memories from both our conscious and subconscious minds. We must push them down deep, knowing they may never be retrieved. This is a soldier's precursor to Post Traumatic Stress Disorder — and doomed relationships.

I'm not proud of the man I become in soldier mode, but it makes me effective at my job and keeps me alive. I just hope Tova understands what she is about to see is an act of war and not the real me.

After several deep breaths, I go through my visualization. I envision the splitting of the protective cover that shields my body. It peels away like a snake shedding its skin to open for new growth. I emerge from the old skin, kick it away with my boots, and flex the muscles that cover my new, rubbery, tough skin. After removing emotion, I feel the change immediately. I'm standing a little taller, breathing a little deeper, walking a little faster, and thinking a little more clearly. I flare my nostrils and push out every bit of stale air in my lungs. I punch my chest with both fists. I am ready.

As we step up to the portal, Seneca calls us to attention and lays out the plans. "The tour is over, and we are ready to begin our training. In seven days, you will be on Earth. Your week of training will be short, but intense. On the final day, you will meet with Archangel Michael for an assessment. He is going to direct your physical preparedness for this assignment. As you have been told, Michael hand-picked each of you for this Mission.

"Excuse me, Seneca, but these awesome bodies are already in great shape." Liam says with a smile. "If we went to Earth just as we are right now, I would have to register mine as a lethal weapon."

The group laughs as Liam runs through some Mr. Universe poses.

Seneca laughs. "Yes, Liam, each of you is in great shape. But there are many levels and types of fitness. Beyond building more stamina and muscle on top of what you already have, Michael wants you conditioned in flexibility, the martial arts, and yoga."

From the back of the group, Seiko comes alive when she hears this. "That is a great idea! I was a big yogi on Earth. It gives you great mental focus and body awareness. It will make us better for sure."

Sterling objects. "Wait — Seiko, if you like yoga so much, why haven't I seen you practicing it since you arrived? And, of course you like yoga — you are a girl. Plus, your Japanese ancestors invented it. You are built for it. Big guys like us don't need yoga or martial arts to protect ourselves."

Seiko is offended by Sterling's comments. "That is not true. Yoga originated in India. Martial arts and yoga are not about using muscle mass to defend and attack. They are about controlling your thoughts and breathing to increase your body awareness and flexibility. They are even about using agility to escape, and even neutralize, your enemy. Tell them, Seneca."

"Okay, let us take the intensity down a notch. We are on the same team here. Liam and Sterling, Seiko is right. The preparedness plan is being handled by Michael who, by the way, is one yogi who has never backed down from a fight. He is the one who designed the fitness program, including the types of exercise arts to be used. He wants you to train together so you can become familiar with each other's moves and strengths. It is possible you are going to be doing some intense cave climbing. If so, a limber body is a must. I want your word you will do what he asks. Sterling?"

"Sure."

"Liam?"

"Absolutely!"

"Great. Now, two more things I need to cover before we leave. First, the Mission will take place in Jerusalem. The training will take place in a reproduction of Jerusalem. It was built in a gravity pod and set in an outlying area of the Milky Way galaxy."

"What is a gravity pod?" Seiko immediately zeroes in on the science.

"It is enclosed space where a gravity equal to that of Earth is applied. This one was designed to simulate the terrain of Jerusalem. You will be conditioned in a setting identical to the actual city — including the heat, humidity, and sandstorms common in the area. Training in the pod will prepare you for the lay of the land. It will also give us the privacy we need for your training."

"Why do we need privacy?" Kimmy asks. "Aren't all the residents of Heaven aware of the Mission?"

"The challenge is Lucifer. She is working hard to gather information on this team as well as our battle tactics. She already knows about Grayson. His death tipped her off that we were ready to make a play for the Keys. This, in turn, tipped her off to Almighty's timing for the end of the Earth. We do not want her to figure out your strategy, or your superpowers, before you use them on Earth."

MALLOW SHERIDAN

42.

SUPERPOWERS

"What? Wait...*superpowers*?" Tova's voice pitches high.

"Yes. It seems we have arrived at the second thing I wanted to cover before we leave. Each of you was equipped with a superhuman power when you were born. It is not limited to the seven of you — every human is equipped with at least one superpower. Most have never developed them because man lacks the discipline, concentration, and self-assurance necessary to bring them to the surface and, more importantly, under his control. Man can be short-sighted and focused only on the things in front of him rather than on the powers within."

"Preach!" Liam punches his fist into the air.

"How is it possible for people have superpowers and no one figured it out? This seems implausible, Seneca." Sterling crosses his arms. It is easy to see that he is doubting what Seneca just told us.

"Some *did* figure it out, Sterling; but when they demonstrated their powers, they were often accused of witchcraft or trickery. Many were labeled as 'freaks.' Jesus demonstrated all seven superpowers when he walked on Earth. He personally showed us how to use them. His acts were often referred to as miracles, making them seem out of reach for humans; but when Jesus left Earth, He told His disciples they could do the very same things, and even greater ones. We chose not to listen, and we chose not to believe.

"Now is the time for you to dig deep and connect to your inner strength. You need to remove every bit of doubt so you can use and control your superpower. I will reveal to each of you which superpower you have always had. By the time you stand in front of Michael, you will need to be ready to demonstrate it for him."

All seven of us stand in front of Seneca with our mouths hanging open.

Before we can put together a group protest, he starts talking again. "Here we go. Liam, you have the power of *shapeshifting*. You can transform your physical appearance so convincingly that you cannot be recognized. You can alter your skin color like a chameleon and change your posture from young to old with ease. Only those who know you will be able to identify you by the nuances of your movements and voice. Jesus used this power to evade arrest many times up until the day He willingly surrendered Himself. The Jewish soldiers knew He had this power. This is the reason Judas betrayed Jesus with a kiss — the guards wanted a sign they were arresting the right man."

Liam's fidgeting stops as he stares at Seneca in disbelief.

"Kimmy, you have the power of *strategic imagination*. You can see solutions for any problem. You can find a way to escape any imprisonment — even those that originate in the mind. You will be able to visualize ways to capture and escape your enemies. You can solve problems by using simple things around you. Jesus did this when He fed the five thousand with five loaves of bread and two fish."

Kimmy lets out a "Yeah, Baby!"

"Seiko, you have the power to *levitate*. You can rise above gravity and move short distances. Not only can you lift yourself, you can lift other people and objects with your focus. Jesus levitated when He walked on water and calmed the sea for His disciples. He showed Peter how to use his power of levitation by inviting him out onto the sea. This served to prove that some humans are capable of levitating."

Seiko flaps her arms like a bird and smiles at the team.

"Sterling, you have the power of *telepathy*. You can exchange information with another person by using your mind. This power probably contributed to your success as a trial lawyer. You can send data and guidance from afar. Once you connect with the enemy and get him to trust you, you can insert confusing information into his mind. Jesus demonstrated this power many times when people came to Him for help. He could tell them what they were thinking and expose the things they were hiding, The woman at the well was astonished Jesus knew she had been married five times and was living with yet another man who was not her husband. She wisely opened her mind, followed His advice, and launched a huge ministry. No doubt, she trusted His words because He could communicate with her in a way that others could not understand. He kept leading her to the truth. You have this ability."

Sterling gives Liam a fist bump.

"Tony, you have the power of *exorcism*. You can identify evil spirits in others and can empower the host to oust them. Jesus cast out many evil spirits that were holding people captive. This is a lost art. Many people are controlled by evil spirits, and many evil deeds are done by evil spirits working from inside a human host."

Tony nods and gives Sterling a nod. "Good. I like it."

"Tova, you have the power of *healing*. Jesus healed in many places and circumstances where people doubted His power. Like you, His compassion was strong. He was never afraid to hug people who had leprosy or to touch people who were hemorrhaging blood. He could also heal people from afar if their faith was strong."

Tova smiles sweetly up at me. I am not surprised by her superpower.

"Grayson, you have the power of *teleportation*. You can remove yourself from one location and place your entire body somewhere else. As the Mission begins, this teleportation ability will allow you to move anywhere on the planet. Jesus was able to teleport Himself and His disciples in a boat. After He calmed the sea, they immediately reached the shore where they were headed. Philip also traveled by teleportation on one occasion from the wilderness to a city thirty miles away.

"If each of you thinks back, you will remember a time as a child when you believed you had the very superpower you possess. Over time, you gave up believing you could use it. The powers lie dormant within you. The time has come for you to do something amazing with them."

I look around the room at my teammates. It is obvious everyone is surprised, but flattered, to receive this information. After a minute of silence, during which we all look at each other and think about what these powers might look like, Liam begins to laugh. His deep, hearty laugh takes us all in. Soon, the entire group is laughing, including Seneca. I'm sure, like me, we are each thinking of a time when this information could have come in handy.

43.

JERUSALEM

January 11, 2029, Gravity Pod, Milky Way Galaxy

A soldier is trained in many things, but time travel is not one of them. Seneca says it's not really "time travel," it's "dimension change." Either way, I'm confused by what transpires when I step through a portal and am completely removed to a different place. The portal to the gravity pod is different from the others I've seen. In the intra-Heaven portals, we stepped through a misty fog and that was it. This portal is like a black hole. There is absolutely no light inside — not even at the end of the tunnel.

The team goes in one by one. I watch Tova step through. The darkness swallows her whole. I take comfort in the fact that Seneca went through first and is waiting for her on the other side. He asked me to stay behind to see that everyone makes it through. I'm not sure exactly what he meant by this request. On other covert operations in my past, it meant, "Make sure no one deserts."

While I wait my turn, my mind returns to the superpowers. Interestingly, Seneca told me I can teleport. I remember times playing Hide and Seek with my father when I would pretend, I could change hiding places without him seeing me move. It's likely my father was playing along when he would go to the last hiding place I just left and act surprised that I wasn't there. He would do this for about ten moves before he "found" me. I wanted this superpower for a reason. Seneca says it's because I subconsciously knew I had it all along.

Liam catches my attention and brings me back to the present with a wave of his hand. Ever the character, he turns and gives me a mock salute as he heads backwards into the portal.

Now that he is gone, I'm alone. Normally, this would be concerning, but it seems as if this new body and the things I've learned about the future have relieved me of the fear of the unknown.

As I take a final look around before I step into the portal, I'm curious about the full potential of this new brain I've been given. Since it is free of defect and illness, it seems plausible that I can do so much more, like teleport. I noticed the powers Seneca identified in each of us are "mind over matter" powers. I can believe humans fail to use the full potential of their brains. I utter a simple "Incredible" and follow Liam into the darkness.

When I emerge from the portal, I find myself standing in a red desert. The sun is directly overhead making the heat almost unbearable. It's so bright I find it hard to see the others. I put my hands up to shield my eyes and find the other team members are doing the same.

Seneca speaks. "Welcome to the gravity pod. We have been preparing this place for some time now. Almighty created it and let the hosts of the heavens do the decorating. It is an exact replica of the city of Jerusalem and the surrounding areas. This is exactly how it looks and feels today."

"Wow! How big is this place?" Sterling is starting early with the questions.

"It is approximately five miles by five miles. It is mostly made up of desert that surrounds the city. We are standing just outside Eastern Jerusalem. This is where the great controversy over ownership of the city is taking its toll on the people. This will be the launch site of the Great War. I am beginning our tour outside the city because many of the tunnels that run under Jerusalem open out here. They were, and continue to be, escape routes from the Temple of Solomon. Some tunnels open in the caves of this hillside, some open under the shielding of a boulder, and some open into landmarks that act as camouflage. You would do well to split up and tour the area to map out these openings and become familiar with them before the Mission. You may need that information later.

"I can plot our findings out on a map for the group." Seiko offers her organizational skills. "I could stay here in a neutral spot while the rest of you explore the territory and report back here so I can assimilate the data. Seneca, what was the need for an escape route from the Temple? How many vein lines do you think are here?"

"Good questions, Seiko. The tunnel system served as an escape route for the Jewish priests as well as a hiding place for the gold and other treasures normally kept in the Temple. There are twelve vein lines that break off the main underground corridor below the Temple."

"When you say, 'the Temple,' are you referring to the newly-rebuilt Temple in Jerusalem? The one the United States defended to the United Nations? Didn't it pretty much wipe out ten years of Israel's budget while costing America the respect of the rest of the free world?" Liam asks.

"Yes, one and the same. However, your description of the events might be slightly colored by cultural biases." Seneca winks at Liam.

"You have to overlook Liam's exaggerations, Seneca. They are fairly common in stories told by Idealists." The group joins in Sterling's laughter.

"Ha, ha," says Liam. "At least Idealists have vision enough to stretch the story to the next level. That is better than holding everyone back with the doomsday outlook of your average Strategist. Right, Sterling?"

"Well, that depends of whether or not you need a realistic assessment of a situation that is as critical as a war or writing a children's storybook."

"Okay, guys, simmer down. Save that passion for the enemy; you are going to need it. Once you know the history of this city, you will understand the need for the tunnels. Let me run through some stats. During its long history, Jerusalem has been destroyed twice, besieged twenty-three times, and attacked fifty-two times. It has also been captured and recaptured forty-four times. King David took the city from the Jebusites and established it as the capital of the United Kingdom of Israel. His son, King Solomon, commissioned the building of the First Temple.

"In 66 A.D., the Jewish people rebelled again the Roman Empire. Four years later, in 70 A.D, Roman legions under Titus retook and destroyed much of Jerusalem and the Second Temple. The Third, and current, Temple took a decade to complete under the guidance of the Jewish Parliament and the priests who make up the Sanhedrin. The United States played a big role in funding the rebuilding of this Temple as well as protecting the city during the reconstruction period.

"The Muslim center of worship, The Dome of the Rock, is on the same grounds. This is part of the U.S.-inspired peace treaty between Israel and Palestine. As it is now shared holy ground, citizens of all nations are allowed access to the property. Until 2021, only Muslims were admitted to the Dome of the Rock. The change was accepted as the world reopened after the COVID-19 pandemic, but many Muslims resent the new treaty. They still want to build their state of Palestine on this land. This tension continues to stretch the patience of the Israeli soldiers who are charged with keeping the peace.

"This city is considered a holy city by three of the world's largest religions: Islam, Judaism, and Christianity. In Sunni Islam, Jerusalem is the third holiest city after Mecca and Medina. According to the Koran, Muhammad made his Night Journey from here to speak with Allah. The Christian Bible identifies Jerusalem as the city where Jesus was crucified. Judaism has its entire religion centered here.

"Though both Jews and Arab Muslims date their claims to the land back a couple thousand years, the current political conflict began in the early 20th century. Jews fleeing persecution in Europe wanted to establish a national homeland in what was then an Arab and Muslim territory. The Arabs resisted because they believed the land was rightfully theirs.

"In 1948, the Provisional Jewish Government proclaimed a new State of Israel. On that same date, the United States recognized the Provisional Jewish Government. A battle ensued. After an early United Nations plan to give each group part of the land failed, Israel and the surrounding Arab nations fought several wars over the territory. The United Nations voted to admit Israel as a member on January 31, 1949. The wars of 1948 and 1967 put us where we are today.

"The status of Jerusalem remains one of the core issues in the Israeli-Palestinian conflict. The international community, including the United Nations, still refuses to recognize Jerusalem as Israel's capital. The city hosted no foreign embassies until 2018. The United States, under the leadership of President Donald Trump, approved and supported the moving of the Embassy of the United States from Tel Aviv to Jerusalem. Much to the surprise of the U.S., only a handful of nations followed its lead. However, with the U.S. move alone, Israel has moved forward with its determination to keep the city united. All branches of the Israeli government are in Jerusalem including their Parliament, the residences of the Prime Minister and President, and their Supreme Court.

"All of this controversy is coming from a nation with a population of only twelve million people. About seventy-five percent of the nation is Jewish, twenty-one percent is Muslim, and four percent identify as Christians. Though the Palestinians and the Israelis have agreed to share the Temple grounds, and a peace treaty to that effect was signed, the conflict is intensifying under the surface. Other nations of the world are choosing sides and getting involved to protect various interests. On top of that, nearly 3 million Jews have moved back to Israel in the last decade. Jerusalem is overpopulated, which angers

Palestinians as they watch resources being used up. All this is leading to the Great War."

"How much time do we have before this war?" Sterling sounds concerned.

"About forty-two months. Three and a half years."

I decide to focus the team with direct questions. "What specifically are we to do with this time and these tunnels? What is our exact assignment?"

Seneca motions us to move into a concave of the rocky banks. It offers us a little protection from the sun's direct rays. He sits on a boulder, and we surround him on the red soil.

"One year after the Israelite's exodus from Egypt, the Ark of the Covenant was created according to a pattern Almighty gave to Moses. It was a wooden box about the size of a coffin and was built for the purpose of holding the two stone tablets that Moses brought down from Mount Sinai.

"The Ark was carried in front of the Israeli army. It has been said that any army that carries the Ark in front of it is invincible. There is no reason to believe the Ark's power to influence wars has ended. It would be quite the treasure for any nation as the world heads towards a third World War. This should make the need for secrecy clear to you. We cannot lose the Ark to the enemy. Though the box was built to carry two stone tablets, other items were eventually placed inside it for safe keeping."

"I know this story," says Liam proudly. "It was in the Indiana Jones movie."

"Yes, Liam, that movie was loosely based on a fictional rescue of the Ark of the Covenant. Just imagine, you could accomplish what Indiana Jones failed to do." Seneca lets out his hearty laugh.

I recall some of my Bible trivia as Seneca laughs. "I know something about this. The stone tablets are carved with the Ten Commandments. Aaron's rod, which has magical powers, and a pot of manna, which is the food Almighty rained down from Heaven to feed the Israelites in the desert are also in there."

"Correct. You might recall Moses said he has a personal interest in this Mission. He wants the Ark of the Covenant, and its contents, home with the Saints. Later, a fourth item was sealed into the Ark of the Covenant. Though we want to rescue all the items, and the Ark, we are most in pursuit of the fourth item."

"Which is?" Sterling asked with trepidation.

"The Keys of Death and Hades."

"What? Why are they on Earth?" Liam shifts from jovial to serious.

"When the Romans were on their way to destroy the Second Temple, the Archangel Michael appeared to the Head Priest to foretell of its destruction. He brought with him the Keys of Death and Hades as a symbol of Almighty's promise that the Temple would be rebuilt a third time and that the new one would never be destroyed. Michael instructed the priests to seal the keys into the Ark of the Covenant and hide it within the tunnels."

Liam paces, and his voice cracks as he speaks. "Aren't these keys kind of important for locking up Lucifer and ending her reign on Earth?"

"Yes. Almighty must have these keys to lock her away for one thousand years."

I need to refocus the group. "What happens if we fail?"

Seneca's face is serious. "Should the keys fall into Lucifer's hands, she will be allowed to remain in control of Earth for one thousand years in addition to the seven years of the Tribulation. The Great Game stipulates that if this happens, Almighty cannot intervene to spare His children from her wrath."

"What is this 'Great Game' to which you keep referring?" Seiko asks.

"The Great Game is the story of everything — how it came to be, why it came to be, and the ultimate story of good vs. evil. The Great Game is a contest, of sorts, between Almighty and Lucifer. There are rules and stipulations — and some compromises."

"Compromises?"

"Yes. Almighty was sometimes forced to adjust the path to His final goal due to mankind's decisions to go its own way. I cannot tell you more about the Great Game than this."

"Why not?"

"Quite honestly, I have told you everything I know. The rest would be conjecture on my part. I will know the rest of the story at the same time as you. Archangel Gabriel is coming here before you depart for the Mission. I was told he would reveal to us some of the finer details of the Great Game that will shed some light on your journey. Though some of us know about the existence of the Great Game, the details are sealed in the Holy Atrium. I was told that our assignment is to rescue the Keys at any cost."

The soldier in me is getting intensely aggravated. I refuse to lead people into a situation where secrets are kept.

"'Any cost?' What is the risk here, Seneca? What happens if we are captured?"

"If you are captured, you will be held in prison, or you might be on the run. It may be a combination of the two. If this happens, you can still use your superpowers, so you certainly would not be helpless. At the meeting held between Almighty and Lucifer at the end of the Tribulation, you would be released to return to Heaven. I know it is not the promise you hoped for, but Almighty will be relinquishing His power on Earth for these next seven years. That means He cannot rescue you."

The team goes silent after hearing Seneca's last declaration. I'm disheartened to see we've been drawn into this dire situation.

This scenario is a constant of war, but the soldier in me rises to take control. "Understood! Okay, we need some more specs. Who's protecting these tunnels?"

Seneca beams at me with pride in his eyes. He understands that, with my last statement, the power of leadership has subtly transferred to me. He knows I'm ready to lead.

"Israeli troops are protecting the people and the cave openings — at least the ones that have been found. Many other openings have yet to be found.

"On the inside, servants of the priests provide protection. No weapons can be taken inside the holy areas, so they are stored in the tunnels below the temple. It is the perfect location for easy access by the servants in case of an invasion. Should you find yourselves cornered in the tunnels, look to the walls for encoded Jewish markings. These will show you where certain weapons are hidden. Then dig. Seiko knows the language well."

"What kind of weapons do they have?" I ask.

"There are many Uzi guns and Desert Eagle pistols stored in the holding boxes. In other places, you will find tear gas, grenades, and pepper spray."

"Are we being armed?"

"I see no need."

"Are we being given any technology?" Seiko asks.

"You will not be able to use technology as it now belongs to Lucifer. It has been compromised and you could be traced. It will be as if you are stepping back in time. Still, you will not need to be armed. You are taking enhanced bodies, combat training from Michael, and your superpowers with you. Should you be injured, you will heal immediately. Your new bodies regenerate."

"Before another question can be directed to Seneca, I refocus the group once more. "Seneca, I assume there is a housing and training facility for us in the city."

"Yes, there is."

"Troops, we are heading to the city now. We will return to map out the tunnel system. Seiko, you will move forward with mapping the data for us when we return. Training begins as soon as we change into whatever uniform has been provided for us. Let's go."

DEMON GAMES I

44.

WARFARE

January 18, 2029, Gravity Pod, Milky Way Galaxy

After their meditation time, the team reports to the gym. It's the crack of dawn in the gravity pod, and the training sessions are going well. Just as we have done for two weeks of Earth time, the seven of us rotate in rounds on the equipment, weights, mats, cardio, and yoga room. Archangel Michael arrives today. I think we're ready, except for the superpowers. I've been giving the team two hours alone each day to work on their individual powers. We don't talk about the results, but I'm pretty sure we're all feeling intimidated. As much as I've tried, I haven't seen any progress with my teleporting. My hope is that Michael will show up and unleash these powers for us.

I had forgotten how much I enjoy leading physical training. Knowing I am training a team for a mission set by Almighty Himself is surreal. This time, preparing for combat really does feel like I am going to help save the world. It took coming to Heaven to see my life was always on a pre-determined path to have me here at this exact moment. There isn't anyone on Earth who wouldn't like to know their life has a divine purpose — and is perfectly timed. Someday soon, they'll know, but before that - comes the Great War. Our team won't be a part of World War III, but we will undoubtedly see some bad stuff. It's my job to have them as prepared as possible.

Though I am working with each of the six warriors, I admit I most enjoy watching Tova go at the punching bag. She is every bit the tough person I knew her to be on Earth. I want to spend every minute with her. I find it odd this   has transferred to the other side. I am beginning to suspect love truly *is* eternal. I can think of a lot of people on Earth who are going to be excited about this part of Heaven. If this mission ends with me being able to see Tova every day for the rest of eternity, I will live forever as a happy man.

"Hello, Warriors, I need your attention." Seneca's voice echoes across the training room.

All seven of us halt our workout regimens and gather around him.

"First, congratulations on your physical preparedness. You are all in great shape. You are harnessing the power of your new bodies and, hopefully, learning how to use your individual superpowers. It seems as if even the Yoga is being taken seriously." Seneca winks at Seiko who is grinning big.

Laughter spreads through the group.

"There are only two days left before you begin your Mission to retrieve the Keys. The enemy is preparing troops as well, but they will be no match for you. Please, have a seat."

Seneca directs the seven of us to an open area of the gym. There are chairs circling him and a hologram square floats in the center.

"Today, I want to begin another part of your training."

"There's more?"

"Yes, Sterling, there's more." Seneca smiles at Sterling. He seems to be enjoying the outbursts of our most vocal team member.

After a quick laugh, Seneca refocuses the team.

"As in any war, there will also be intellectual warfare. In many of the great wars of history, intellectual warfare was far more debilitating than physical combat. I am sure Grayson can attest to the effectiveness of these tactics. You are going back to Earth where war is practically a sport. Intellectual warfare comes through propaganda, mirages, traitors, misdirects, outright lies, distortion of senses, and even false surrender.

"I'm sure each of you is familiar with the story of the Trojan War and the gift horse sent to the city of Troy. After ten years of failed attempts to enter the city, the Greek army constructed a huge wooden horse. They left it on the beach as they sailed away in apparent surrender. The army of Troy opened the gates and pulled the horse inside. Thinking it was a gift for victory, they started celebrating. The horse was filled with Greek soldiers who crept out of a hidden trap door late at night, opened the gates for the rest of their army — which had sailed back to shore in the dark — and began its attack inside the city walls. The city was destroyed in a matter of hours."

"So, what are you saying? We should be wary of looking a gift horse in the mouth?" Liam's laughter quickly spreads through the group. Even Seneca joins in.

"No, Liam. You are mixing metaphors. This story did not actually happen, but the tactic used makes for a great teaching point of battle strategy. The war tactics you will see on Earth will be epic. We do not know what to expect. The enemy has had thousands of years to prepare. We will be monitoring things from the 10th Dimension and will do everything we can to communicate as you advance."

Seneca stops talking and pulls up a seat directly beneath the hologram. He looks around the group — looking into each team member's eyes. "Before Archangel Michael takes over, I need to walk you through the rules of engagement and explain some of the psyche of Lucifer."

"With all due respect, Seneca," says Sterling, "we have seen the holograms of Lucifer. She looks harmless to me. She is a tall chick with fighting skills, for sure; but mostly, she seems like your run-of-the-mill bad girl with a hot bod and an attitude to match. Weird stinging tail aside, her fiercest weapon seems to be her entourage. Those demons are nasty!"

"Sterling, if you are going to help man come out of this alive — and by alive, I mean free from literally existing in Hell on Earth for one thousand years — you have to open your mind to receive the information I'm trying to provide for you. Lucie is dangerous because she attacks the very organ that can convince you she is not a threat — your brain. I assure you Lucifer has taken down greater men and women than those in this room. I do not want to demean anyone, but there is not a single person sitting here who can defeat her on their own. This is the reason for the team. It will take the combination of your talents to have enough power to outwit her and recover the Keys. Allow me to demonstrate one way she can gain control of your mind."

Seneca stands and walks over to Sterling and closes his eyes. He waves his hand in a circular motion over Sterling's head. Within seconds, Sterling jumps to his feet and begins screaming profanity. He starts swinging his fists and punching the air. He seems to be fighting an invisible force. He is kicking and threatening someone named Jack. His screams turn into cries for help.

The rest of us look at each other in horror.

"It is a mind game," whispers Tova. She stands. "Seneca, stop! He is in pain! Stop it now!"

Seneca waves his hand and Sterling falls to the ground, gasping for air between sobs. He covers his eyes with his hands.

Tova runs to him and cradles his head in her lap. "Why did you do this? He was not hurting anyone."

Seneca extends his hand to Sterling and helps him to his feet. He puts his arm around Sterling's shoulder and helps him back to his seat

Sterling is fighting back some final tears.

"I am sorry I had to put you through that, Son. Tova, he will be fine — thank you. You can go back to your seat.

"Sterling, you did not deserve what happened to you when you were a defenseless child. You did not deserve to relive it here. You are a very brave young man. Your daily struggle to protect your mother from domestic violence was an ugly chapter in your life, but it was an important one. You saved your mother's life, and you grew into a fine man who spent his life protecting people bullied by the court system. Around Heaven, you are a bit of a legend. This is the reason you were selected to be on this team."

Seneca pats Sterling on the shoulder and begins walking slowly around our circle of chairs. After looking at each of us one by one again, he continues. "This has always been one of Lucifer's weapons. She cannot read your thoughts, but she knows your history. From this, she can surmise your greatest fears. Sterling, may I share your story?"

Sterling nods and looks at the floor.

"Sterling was a victim of child abuse. His father died before he was born, and his mother remarried when he was two years old. By the age of five, his stepfather, Jack, was hitting him and his mother whenever he was drunk — which was most nights. This went on for five years. When he was ten, Sterling shoved Jack back to keep him from strangling his mother. Jack fell down a flight of stairs and broke his neck. He is not in Heaven.

"Sterling was not really seeing Jack just now; however, his senses were convinced Jack was here, and he was convinced the experience was very real. What I did just now was conjure up Sterling's greatest fear. Through mental trickery, aka telepathy, I was able to cause him to see Jack and feel the fear again even though the rest of you could not see or hear the abuser. This is what Lucifer does so brilliantly. She has been doing it throughout the ages. Just as one of Almighty's children is about to take a risk on something good, or make an important life decision, she manipulates conditions to push their fear to the forefront of their thoughts and renders them helpless. I know each of you has seen this in your own lives.

"It will not take Lucifer long to figure out who is on this team. Once she knows your names, the demons who know you best will fill her in on the highlights of your life stories. From this, she will assume your greatest fears. As I mentioned earlier, she already knows about you, Grayson. She has demons placed near the entry to the Fourth Dimension. They hang out there to hear what is said by the angels and spirits who pass over. When she learned of your diversion from entering St. Peter's gates, she knew. Since then my sources tell me your data has been thoroughly researched.

"Expect her to use the information she collects against each of you individually. Here is the thing you most need to understand: You will not be able to see each other's terrors. You do not have access to the information the way she does. The only way you can combat this as a team is to talk to each other. Share your deepest fears while you train here and head to Jerusalem. You will have to be willing to be vulnerable. By the time you get to the end of the Mission, you are going to know each other at the deepest level. Trust each other. Believe each other's intuition — no matter how outrageous it may seem at the time. Do you understand?"

Seneca looks to each of us for physical affirmation. Once he secures our buy-in, he speaks to the hologram, "Give us a history lesson."

45.

HISTORY

The hologram comes to life. We watch stars appear in the darkness and then a fast progression of something taking shape. I'm not sure exactly what we are seeing. I'm half watching the image and half watching Seneca as he paces.

"You are watching the formation of the galaxy that is home to planet Earth. Scientists refer to this galaxy as the Milky Way. Soon, you will see the sun star and the twelve planets that circle it coming into formation."

I glance at our group scientist, Seiko.

She already has her hand up. "Excuse me, Seneca — twelve planets?"

Seneca walks towards her seat. "This is going to be an interesting day for you, Seiko. There are many scientific revelations coming your way. Do not take it personally if you learn a thing or two. Science on Earth has been evolving since the beginning of time. Your profession has done a fine job of discovery even as the governments of Earth try to get you to sell out. Yes, there are twelve planets — one for each of the twelve tribes of Israel."

"And, what would you say to my astrophysicist friends back on Earth who say they have only identified eight planets and one dwarf planet?"

"I would tell them to keep looking." Seneca gives Seiko a big grin.

"You're enjoying this, aren't you?"

"You know, Seiko, that is exactly what Grayson asked me the first day he arrived here. I will answer you the same way I answered him. Yes, Ma'am, I certainly am."

"It is so beautiful!" Kimmy runs her fingers through the light image. "Almighty sure used a lot of colors in His creation. If my art buds were here, we would mentally dissect the colors for you. I wish they were here to see this."

"Be careful with your wishing. You have more power to make things happen here than you did on Earth. You are closer to the source — if you catch my drift." Seneca smiles.

Kimmy laughs at Seneca's humor. "I understand."

Seiko is also impressed. "This image is amazing, Seneca. I want to put it on slow motion and study it detail by detail. I think I could spend years studying creation and all the laws of nature and physics at play."

"You will have plenty of time for that after the Mission. In fact, there is a group of scientists in Heaven who do little more than study this model. They enjoy connecting the dots of 'string theory.' I will introduce you to them once the dust settles after the Mission."

"This is another 'pinch me' moment — it is too good to be true." Kimmy is gushing over the model.

Seiko's eyes do not leave the spinning image. "May I ask a question?"

"Sure."

"What was the timespan of the Evolution? Wait, I guess the proper question is, what was the timespan of the Creation?"

"There is no need to correct your question, Seiko. You can use the 'E-word' here. We do not mind. That is one of the top ten questions asked by people who arrive here. Evolution and Creation coexist. The time span is irrelevant. When Almighty spoke the original matter into existence, time did not exist. He caused the 'Big Bang' that set things in motion. On Earth, scientists have used various tools to establish a time measurement method. Those are certainly helpful for understanding cause and effect — as well as how all matter interacts — but it is not necessary to prove Creation. Simply stated, the 'Big Bang' is Creation, and surviving is 'Evolution.' You are watching a reproduction of Earth's evolution right now. Soon, you will see the first animals and humans."

Seiko steps closer to the image. "I am going to jump in here if that is okay. Who has the numbers right? The scientists who say this process took millions of years or the creationists who say it took six days?"

"They are equally correct. Remove time from the equation. The earliest parts of Evolution occurred outside of the space-time continuum. Earth's scientists have the sequence of Evolution figured out. The timeline is not as important as they think. The laws of physics were established by Almighty, but they were not applied until the fourth phase of Creation. Time was applied after the firmament of the galaxy was created.

"Almighty continued to exist outside these laws, but man would eventually measure time by Earth's relationship to the movement of the sun and the moon. No one can deny evolution. Every molecule on Earth, as well as in the galaxy, continues to change and evolve. It is how we survive extinction and thrive in challenge.

"The survival of the fittest is an ever-running model. The galaxy is very efficient when it comes to expending energy. When it comes to humans, it does not support superfluous body parts. If an organ is no longer needed for survival, the body will stop producing it. An example would be wisdom teeth. As the diets of homo sapiens changed from raw meats to grainy vegetables, their jaws got smaller. Two generations ago, the third molars, or 'wisdom teeth,' were often impacted. The smaller jaw line left no room in the mouth for the last set of molars. They locked in sideways and had to be surgically removed. Eighty-five percent of adults had their wisdom teeth removed in those years. Jump ahead one generation, and you find that twenty-five percent of people did not develop one to four of their wisdom teeth. In the next generation, they pretty much cease to exist. This is evolution."

The image in the hologram keeps spinning and coming into focus. The planets move to the underside of Earth and disappear from our view. The Earth is the only thing left on the hologram. It keeps molding and changing like a clay model on the potter's wheel. Waters form around a single body mass of land with little topography. Most of the land is even.

"Maybe this is where man got the idea that the Earth was flat," Liam jokes.

Through the 3D imaging, we zoom through the Earth's atmosphere. Our view tightens further to a beautiful garden with streams of clear water and the greenest plants I have ever seen.

"I have got five dollars on this being the Garden of Eden." Sterling is back to himself, and back in the conversation. I, for one, was missing his sarcasm.

Adam and Eve walk and talk as they share some fruit from a shrub. They are completely naked. We watch the scene unfold. From where Liam and I stand, only their bare bottoms are showing.

Liam calls out to Tony on the opposite side of the hologram, "Hey, Tony, want to switch sides?"

The whole group laughs hysterically.

"What? Oh, come on!" says Liam. Every person in this room wants to see what the perfect man and woman look like. Do not even pretend you are not curious to see if they have belly buttons."

After a hearty laugh, Seneca sums things up: "It is beautiful to watch Creation happen in front of your eyes," chides Seneca. "I never grow weary of it. I wanted you to see the sheer power of Almighty. He is capable of breathing all of this into existence."

"We are interrupted by a blast of bright light in the room. It cuts into an open area and hits a spot on the floor like a sword. Immediately after the light, we hear the roaring of thunder.

"Is there a storm in the area?" Kimmy asks as she turns toward the light.

"No, this is our notification that Michael is approaching." Seneca lowers onto one knee and bows his head to the spot where the light is touching down.

The team looks at me in bewilderment. "I guess it's time to show our respect for His Highness, Archangel Michael. Everyone, please bow."

I give the strangest order of my career - to troops preparing to save the world – using superpowers we didn't even knew we had. I can't imagine it getting any more surreal than this.

MALLOW SHERIDAN

DEDICATION:

For my son, Grayson, who never doubted this book needed to be written.

SPECIAL THANKS TO:

Janet Mallow

Kevin Brooks

January Woods

Sandy Land

BOOK EDITORS:

Kristin Dunstan & Ashley Godfrey

ALSO, IN TRILOGY:

DEMON GAMES II: GAME OF EVIL

DEMON GAMES III: NEW WORLD ORDER

800-633-4227